The Counting House

Christina Croft

First Edition. 2006

© *Christina Croft 2006 All rights reserved.*

Cover photographs:
© *André Hilliard 2006*

ISBN 978-1-4303-0988-8

www.christinacroft.com

Acknowledgements

Many thanks to my parents,
Josephine and Edward Croft for their
patience and support.

Sincere thanks to
Sarah Bull
for her unwavering encouragement
and support over many years;
to
Dominic Bull
for the author photographs,
and his artistic guidance;
and to
André Hilliard
for his website design and permission
to use his cover photographs.

And heartfelt gratitude to
Cheryl Hilliard
for her constant inspiration, guidance
and kindness.

Chapter 1

By day the churchyard was safe and free from ghosts but the lodge by the gate was a Maximum Red Alert Zone. It was old and dilapidated, waiting to be pulled down and the builders' sign on the door warned trespassers to *KEEP OUT*. No one ever came or went and the grey net curtain in the upstairs window never moved.

I leaned my bike against a headstone and crept through the knee-high ferns, then throwing myself onto my belly to avoid being seen from the church, crawled like a commando through the builders' gritty sand until I reached the window ledge. Brown paint had chipped away from the wood revealing traces of blue. It might have been a bright house once - a happy, children's house - but now it held only ghosts and spiders weaving webs down the window pane.

I stood upright and on tiptoes pressed my face to the glass; torn newspapers littered the naked floorboards and a broken stool lay in pieces near the wall. Flakes of paint prickled the skin beneath my fingers as I raised myself onto the ledge and gazed at the candlestick on the hearth. This was the Holy Grail that would win me the prize of a bottle top tied to a string. It was a matter of honour: the glory of a medal and the treasure of James' smile.

The door didn't creak as it opened but a musty, dusty smell caught the back of my throat as I scurried into the room where the candlestick stood. Shaking, I dared myself to go forward and knelt to wrap my fingers around the cold metal.

Then I saw him.

I saw him and he was watching me. From the farthest corner of the room an ugly image in a wrought gold frame caught me in an evil stare. Dark demonic eyes bored through my body and followed me when I tried to move away. Drops of deep black blood dripped from his fingers where he held a splattered heart in an outstretched hand. Every muscle stiffened to a tight uneasy pain across my shoulders as I read the gold lettering at the bottom of the frame:

Most Sacred Heart of Jesus I place all my trust in Thee.

It wasn't Jesus. It was Satan from the Children's Bible.

"The devil is a master of disguises," Auntie Philomena had said, "He comes like a wolf in sheep's clothing. We must always be on our guard."

Clutching the candlestick, I flew through the hall leaving the front door wide open and a trail of sand trickling from me like blood. I jumped onto my bike ploughing tracks through the unmarked graves, and sped out of the churchyard, praying in each gasp of breath,

"Jesus, Mary and Joseph, save me from the devil. Jesus, Mary and Joseph, save me from the devil."

But the devil had seen me and now he would follow me home.

"The devil is a roaring lion," Auntie Philomena had said when she came to baby-sit.

She stood by the door and waited for us to undress.

"Come on! Come on!" She clapped her hands teacher-fashion and hurried us into bed,

"That's right. In you get and then we'll say our prayers."

"We say them in our heads," Jessica said.

"The family that prays together stays together."

Auntie Philomena stood in the lamplight with her right arm outstretched, her left hand pressed to her flat stomach. *"In the name of the Father and of the Son...."*

I hated it. It was embarrassing. Jessica wouldn't say the words and I glared at her when Auntie Philomena closed her eyes.

"Angel of God my Guardian dear," I said it louder and bared my teeth at my sister. *"Ever this night be at my side to light and guard, to rule and guide, AMEN."* I shouted the 'amen' as a definite full stop and Auntie Philomena opened her prayerful eyes. I closed mine and smiled piously.

"That's better," she sat down on the edge of Jessica's bed, "always remember your night prayers. The devil is a roaring lion; you never know when he will strike. The greater the saint, the greater the temptations the devil throws in his way. Why should he bother to trap sinners when he already has their souls? But to watch a saint fall! *That* would be his triumph."

Jessica sighed and rolled over, pushing her head beneath the blankets until all I could see was a mesh of golden curls.

"Like nits," I said, "they only go on clean hair."

"Like a roaring lion!" Auntie Philomena growled.

I thought of the devil's horns in the Children's Bible and fumbled beneath the pillow for my rosary beads, "If he comes in disguise, how do you know it's the devil?"

"By his feet," she said with infallible conviction, "he can't disguise his feet! That's why Our Lady always appears with her tiny feet showing beneath her dress. Now you go to sleep like good little girls while I check on Peter."

She switched off the lamp and closed the door, shrouding the room in darkness. The devil, like a roaring lion, prowled under my bed. I trembled and tied the rosary beads round my hand.

"Jess," I whispered, "I'm scared of the devil."

"Don't be daft," she said, "go to sleep."

If I were a sinner the devil wouldn't want me. I hung out of bed and whispered through the darkness, "Bloody, bloody, buttocks and bosoms."

He wouldn't bother me now.

It was an amber afternoon; the leaves were waving from the apple tree like a washing line of green socks above the chatter of children gulping blackberries on the grass.

"Guess what I did!" I dumped my bike and flew across the lawn with my arms outstretched in triumph.

"We know what you did," Jessica flicked her curls with dainty fingers. "You dug a hole round the shed and you're not allowed to play out."

James, sprawling beside her, began to smile.

"A moat!" I said, "It was a moat, not a hole."

"A moat without water? A moat around a shed!"

James' brown eyes met Jessica's and they sparkled. I stepped between them and stared into his face.

"I went into a Maximum Red Alert Zone on my own."

He didn't look at me. He reached to trap a butterfly floating to the purple-pink buddleia.

"I went into the haunted lodge."

Alan grunted and Peter raised his head.

"I saw the devil!"

Peter's eyes were wide with interest now.

"I've brought the candlestick to prove it."

He stared, "You got the candlestick?"

"Look," I lifted my T-shirt and pulled out the trophy, "and when I got it the devil saw me and chased me out of the house."

Alan drilled his finger into a worn patch on the apple tree and prised off a piece of bark, "Liar!"

"Look!" I waved the candlestick in his face.

"That's a different candlestick. The one in the lodge was gold. That's just brass."

I tugged my brother's arm, "Tell him, Peter. It's true!"

Peter took the candlestick from me and turned it around in his hand, "Yes, this is the one we saw through the window."

"Can I have a medal?"

The sunlight shone on James' jet-black hair and, shielding his eyes with his hand, he looked up at me, "Did you really do it?"

"Cross my heart."

My ribs throbbed in anticipation of glory and the feel of his fingers as they placed the medal around my neck.

"Okay, you can have a medal but you'll have to wait. I've not brought any with me today."

Jessica looked at him and flicked her curls, as I flicked a greenfly from my leg, pretending not to care. He shuffled closer to her and his fingers crawled towards her like an insect through the grass. I looked away and wondered why he loved her.

He had loved her all my life. He loved her before I was born. He loved her since the day he and his brother, Alan, moved into the big house next door to my Great Auntie Lucy's. And she told me he would love her until the day he died.

The sand inside my shorts prickled my bottom. I fidgeted with the elastic and waited for something to happen.

Suddenly James stood up, "Let's play Crusades. I'll be Richard the Lionheart."

We ran to the shed for swords and arrows while Jessica leaned against the apple tree waiting for James to tie her hands, "I'll be the hostage. You'll have to rescue me."

He couldn't help but love her; she was so pretty and so dainty with red ribbons in her hair. In spring she made perfumes from pink blossom in a jam jar and their scent filled our bedroom. She dabbed it on her wrists and, carrying her little parasol, walked among the primroses humming songs she'd learned in school.

Peter threw out a pile of brown sacking from the underside of an old bed and we donned it as knightly tunics before scrambling in a box for shields and weapons. Jessica didn't need a sword or costume; she already had the ribbons of a lady.

"Can I be a king?" I said, but James commissioned me as Captain of his bowmen.

"Follow me and I'll tell you when to shoot."

I pulled back the string of my bow and sent an arrow flying into the hawthorn, "For England and Saint George!"

"Help! Help!" cried the hostage in Hollywood tones.

I ran towards her; this time she wasn't going to fall into his arms and burst into tears when the Lionheart saved her.

"Go away!" she huffed as I started to untie the rope.

The Saracens seized our castle and every man was needed to sustain our defence. I abandoned the hostage and fired my last arrow into the rhododendron bush before decapitating a few flowers with my sword.

"Come on," the Lionheart cried, "let's storm their drawbridge!"

"I'll get my arrows," I said and felt the wound of his angry glance.

"I said I'd tell you when to shoot."

We pierced the air around Alan who stood motionless by the shed.

"Do something! There are enemies in the moat."

"Shut up!" he flicked a woodlouse at me.

"Save me! Save me!" the hostage wailed.

King Richard abandoned his command and galloped towards her. I watched him go and, waving my sword, plunged the heathen horde into the moat.

The gate opened and the sudden intrusion of an Infidel wrecked the whole enchanted world. There were no more castles and knights, only children on the grass.

Peter ripped off his tunic and threw his sword behind the hedge.

"Hi, Uncle Max," he walked across the garden, pretending he was too old to play, "are you looking for Dad?"

"No," Uncle Max stuffed his hand into an inside pocket, "I'm looking for Georgie."

"Me?"

"I found something of yours." He crouched to my height and a gold tooth flashed from his smile, "I found it in our garden while I was cutting the grass."

"She's so hopeless," Jessica said, slipping her hands from the rope, "she leaves her things all over the place."

Jessica took care of her belongings; she was so neat and tidy that she drew an imaginary line across the middle of our bedroom to separate her neatness from my mess.

"You're lucky it didn't go in the motor mower." Uncle Max said.

My heart sank when he pulled out my secret notebook. I hoped he hadn't read it:

"POEMS AND SONGS BY GEORGINA MEADOWS"

"I'm fond of poetry;" he said, wiping his hand over his bald head, "we learned them all by heart when I was at school, '*Half a league, half a league, half a league and on...*'" He smiled to himself then at me, "You want to keep it up! A bit hard to read your writing in places, but the bits I could make out were smashing."

"She's always in trouble at school for her untidy writing," Jessica said, "she doesn't take enough care over it."

"There you go then," Uncle Max handed me the book, "I'll call in and see your mother. I've brought her some eggs."

I lifted my tunic and stuffed the book into the elastic of my shorts.

"What's in it?" Alan said.

"Nothing."

"He said poems."

"She tries to make up songs," Jessica laughed, "but they all sound the same."

At night when we took turns to sing ourselves to sleep, Jessica always chose a song she learned in school.

"You can join in the chorus," she said.

She sang *The Ash Grove* slowly, pronouncing every word syllable by syllable to make her turn last longer. When she reached the line 'streamlets meander' she pretended to have forgotten what came next so she could sing it again: *'stre...ee...am...lets mee...aa...ander."*

"If you forget it again, you'll have to stop."

"Don't interrupt," she snapped. "I'll have to start from the beginning again."

There was no chorus and I thought I'd fall asleep before my turn came.

"My song," I said, "is a very sad song about the war."

"Not *Keep The Home Fires Burning* again."

"It's a song they used to sing when Auntie Lucy was a little girl during the Wars of the Roses."

Mum's Auntie Lucy sang with a Lancashire accent which so impressed me I tried to imitate it,

"Keep the yome fyrres burrning."

Jessica laughed.

"It's not funny. It's sad. There was a lady called Mary Ellen and she was in love with a handsome soldier called…James. He went to war in a place called Roses and was shot with three arrows. Mary Ellen was so sad that she died of a broken heart and as she was dying she sang this song. 'While yerr 'arts arrre yurrrning…'"

A snuffle came from Jessica's bed. She was crying; my singing was beautiful.

"Let's see your book," James said.
"No."
"Suit yourself."
"Come on," I galloped back to the shed, "let's capture Saladin."
Jessica sat on the grass, "I'm bored with Crusades. It would have taken ages for you to rescue me."
James leaned over her, "You were very brave. You deserve a medal for courage," and, putting his hand into his pocket, he pulled out a bottle top tied to a string.
I stared in disbelief, "You said you…."
"Sorry about that, Georgie. I forgot I had this one."
I didn't argue. I drew a pattern in the soil with the tip of my sword and wondered why he loved her. She wasn't brave or daring. I ran with him, dug trenches, built castles and slew enemies while she made her perfumes in jam jars and tied ribbons to his lance.
I swung on her shoulders, "Come on, it'll be teatime soon. Let's play something."
I shook her and the book slipped from my shorts. I jumped to pick it up but Alan had snatched it and threw it to his brother.

"It's *mine!*" I leaped up at them as they held it over their heads.

They ran about the grass passing it between them like a rugby ball until they came to the wall of the extension where they huddled in a scrum and fingered my poems:

'*A song for James*', '*The Hero*' and '*I love the Lionheart*' Line after heartfelt line of my most secret sacred dreams: his eyes, his hair, his smile, and my undying love.

They laughed at my spelling, my joined-up writing and forced rhyme. Alan shrieked with delight and read the lines aloud until I felt hot tears burn my eyes. I fidgeted desperately with the elastic in my socks and pretended to laugh.

"Listen to this!" Alan yelled.

"I didn't mean it! I didn't mean any of it! It's all just things that Jessica says. It's Jessica! She's in love with James. That's why she cries all the time."

James stopped laughing and glared at me with anger in his eyes, "That's a nasty thing to say."

"She does! She writes everything you say in her diary and she cries all the time so you'll put your arm round her."

He shook his head and turned away, "I didn't think *you* could be so cruel."

Alan flung the book into the bushes and I scrambled after it, trying to straighten the pages.

"It's nearly tea time," James said. "We'd better be going."

He and Alan disappeared up the drive and Jessica followed Peter into the kitchen. I hoped I'd never see any of them again.

I lay down on the grass and rolled over and over until I reached a trench where I curled up and cried. I hated James; I hated his silly hair and sissy voice. I mouthed his words scornfully, "I didn't think you could be so cruel."

I picked up my sword and considered playing the Roman and plunging it through my heart. Then they'd be sorry. Jessica would cry at my funeral and James would kneel by my grave whispering that he had always loved me best of all.

The soft soil where Dad had filled in my moat trickled into my shoes and gathered between my toes. I climbed into the shed where woodlice crawled across the beams, and sat among the insects, wiping my tears on my T-shirt.

I saw my dirty shorts, my sand-scuffed shoes, my silly sackcloth tunic, "I hate me. I hate me! I'm horrid and cruel! Bloody poems, bloody silly girl who looks like a boy, bloody James, bloody Alan, bloody Jessica…BLOODY BLOODY BLOODY!"

The shed door opened.

"What are you doing?" Peter said.

"Nothing."

"Are you crying?"

"I've got soil in my eyes."

"It's tea time," he sounded sorry. "Mum told me to come and get you."

"I don't want any tea."

"We can play out again later. You can have the castle and I'll…"

"It's not a castle, it's a shed. It doesn't even look like a castle," I kicked the wall, "and they're not swords, they're sticks." I snapped the cane across my knee, scratching the skin but concealed the wince. "You couldn't kill anyone with them. You couldn't really *kill* anyone."

"It's a game," he said quietly, "you're not meant to kill for real."

"One day I'll get a real sword and chop off their heads."

"My head?"

"No," I followed him to the house, "not yours. James's and Jessica's and Alan's."

Eggs. Tea was a huge pile of scrambled eggs dotted with chopped tomatoes. I bordered my plate with the little red bits and spread the yellow gunge with the side of my knife, flattening it to make it disappear.

"Don't pick at your food," Dad said.

"I don't like…"

"EAT IT!"

He'd already finished and Jessica was primly taking her last forkful.

"I hate egg."

"You should be grateful you've got something to eat. Think of the starving children in Biafra."

I shuffled the egg around the plate, "You can send them this."

"No more sweets for you," Dad said.

I hadn't had any sweets.

The egg was cold and slid down my throat like an eel. Every mouthful made me retch and Jessica's 'I've eaten all of mine' expression made me feel sick. I opened my mouth as widely as I could and showed her the soggy, half-chewed egg.

"Georgie!" Mum's heavy hand came down on my thigh, "Don't be disgusting."

"Mum," Jessica said, "Georgie stole a candlestick from church."

A sharp portcullis fell down in front of Mum's eyes.

"I didn't steal it. I found it! I found it in the lodge."

"What were you doing in the lodge?"

"Nothing. I just looked in on my way back from Auntie Lucy's."

"You'd no business being in there, *trespassing*."

"And stealing!" Jessica beamed.

"I didn't steal it. I borrowed it."

"I didn't know we had a thief in the family," Mum said.

"When you die, you'll go to hell for stealing from church," Jessica gloated.

"You'll go to hell for telling lies."

"Be quiet," Mum said, "eat your tea."

The more I ate, the bigger the egg mountain grew. I wanted to see it splatter over my sister's pretty curls and smug expression. I took another mouthful and chewed but the muscles in my throat refused to swallow. I could see the little yellow bits sticking to her hair and her face all squashed like a plum.

"Stop playing with it," Mum said, taking the other plates to the sink.

Nothing they might do, no punishment could outweigh the sheer joy of seeing this yellow gunge slapped across her cheeks.

The fork was laden, the ammunition ready. If I pressed my fingers, just so, against the prongs and aimed a little higher…

"Mum!" she squealed like a wounded rabbit.

Peter stared in amazed admiration and I laughed until tears welled in my eyes. I laughed when the heavy hand came from nowhere to drag me from the table and I laughed until the flat palm slapped against my leg.

"Get a cloth!" Mum jerked me to the sink, "And when you've cleaned that up you can wash Jessica's blouse."

"She's spoiled it, she's spoiled it and it's all in my hair!" Great tears dripped from Jessica's blue-black eyes.

I brought the dishcloth and rubbed it over her face. It stank of egg and cabbage and she cried all the more.

Dad took my plate into the garden, "If you're going to behave like an animal, you can eat outside."

They put me on the doorstep and closed the back door. The soggy egg had set solid and a sticky skin covered its surface. I took it to the rhododendron bush and scraped it into the soil then sat down on the step until Mum came to bring me in. She stood me on a stool at the sink where for half an hour I scrubbed at Jessica's blouse. It wafted on the washing line like a triumphant banner in the breeze and Peter came into the garden and smiled.

He fished an old *Sqweezy* bottle from the bin and filled it with water. He squirted me a few times so I found a plastic bag and made a water bomb to throw at him.

"Let's squirt Hoagey's washing," he said.

Mrs. Hoagey lived next door; she had a tree with bigger apples than ours, "Don't eat them," she said, "they're baking apples. They'll give you tummy ache."

Alan often ate them and he was never sick.

The jet from the *Sqweezy* bottle wasn't strong enough.

"We could climb onto the roof and shoot from there."

The roof of the extension was flat and in winter the rain came in. I climbed up the drainpipe, curling my foot between the bracket and the wall but Peter's feet were too big.

"We need a rope," he said, " I know! The judo belts! We could tie them together."

In term time we had judo lessons in a basement gym. A boy held out a tube of sweets to Jessica, "Would you like a *Toffo?*"

His hair was thick and curled around his face like the picture of Narcissus in Peter's book of *Myths and Legends.* His lips were so red I thought he wore lipstick. I smiled at him but he didn't offer me a sweet.

Thud…slam…thud…slam: we practised falling on the mat one after another. We lined up by the lagged pipes waiting for our turn: black belts first, then brown, right down to whites. Jessica never moved beyond whites. I looked down the line and counted the people between us. I stroked my orange belt. I was better than Jessica at judo.

The others were men or older boys who never hurt us but let us throw them. I knew they let me do it but I felt proud to see them conquered on the mat. Jessica grew tired of judo and said she wanted to leave but I persuaded her to stay.

"James is going to start judo," I lied.

We were the only girls and I was better than she was.

I lay across the beams where the roof was strongest, and looked down at Hoagey's drive. It was covered in black tar speckled with little white stones that looked like fish in the river at Bransden Wood where the grey-green water trickled and bubbled over pebbles. It was deep in parts but towards the bank only reached my shins. I pretended it was a moat and I was swimming to the castle.

"I've got Jessica's belt too," Peter whispered up to me.

"Does she know?"

"No."

"Good. Throw them up."

I tied them together in thick knots and lowered them down.

"Tie your end round the drainpipe and hold on really tightly," he said.

He tugged at the bottom and swung a few times to test the strength. I tied the end around my waist and he began the ascent. He was lighter than I'd expected and when he reached the top we shook hands.

"Shoot at the pink things," I said, "it shows up most."

Hoagey didn't come outside for ages then she started to bring in the washing. It was wet and streaky from the dirty spray. She looked up at the sky and around the garden but we lay flat so she couldn't see us and we laughed when she'd gone.

"Let's stay here all night," I said.

"They'd find us."

"Not if we keep our heads down." I looked at Peter and giggled, "I'm not going in tonight."

"They'll send for the police if they don't find you."

"Georgie!" Mum called from the back door, "Two more minutes. I'm running your bath."

I hated being called inside. I never wanted to leave the garden but when I first climbed out of the bath I felt so warm and clean and cosy. It was cold for a second between leaving the water and snuggling into the fluffy towel when Mum hugged me dry. Jessica sat on a little blue chair pulling faces. I made the water dirty, she said, and I made her get out first; I always did. She said it wasn't fair.

"I'm staying out here all night," I told Peter.

He leaned over the edge to see if anyone was coming. "They'd go mad if they knew we were up here."

The *Sqweezy* bottle rolled across the roof and landed with a thud on the concrete below.

"I'll get it," Peter said.

I tied the ropes around my waist to lower him down and he slithered to the edge.

"Wait!" I whispered, "I haven't tied it to the drain."

He didn't hear me.

"Don't go yet!"

He'd already gone. His fingers were clutching the edge of the roof when I heard the back door open again.

"Come back! Someone's coming!"

The door closed and I peeped over the edge. The rope slipped from my waist. I caught it in my hands but it burned my skin as it slid through my palms.

"Peter!"

He didn't scream or make a noise.

Thud…slam…the basement gym. He lay on the concrete below. I slithered down the pipe and called his name. I touched him and shook his shoulder, pouring the dregs of water from the *Sqweezy* bottle over his head but he didn't move. I thought he was playing then I thought he was dead. His arm was stretched out beside him and his legs twisted underneath. There was blood on his face, *real* blood.

    Auntie Lucy arrived before the ambulance, a ragged cardigan slung over her flowery dress, her great bosoms bouncing as she marched down the drive.
    "Don't move him," she said authoritatively, "just put a blanket over him."
    When the ambulance arrived with its blue light flashing, a small crowd gathered at the gate. I stood on the drive and watched two men in uniform stride towards Peter. They wrapped him in an orange blanket and strapped him to a stretcher with sandbags round his head. Mum and Dad followed him into the ambulance and we watched it disappear. Auntie Lucy put her arm around me and whispered something soothing. Everything would be alright now that Auntie Lucy was here. Auntie Lucy never raised her voice but spoke with a firm conviction that made everything secure.
    I sat on her knee in the dining room and sipped a cup of milk. The clock ticked loudly and nobody said very much. I tried to stop crying. I knew he wasn't dead. I knew it in my heart, my skin, my teeth. When I hugged Auntie Lucy I knew Peter wasn't dead. Mum hadn't phoned and it was ten o'clock.
    I lay in bed and thought about the moon, so far away yet almost near enough for me to reach

out and touch it with my hand, put it on my tongue and taste a sticky toffee; a sweet I would suck for a while then spit into a tissue.

No, Peter wasn't dead. I'd make him a medal, buy him a comic, write him a poem. Peter wasn't dead.

"Please God, I'll never be naughty again. I'll eat eggs. I'll always be good. *Please* God, don't let him die."

"Are you awake?" Jessica whispered.

"Yes."

"I'm scared."

"So am I. Can I come into your bed?"

"Yes."

She smelt of soap and bubble bath. We cuddled each other and our tears mingled on my cheek.

Chapter 2

Nobody was angry. Nobody shouted or blamed me. That was the hardest thing. If only they'd said it was my fault I'd have cried and then it would all have been over. Instead it dragged on for days and weeks and months.

Two women were talking in a shop:

"Poor kid, he broke his back."

"He'll never walk again."

"He's lucky to be alive."

I blocked my ears and wished that I were dead.

"Mum," I said, "will Peter never walk again?"

She stroked my hair, "We just don't know."

Maybe he would. 'Maybe' or 'perhaps' meant 'yes', like 'wait and see'. Mum never 'didn't know'.

I didn't want to see him in the hospital.

"Will he remember me?" I said.

"Of course he will," Mum smiled, "and he'd love to see you."

His face was pale and his hair was matted on his head. I knelt on a chair to look at the deep red scar on his cheek.

"Wow! You look like a real knight now."

Jessica peered at him from the foot of the bed, "Does it hurt?"

Peter didn't answer.

The boy in the next bed had bandages over his eyes and he moaned and flapped his arms like a wounded sparrow.

"What's up with him?" Jessica whispered.

"He had an operation. They pulled out his eyes and put them on his cheeks to cut them open."

"They didn't!"

"Yes they did. He told me."

The nurse put a thermometer in Peter's mouth and tousled his hair, "Isn't he a brave boy?"

He pretended to smile.

"I'd hate to be in hospital," I said.

Uncle Max arrived in the afternoon, sucking his cheeks into hollows like flying saucers.

"There you go!" He held up a present.

Peter undid the wrapping and held a cardboard cylinder to his eye.

"I see no ships!" Uncle Max laughed.

"What is it?"

"A kaleidoscope. When you look into it you see whatever you want."

I wanted to see Peter walk again but saw only black silhouettes like a mass of crawling ants.

As soon as he heard Auntie Philomena's voice, Peter pulled the sheet over his head.

"Tell her I'm dead," he said and I laughed.

She placed a consoling hand on Mum's shoulder, "I lit a candle for him in church. How is he today?"

Peter lay as still as a corpse beneath the sheet.

"Much better," Mum said, pushing me off the chair to make room for her aunt.

"I've brought him a present."

Auntie Philomena placed a children's prayer book on the locker. She looked around the ward and clutched her handbag with both hands. "My father died in this hospital," she said.

"James' mum died here too," Jessica said with tears in her eyes. She didn't remember James' Mum who died before I was born, but she'd seen her photograph and said she was a beautiful princess.

When Peter came home after Christmas I made him eight medals out of bottle tops and spread them across his bed. Dad carried him upstairs and sat him on a chair. He looked alive but his legs didn't move.

"Welcome home!" Jessica kissed him but he rubbed his hand across his cheek to wipe away the kiss.

I said, "I'm glad you're back," and he smiled.

James' Dad bought Peter a Scalextric. We set up the track on the kitchen table and watched the red car whizzing round and around.

"I'm going to be a racing driver when I grow up," Alan said. He looked at Peter's legs and said it again.

In March Mum pushed Peter's chair into the garden.

"What shall we play?" Jessica said.

Alan looked at Peter, "Let's have a race."

James shoved his brother in the back.

"We could play Crusades," Peter said.

Jessica looked at him with pity but Peter rubbed his hands over the wheels of his chair, "Kings ride in chariots."

A light dawned on James' face, "There's a go cart in the shed. Peter can be the King of France and I'll be Richard the Lionheart."

"Can I ride on the back as your squire?" I said.

Jessica looked at me and pouted but I'd asked first and, climbing up behind him, I clung to his waist. For over an hour we fought the finest battle ever. James pedalled quickly until the grass and paving stones spun past my eyes. I held a sword in my hand and tried to catch the bushes as we sped around corners. We shouted and yelled and took the castle from the heathen.

Peter's chair was faster than the go-cart. He held a lance beneath his arm and charged at the rhododendrons, unaware of Alan cowering in the bush waiting to throw a worm. The lance struck Alan's shoulder, knocking him backward into the soil.

"Idiot!" he cried, "You bloody stupid *cripple!*"

Everything stopped. Even the birds stopped singing and I heard the same silence I had heard between Peter's fall from the roof and the thud slam onto the concrete.

I leaped from the go-cart with a loud roar and hurled myself onto Alan, forcing his face into the soil. He was bigger than I was but anger strengthened my muscles and the speed of my attack gave me advantage.

"You're the idiot!" I yelled, "You're the bloody stupid idiot!"

He roused himself from the shock of my fury, "Get off me you little witch! You brought the devil home with that candlestick!" He seized my wrists as I tried to punch his face. "Don't blame me!" he screeched, "It was you who broke his back!"

I wanted to hurt him. I wanted to make him scream. There was nothing in the world except my anger and his face. He rolled on top of me and I wriggled to break free from his hands. My arm flew out of his grasp and my fist shot towards his eye.

"Georgie!" Jessica shouted and James flew across the lawn.

"Get out!" he kicked his brother onto the grass, "Go on, get lost!"

Alan crawled like a slug from the garden.

James, his face red with exertion, turned to Peter. "I'm sorry," he said, "ignore him; he doesn't know anything."

Peter didn't speak but let the lance fall onto the grass and steered his chair towards the back door.

"Where are you going?" I said.

"I don't like this game anymore."

Peter sat at the dining room table reading his *Look and Learn.*

I knelt on a chair at the opposite side resting my chin on my hand, "Alan's an idiot. He doesn't know anything about anything."

Peter shrugged and turned the page. I looked at him through the fruit bowl that had been in the family for three generations. It was huge and round and made of crimson glass and when the light shone through it, the wall behind glowed like a summer sunset. I put my face to the glass, turning Peter's hair bright red.

"Do you want to play a game?" I said.

"I'm reading."

"I don't think we should let Alan come round here ever again."

I lifted the bowl to my eyes and made his cheeks crimson. When I put it down it spun by itself on the polished table.

Peter looked up, "Hey! That's good." He reached for the bowl, spun it and it danced on the wood throwing shafts of light like tiny flashes of lightning onto the ceiling.

"Do it again!" I said.

He did it again and again, faster and faster like a merry-go-round. It spun so quickly and danced in a frenzy, hurled itself against the wall and shattered into a million slivers on the carpet.

Mum flew into the room, "NO!" Her voice ran through me like a metal blade, "I can't leave you alone for a minute!"

I jumped from the chair, out of reach of her hand.

"What on earth were you doing?" She snatched his *Look and Learn* to gather the shattered pieces.

Peter's face was serious and defiant; he watched her collect the shards with sheer contempt in his eyes.

"For heaven's sake," he sighed, "it's only a bowl."

She turned, "Don't you *dare*..."

"It's only a bloody bowl!"

In an instant her hand came down across his face. She stopped for a second as though uncertain what she'd done, then silence spread through every corner of the room.

The shock in Peter's eyes turned into rage. His face burned redder than I'd seen it through the glass. His breath came loudly working up to a scream, "It's only a bowl, for God's sake! It's only a damned bloody bowl!"

She seized his chair and pushed him from the room, slamming the door behind him and he shrieked as though in pain. I winced and heard the wheels roll quickly down the hall. He was crying. Some seconds passed. The front room door slammed and loud music came from the piano.

He was right. Mum knew he was right; it *was* only a bowl and Peter's spine was smashed. I moved closer to the table and, trying to please, touched a fragment of glass.

"LEAVE IT!" she yelled.

I ran out of the room and blocked my ears. I tapped on the front room door.

"Peter, it isn't fair."

"Go away." He thumped the black keys on the piano.

"She's sorry she hit you."

"Go away!"

I ran upstairs and kicked the side of my bed.

Peter didn't play outside again. He locked himself in his room strumming the strings of his guitar and singing to himself when he thought no one could hear. I took the microphone from a tape recorder and stuck the end of the wire into the elastic of my shorts. I danced around the lounge miming to Dusty Springfield: '*You don't have to say you love me just be close at hand...*'

Jessica laughed and held up the microphone as she bounced up and down, '*Love is just like a merry-go-round with all the fun of the fair...*' we laughed and she sang it again.

Mrs. Hammil came to teach us the piano and Peter worked his way from scales to sonatas but it frustrated him being unable to use the pedals so Auntie Lucy had bought him the guitar. Jessica practised Czerny's exercises and I scraped my way *A Tune a Day* to some semblance of a melody on the violin.

"Listen to this!" I poked Jessica in the ribs with the sharp end of the bow.

"Not *that* again." She put her hands to her ears.

"*Keep the Home Fires Burning.*"

I tried to sing as I played but the chin rest banged on my jaw. I put the violin back in its case and took the bow into the garden where I snapped the horsehair trying to fire an arrow. I slid the broken bow beneath my mattress and took the violin to school, returning the next day with the tale that the bow had vanished at playtime and Miss Keppel was 'looking into it.' Some weeks passed before Dad asked about it.

"I got it back," I said, "but it's broken."

"Who did it?"

"They don't know."

"I bet it was Barry Saxon," Jessica said.

She hated Barry Saxon. He had nits and one day in the cloakroom when she reached to collect her coat, his hair brushed against hers. Later, in the bath, Mum's face turned white with consternation as she poured water over Jessica's hair. She pulled me from the water and with long, probing fingers, examined my head.

"Get ready for bed," she told me urgently, "I need to talk to Jessica."

I listened at the bathroom door and heard my sister squeal on hearing of Mum's discovery.

For the next fortnight we bathed separately and every day the same strong smell came from Jessica's head.

"I can't come near you, you're dirty," I said. "you've got nits."

"They only go on clean hair. They wouldn't come near you!"

She cried as Dad dragged the metal comb through her ringlets and I sat on the washing basket smiling at her puckered lips and tears.

"They'll have to cut all your hair off and you'll look like Uncle Max."

"Silly baby!" she said.

"Anyway, I know what happened to Uncle Max. He wouldn't go to the barber's and his hair grew in long curls so one night when he was asleep, Auntie Lucy sneaked in with some scissors and cut it all off."

"Fibber."

"It's true," Peter said, "Auntie Lucy told me."

"James," I said, "Jessica's got nits."

"So what? Alan's got worms from eating Hoagey's apples."

On the corner of a tatty parade of shops stood *'BILLINGS' MODEL & TROPHY SUPPLIERS'*. In the window golden cups and statuettes stood on miniature pedestals with spaces left blank for names to be engraved. Beneath them were battalions of blue and red clad soldiers of every regiment: infantrymen with pikes, cuirassiers with shining swords, musketeers, horse guards and Coldstream guards, fusiliers and grenadiers. The entire Charge of the Light Brigade, complete with cannon and regimental flags, was staged in a large glass case.

I pressed my nose to the glass and looked at the rearing horses and officers swinging their swords above their heads. They were beautiful and colourful and way beyond the limit of my pocket money, but for ten new pence I could buy five plastic men in khaki. Some were standing to attention; some were crawling with their rifles held in two hands before their faces; others knelt with bayonets fixed to their guns.

Mr. Billing let me stand for hours in his shop, gazing at the figures and deciding which to buy.

"Hurry up!" Jessica yawned, "We haven't got all day."

"Take your time, sonny," Mr. Billing said.

I blushed when Jessica giggled, "She's a girl."

Mr. Billing peered over his half-spectacles and looked me up and down, "I'm sorry," he said.

I fidgeted with the coins in my pocket.

"Everybody makes that mistake," Jessica smiled, "because she does look like a boy."

I soon amassed an army and with Dad's red ink and fake grass from the green grocer's, I staged the whole of Agincourt and the Somme. The anachronistic rifles and rounded helmets of American marines didn't detract from the glory of the bloody battles taking place beneath my hands.

The kitchen sink was a river where Guy Gibson dropped wooden bobbins as bouncing bombs and the plate rack was a castle from which my wounded soldiers fell into the moat. Peter wheeled his chair to the sink and flicked paper missiles from a lolly stick with an elastic band. Plop, plop, plop my heroes dived into the water and the battle gained the excitement of our old Crusades.

Jessica didn't want to play that game. We ruined the wooden bobbins she was saving to make cork wool teapot stands for birthday presents.

"Watch, James!" I dropped a fork between the wire of the plate rack into the ribs of a hapless rifleman, "It's a portcullis."

Alan picked up the wounded figure and turned it around in his fingers and read the plastic stand, "U.S. Marine? They don't have castles." He dropped the soldier onto the draining board and followed the others out of the kitchen.

I went upstairs and made a list of my soldiers, giving them names and ranks and for each of those who had fallen into the moat I wrote a telegram like the one that Auntie Lucy had received to say her husband was 'Missing Believed Killed' in some dark muddy shell hole on the Somme.

Music wound its way upstairs. Jessica was singing at the piano while Peter strummed his guitar. I put my head out of the bedroom door and listened. James wasn't singing but I could hear his voice urging them on. Avoiding the creaking floorboards on the sixth and seventh stairs, I slithered along the banister and put my ear to the door. The piano was silent now and the only sound was Peter singing an old folk song and his fingers gently plucking the strings of his guitar.

I stood alone in the middle of the garden and tried to find a castle but could only see a shed. Daily, inch by inch, the vision faded; shark-infested oceans lost their terror; battles soon grew tedious; it was hard to play alone but I couldn't let it end. I wouldn't let the enchantment disappear.

Mum came to hang out the washing, "What's the matter?"

"Nobody wants to play."

"Do something else."

"Like what?" I followed her into the kitchen.

"Draw a picture."

I huffed and put my chin into my hands, "Can I have a horse?"

She stuck a cabbage in a colander and put it under the tap, "What for?"

"To ride."

"Where would you keep it?"

"In the garden."

"It's not big enough. They need a lot of room."

"Beverley Winter's got a horse. She goes riding every Saturday. Can I go riding?"

"It costs a lot of money."

"Peter could come with me. Beverley Winter says that lots of people in wheelchairs go riding."

"Here," she scattered a bag of peas across the table, "shell these."

"Then can I have a horse?"

"We can't afford it."

"I'll do without pocket money."

"They cost hundreds of pounds."

I squeezed the peas from the pods, "I'll save up."

In my treasure box of old coins there was one engraved 'Victoria Regina.'

"What date is it?" Peter said, "It might be valuable."

I rubbed my finger over the worn Britannia, "1896."

"There are only four 1933 pennies in the whole world," he said.

"This might be the only one from 1896."

I polished it with Brasso and took it into the front room where Dad sat drinking tea with Auntie Lucy.

"Dad, is this worth a lot of money?"

Auntie Lucy opened her handbag and pulled out a purse, "Here," she emptied a pile of old coins onto the coffee table, "you can have these."

"Wow! Thanks!"

Four farthings, three silver threepenny bits, some ha'pennies with ships on the back and an 1890 penny. I gathered them in my hands and took them to Mum, "Is this enough to buy a horse?"

"No."

I stuffed the coins into my pocket, "Can I go out on my bike?"

She nodded, "Don't go far."

The devil's candlestick lay in the corner of the shed where I left it the day that Peter fell from the roof. It was the cause of all misfortune and but for want of courage I should have taken it back sooner. If I replaced it now the devil might lift his curse; I'd find a horse and Peter would walk again.

I stuffed the candlestick into my shorts and climbed onto the bike that was bought for Peter second hand. It was purple and rusty round the mudguard and frame and a little pendant flag drooped from a corroded spike. It was bigger than mine and would make my escape easier. Peter wouldn't mind if I borrowed it; he had no use for it now.

"The chain keeps coming off," I complained.

"It will if you pedal backwards!" Dad said.

I took a ball of string from the shed and threaded it round the handlebars, "Yah!" I kicked the spokes of the back wheel and shook the string to gallop down the road.

"Giddy up! Giddy up!" I whizzed through a Red Alert Zone where the beast called Enemy Black was gnawing a rubber shoe. I wobbled in the gutter but kept my balance. It was a boy's bike with a cross bar; I mustn't fall forwards.

"Hi ho, Silver!" I patted the brakes and slapped my thigh on the downhill stretch beyond the new apartments in Poppy Field Court.

Reaching the churchyard I tied the bike to the gate and looked towards the lodge.

"I have come on a quest to combat the forces of evil. I cannot be turned back."

I held the candlestick arm's length in front of me and ventured towards the door but something was different. Barbed wire barred the entrance and a new and bigger sign read 'DANGER! DEMOLITION IN PROGRESS - KEEP OUT!'

I hurried to the window and, pulling myself up on the ledge, tried to look inside but the glass had been replaced by an opaque sheet of corrugated metal. I jumped down from the ledge and ran across the graves. How could I appease the devil now? I scurried into church and dipped my fingers in the holy water, blessing myself and sprinkling it over my head.

"Make the devil go away!" I prayed with all the fervour in my soul.

Years and years before I was born, my grandmother's grandfather, building the church, was hit on the head by a falling slate and died in front of the altar. His wife was given the slate that killed him and he was given an honourable burial in the place where he fell. He lay in the aisle beneath a stone slab on which I stood reading his name and the verse inscribed in the stone:

Of Your Charity, Pray For The Repose Of The Soul Of Bartholomew Benson

I rejoiced when I heard them say, 'Let us go to God's house!'

Above him, floating across the ceiling, wooden angels hovered through the scent of beeswax and dry rot. The stone clicked beneath my feet, a satisfying sound that rebounded on the walls and echoed on the marble altar. I moved slowly down the aisle with the cautious footsteps of a felon approaching the magistrate's bench.

Reaching the front pew, I paused and, kneeling, raised my eyes to the crucifix. The man hanging on the cross was very small; he had to be small to live inside the tabernacle.

"The tabernacle is God's house," Miss Keppel said, "the holiest part of the church."

God's house? I looked at the little green curtain over the door and wondered what was inside. There were probably rooms; tables and chairs, perhaps an upstairs with tiny wooden beds; a doll's house like Jessica's.

The church was silent and the sunlight of a bright afternoon streamed through the blues and greens of the stained glass window making patterns on the aisle like the rainbows in a pool of oil.

I tiptoed up the sanctuary steps and listened to the echo of my sandals on the wobbly stones. Drawing closer to the crucifix, I examined the feet of the figure whose eyes were closed. Blood had seeped from the nail wound, coagulated and dried.

"Please help me," I whispered, "please make the devil go away."

Peter said dead bodies stink and putting my nose to his feet, I sensed the strong beeswax smell that filled the church. It smelt of May processions and benediction - a holy smell, the way I imagined heaven smelt.

I put out a finger and touched the end of his toe. It was solid like wood not flesh, and I wondered if from heaven he could feel my fingers.

I looked at the little tent on the tabernacle and with one finger pushed the curtain aside. A bronze dome sparkled in the candlelight and, looking up at the sanctuary lamp in its red casing, I knew Jesus was at home.

"The light is a reminder of Jesus' presence among us," Miss Keppel told us.

"Like the flag at Buckingham Palace that shows the Queen is at home," I said.

"Wherever you see it burning you must genuflect with the greatest respect."

I genuflected dramatically; I put out my arms as I knelt down and lowered my head like Francis Drake being knighted by Queen Elizabeth.

I rose with a gracious bow and tapped gently at the door of the tabernacle. The only reply was the echo of the tapping on the walls. I tried the door but it was locked and a huge bronze key with a clover-shaped top lay at the side. A fitting key for the house of God; like the key to a castle or a palace. I picked it up and turned it round in my fingers and was about to twist it into the lock when a boom like the voice of God split the silence and my awe.

"What do you think you're doing!"

I glanced at the cross but Jesus' eyes were closed.

"Get down from there! Get down at once."

Mr. Blackland stood at the side of the altar, dressed in his cassock and surplus while a group of boys gathered behind him and stared at me as I did at them. They were dressed identically like miniature Mr. Blacklands.

I scurried down the steps and stood in the middle of the aisle. I would have run away but he had caught me by the shoulder and pressed his fingers like a vice into the bone.

"What were you doing up there?" he said in the broadest Irish accent, "Wait till I see your mother."

I looked at the angelic faces of the boys behind him. They never looked so angelic on the playground: Michael Rushman, Philip O'Keith, Stephen Downes and Jeremy Lawes; they were all in Jessica's class, yet here, in their cassocks, their hands joined in front of them like statues of saints, their faces shone with the radiance of sanctity and I wished I could look so holy.

"Girls have no business on the altar," Mr. Blackland said.

His eyebrows joined in a 'V' and thick black whiskers protruded from his nose.

"I want to be an altar boy," I said.

"An altar boy, is it?" he shook his head as he spoke, "A girl as an altar boy! I never heard such nonsense. Go on, get off home before I call Father Paxton."

The stones in the aisle clicked and clinked as I walked over them. I reached the door and, hiding behind a pillar, peeped down the church.

Mr. Blackland led the boys up the sanctuary steps. They handled the dishes and jugs and jingled the bells. They hung little white napkins over their arms and walked to and from the altar, bowing and kneeling and rising like some country-dance. I *wished* I could be an altar boy.

"I only wanted to talk to you," I whispered to the man on the cross. I pulled a prayer book from the bench for reassurance and opened a page at random:

'Third Station of the Cross: Jesus falls the first time. Consider this first fall of Jesus. His flesh was torn by scourges, his head crowned with thorns and he had lost so much blood...Run now my soul and look on thy Lord and thy Love who bears the cross for thee, hasting to its torment to pay the price of thy great sins...'

Thud...slam...thud...slam...For my great sins... and Peter's spine was smashed. I shut the book and cowered behind the pillar. Tears stung my eyes; it was my fault that Peter couldn't walk and now my sins - my trespassing - nailed Jesus to the cross.

"Forgive us our trespasses," I raised my head and the gentle Good Shepherd met my eyes. His face, blurred by my tears, was smiling at the lamb that nestled in his arm and pressed its head to his breast. How could I have dared to wound so gentle a God?

"I'm sorry," I began to sob, "please make Peter walk again."

I wriggled towards the statue where little blue candles burned on an iron stand. I fidgeted in my pocket for a farthing and dropped it noisily into the slot.

"I've only got old farthings. Will that do?"

"Are you still there?" Mr. Blackland growled from the altar.

I took a candle from the box, "Please make Peter better," the wax dripped onto my hand, "and I'll be good. I'll never be naughty again."

Chapter 3

"I am the Lord thy God who brought thee out of the land of Egypt and out of the house of bondage."

While the boys made Plasticine models with plastic knives on small square boards, we sat like ladies-in-waiting around Miss Keppel's desk, clicking our needles and quietly chanting the steady rhythm,

"In, wrap it round, pull it through, slip it off. In, wrap it round, pull it through slip it off."

Miss Keppel moved among us uttering words of wisdom, "The devil finds work for idle hands. Always keep your hands and your minds busy!"

Her huge nostrils quivered as she surveyed the class, "Gerard Taylor, what is the first commandment?"

He answered without hesitation, "Thou shalt not have strange gods before me."

"Go on," she said.

We carried on knitting, "In, wrap it round, pull it through slip it off, in, wrap it round, pull it through, slip it off."

"Nor any fish or," he looked down and stuck his thumb into the squashy pink snail, "bird or graven image or any insect or anything."

Miss Keppel's great nose came down above him until his neck shrank into his shoulders. A swift hand clipped the top of his head, "For I, the Lord am a jealous God and I punish the father's guilt in his sons!"

She spun around like a whirlwind, "Catherine Gould, the second commandment?"

"Thou shalt not take the name of the Lord thy God in vain."

"In, wrap it round, pull it through, slip it off. In, wrap it round, pull it through, slip it off," faster and faster, building up speed like a train.

I said the words but my hands were out of time. I said, 'Slip it off,' when I was wrapping it round and I knitted a hole where there should have been wool. Catherine Gould's scarf grew longer and longer in a rainbow of bright colours. I wriggled the wool through my fingers, tying the loose ends in knots on the needles. The two rows that Miss Keppel had knitted to start me off grew greyer and greyer but the scarf never grew any longer.

Miss Keppel moved on, calling names at random, "Michael Donnelly, the fifth commandment."

This week she was bound to come to me; I guessed that she would reach me with the seventh. She always omitted the sixth and the ninth and Gerard Taylor said they were rude. I looked them up in the Bible.

"Jessica," I said, "what's adultery?"

"Being cheeky to grown ups."

"That's not rude."

"Being rude to grown ups then."

Miss Keppel's shoes squeaked over the wooden floor and her flowing skirt made a breeze as she passed. My fingers were damp and slipped over the huge plastic needles. I gathered the grubby grey wool on my lap and buried the scarf in my hands.

"Georgina Meadows, the seventh commandment?"

I felt the blood rush out of my face and my hand began to shake. I opened my mouth but no words would come.

"The seventh commandment, Georgina?"

She was standing in front of me, her long bony fingers entwined before my eyes. Her knuckles were red and inflamed and brown spots covered the skin.

I screwed the wool into a ball, "Thou shalt not steal."

One by one her fingers untwined and stretched themselves like an eagle about to swoop on its prey. Her hand was cold when her skin touched mine, pulling the woollen ball from my knee. When she lifted it up her nostrils flared and her thin lips sank into her mouth.

"What," she said, pausing between each word, "is this?"

I didn't know if she wanted an answer so I bent down and pulled up my socks.

"Well?"

"Please may I do Plasticine next week?"

"Plasticine?" the word burst out like an oath.

"I can't knit. My Mum can't knit either. None of us knits in our family."

Her dull eyes widened and her lips disappeared. She took the end of a thread in her finger tips as though it were an insect she could hardly bear to hold and with one sudden movement of her wrist, unravelled the whole creation and dropped it in a heap on my knee.

"You can't knit? Then it's time you learned. You'll stay in at playtime this afternoon and every afternoon until you can."

Her skirt brushed against my legs as she turned away and I looked at the odious heap she had thrown in my lap.

"Thou shalt not steal," and the devil's candlestick still lay with its curse in the shed.

"Beverley Winter," she said, "what is the eighth commandment?"

I sat upright in bed and through the darkness looked across the room to Jessica silhouetted by the glow of the landing light,

"Lie still," she said, hammering her pillow, "you're keeping me awake!"

"I can't sleep. Will you play a game?"

"No."

"I'll say someone in my class and you guess who they sit next to."

"Go to sleep!"

"Shall we take it in turns at singing? You can go first."

She tutted and pulled the blankets over her head.

I picked a scab off my knee and imagined I lay wounded on a battlefield, "Keep the home fires burning, while your hearts are..."

"Mum!" Jessica shouted.

The door burst open and the landing light drowned my bed.

"She's making noises to keep me awake."

Without a word Mum came towards me. Her arm flew out and her hand came down in a thud. She knew it didn't hurt through the blankets, "If I have to come up again," she said, "it'll be harder!"

She left the room in darkness but for the thin line of light beneath the door. Every shadow bore

Miss Keppel's face glaring at me from the ceiling, from the curtains and the wall. I put my head under the pillow and my eyes grew heavy.

"Jess," I whispered, "there's a ghost in the room."

Miss Keppel's face grew bigger and more grotesque until her thin lips sucked me into her mouth and I lay on a bed of knitting needles in a deep dark cave. Her bony fingers reached for my face and their swollen knuckles burst into yards of grey wool that wrapped itself around my neck, choking the breath from my body.

"Thou shalt not steal!" she cried and the devil's candlestick crashed through the ceiling onto my head.

As I lay helpless at her feet, she came towards me, creeping slowly with an evil delight in her dull grey eyes. In her fingers she held a long thin knitting needle like a dagger aimed at my heart. She lifted it high above her head and drove it down with all her might into my hand. Blood spurted like a bright red fountain, spilling over my flesh and dripping down onto my knees. She cackled like the hag from *Hansel and Gretel* and raised her arm again for a second attack. This time she aimed for my face and in one horrific moment I felt its point scrape the film of my eyeball. I screamed and shot upright in bed.

Jessica was breathing deeply in sleep. The thin stream of light had gone from beneath the door. It must be very late if Mum and Dad had gone to bed. My stomach ached and churned and made peculiar rumblings. I rolled onto my side and I was sick.

"Jess," I said, "JESSICA!"

She snorted and pushed her head out of the blankets.

"I've been sick."

She let out a shallow sigh, put on the lamp and came to the side of my bed. "Ugh," she said, "you should have got a bucket," and, wiping the sleep from her eyes, she crossed the landing and tapped on Mum and Dad's door.

"Georgie's been sick."

Everything happened according to the usual routine: a travel rug on the camp bed next to Mum's; a towel on the pillow and a bucket that smelt of strong disinfectant at my head, but I knew I wouldn't be sick again. I listened to the traffic on the road outside and began to smile. There would be no school tomorrow; they'd let me stay with Auntie Lucy and after the weekend Miss Keppel might forget that I couldn't knit.

Music rolled like a wave washing over me and carrying me away to a far off land. Auntie Lucy conducted the massed bands with a feather duster and I marched up and down her sitting room with an umbrella held like a rifle over my shoulder.

"BOOM! BOOM!" she cried as the cannon fired and Napoleon's armies fled. Her giant bosoms bounced unevenly as she swayed to the *Marseillaise*. I knelt on one knee and pulled the trigger of the umbrella aimed at the standard lamp as the last triumphant notes faded away.

Auntie Lucy laughed and dusted the clutter that made her home so special. The room was filled with long-leafed plants that draped from hanging baskets to the floor, tickling my hair when I walked beneath them. Some blossomed into flowers; pink geraniums peeping out of pots, and ugly cacti in dry crumbling soil. She talked to them and gave them classical names: Lysander, Cicero and Livy. The music streamed from a record player: rousing marches, *Pomp and Circumstance, The 1812 Overture* and *Fingal's Cave*. She had a medal in a glass cabinet and a framed certificate on the wall.

"Mrs. Pankhurst herself gave me those," she said proudly.

She'd been a suffragette. She sat me on her knee and told me tales of glory, how she'd been to London to smash the windows of a public hall and spent three weeks in Holloway Gaol.

"We wouldn't eat," she said. "Even when they tried to tempt us with the best food, we wouldn't eat."

I snuggled into her spongy bosom and thought of scrambled egg. "I'd have been a suffragette," I said.

Auntie Lucy knew all about battles; she'd seen so many in her time. When she was a child she watched the soldiers returning from the Boer War.

"Old Jepson put a barrel of beer in the street and all the men had a free gill."

She was only married for six weeks when her husband was killed on the Somme but she never fell in love again. She adopted Uncle Max when he was three and he had stayed with her ever since.

She dusted the ornaments on the mantelpiece and carefully polished her husband's face in the dark wooden frame. He wore a uniform with the badge of a Lancashire regiment and the smile of a proud young hero going to war.

"Auntie Lucy," I said, "what was Uncle Jack like?"

With a sad smile, she studied the photograph, "Like any other young man, I suppose."

"Did you always love him, even when you were a little girl?"

She put the picture back in its place and dusted a pottery 'Souvenir of Scarborough'.

"We were always good friends," she said.

"Did you cry when he died?"

She stopped dusting for a second and stared at me, "What a question!" she said then rubbed the ornaments more vigorously.

I looked out of the window and across the garden to James's house.

"Did James cry when his Mum died?"

"I expect he did."

I looked at the smiling face of the soldier in the photograph and felt a tear burn my eye, "I hope that no one I know ever dies."

Auntie Lucy turned and saw my solitary tear. She sat down in the rocking chair and pulled me into her arms, "Come here!" she squeezed me tightly, "I wouldn't sell you for a shilling!"

She put her hands on my shoulders and held me at arm's length in front of her, "Let's not be getting all maudlin." Her face suddenly brightened, "Do you want to see my medal?"

She lifted it from its case and placed it on my open palms. I ran my fingers over the green, white and purple ribbon then held it against my breast.

"When I grow up I'm going to be a suffragette."

She chuckled and opened the dresser drawer, pulling out a small wooden chest, "Come on, I'll show you my pictures."

I had seen their faces before: the black and white heroines of women's struggle for the vote. They carried banners and waved huge flags and with each one she showed me she told me a story of courage.

I climbed into the rocking chair beside her and snuggled into her thigh, "What was it like in prison?"

"Hard," she said, "very hard, but it was worth it. When something is worth fighting for, you're prepared to suffer the hardship."

Her face so wrinkled and her eyes so cloudy, grew young when she spoke of the 'Cause' and the comradeship she had known.

I followed her into the kitchen when she went to bake some butterfly buns. I wondered if she'd made buns for Uncle Jack.

"I wish I had a magic wand," I said, thinking I might ping his picture and bring him back to life.

"That's easily sorted," she smiled, "I'll make you one."

She washed her wooden spoon under the tap then scrambled through drawers for raffia, tinsel and tape.

I climbed up on a stool beside her, "Will it work?"

"Wait and see!"

While I waited, I planned the wonders I would perform. First Uncle Jack revived, and then Peter would walk again. I'd magic a horse out of the ottoman and turn the shed into a castle. I'd magic myself beautiful like Jessica and magic James to fall in love with me.

"There you go," she handed me the spoon. The tinsel glistened and the raffia swished as I waved it over my head. I ran into the living room, closing the door behind me so she couldn't see.

"PING! PING! PING!" I tapped the photograph.

Nothing happened.

"PING!" I said, "Abracadabra!"

It didn't work. It was just a spoon, but I hadn't the heart to tell Auntie Lucy.

When the sun came out she painted 'VOTES FOR WOMEN' on the side of a cardboard box and I paraded my banner around her garden until I was arrested and put in prison in the porch. I was confined and on hunger strike when Uncle Max came home for lunch. He stuck his head round the back door,

"Are you poorly?"

"No. I'm better now."

"Good. Do you want to play in the stage coach?"

He put two stools inside the shed and sat beside me cracking a cane on his leg.

"Gee up! Gee up!" he called and we rode off into the Wild West dodging the Indian arrows and singing *Wagon Train*.

Uncle Max didn't have a proper job; he worked for different people on different days. Sometimes he helped out on a building site, sometimes he did deliveries for the milkman, or helped Auntie Lucy at home.

"He isn't like a grown-up," James said, "he likes to play marbles and he never goes to work."

"He's great is Uncle Max!" Peter said. "He's better than most grown ups. He doesn't fuss about silly things like the others do."

"Are you still writing poems?" Uncle Max said when we sat down to lunch.

"No, everybody laughed at them."

"Good God!" Auntie Lucy marvelled, "Fine suffragette you'd make if you can't bear a little laughter."

Despite her serious expression her eyes giggled. Uncle Max wriggled his ears and moved his eyebrows up and down to make me laugh. Auntie Lucy looked at him and put her hand over her mouth to conceal her smile.

"Not at the table, Max," she said. "Have you to get back to work this afternoon?"

"Aye, another hour and we should be finished. We've just the clearing up to do."

"Father Paxton will be pleased. He should have had the lodge pulled down years ago. It's been nothing but an eye-sore since old Bellshaw moved out."

"The lodge," I said, "in the graveyard?"

Uncle Max nodded, "You'd be amazed at some of the stuff we found inside: statues, pictures, plates and what have you. We gave the lot to Father Paxton but he told Tom to take what he wanted. There's a lovely Sacred Heart picture that Aunt Philie might like; I could get it for her."

"Bring it and we'll have a look."

"Sacred Heart?" I felt sick again, "It isn't Jesus, it's the devil."

Auntie Lucy put her knife and fork on the edge of her plate, "Who's been telling you stories?"

"Auntie Philomena says that the devil is a master of disguises and he comes like a roaring lion."

Auntie Lucy reached across the table for my hand, "You look pale," she said, "do you feel sick?"

I nodded and she led me from the kitchen into the sitting room where she sat me on her knee and held me in her arms, rocking me gently and humming.

"I'm scared of the devil," I said, "I stole his candlestick and he's coming to get me."

"Nonsense," she said gently, "the devil can't get you! Why do you think God gave you a Guardian Angel?"

"Auntie Philomena says that...."

"Listen," she placed a finger over my lips, "Auntie Philie has some funny notions. She doesn't always think straight. I wouldn't take too much notice if I were you."

"Is my Guardian Angel stronger than the devil?"

"Of course he is!"

"Don't let Uncle Max bring that picture home." I begged.

Auntie Lucy died one night in June. She went to bed with her rosary beads and cocoa and didn't wake up again. She lay in a coffin in the Chapel of Rest with only her face and hands peeping out from the pale blue shroud. The beads entwined around her fingers and the Sacred Heart embroidered on her breast marked her as a Catholic fit for heaven. Her skin was shiny and plastic after the undertaker's art and as I turned to leave the darkened room I saw the coffin lid against the wall.

"Are you alright, love?" Mum said. She hadn't wanted me to come but I insisted and wondered whether seeing a corpse merited a medal.

Jessica waited at home with Peter and Uncle Max whose eyes stared heavily at the T.V. screen. He looked up when we walked in, "Did she have the Catholic shroud?"

Mum nodded and put a comforting hand on his shoulder, "Will you have a drink?"

She poured him whiskey in the best cut glass and he gulped it quickly, staring at the floor.

"She had a good innings," Dad said.

Uncle Max sniffed and I thought he was going to cry. Jessica tugged my sleeve and we left the room.

"What did she look like?" Jessica asked.

I lay on my bed, crossed my hands over my chest and, letting my jaw fall open, tried to make my eyeballs disappear.

"Ugh," Jessica said, "I'm glad I didn't go."

I laughed, but when we were in bed and darkness hid my face, I cried into my pillow for Auntie Lucy,

"Keep the home fires burning," I hummed beneath the blankets, "While your hearts are yearning..."

Uncle Max should never have brought the picture home.

At the funeral we sang *March of the Women* - the rousing chorus of the suffragettes - and closing my eyes I marched with Mrs. Pankhurst to the gates of Holloway gaol.

A warm summer rain beat down on the cemetery, washing the wreath we had placed on the dark wood coffin. The flowers in suffragette green, white and purple dripped over the bronze plate screwed into the lid. I looked at the pile of rubble where the lodge had stood, and cursed the day I had ever ventured inside.

"You're soaking!" James moved towards me and held his black umbrella over my head.

"Here," Jessica thrust her polka dot brolly into my hand, "she can have this."

She swapped it for my place at James's side.

"I'd have been a suffragette," I said.

We sat in Auntie Lucy's house hearing the grown-ups talk of their childhood in a world as far removed from ours as Bronze Age Man.

"Listen to this, this will make you laugh," Uncle Max recounted familiar exploits from his youth. He laughed too loudly and nudged me in the ribs at every punch line. I shuffled further along the settee to avoid his elbow. He poured himself another glass of whiskey and told the same dreary tale in different words.

Peter smiled at him, "Tell us some more."

"Well," said Uncle Max, "did I tell you how P.C. Blackthorn caught me poaching blackbirds' eggs and chased me down the Bunny Run?"

"Yes," I said.

Jessica nudged my other side and I poked my fingers into her ear. She squealed and the heavy hand came down on my thigh.

Uncle Max continued his well-worn story, adding more embellishments with each new glass of whiskey, "Your Auntie Lucy looked him in the eye and spoke with the voice of authority, 'I've had run-ins with better policemen than you! I didn't serve my time in Holloway for nothing!' Wonderful woman, your Auntie Lucy. Wonderful woman."

He let out a loud sob and blew his nose with a sound like a trumpet. I stared at him then looked away.

"Max," said Auntie Philomena screwing the lid on the whiskey bottle, "I don't think this will help," and she started to hum a hymn.

Mum took my hand, "Come on, it's time that you went home."

I looked up at the medal in the glass case, "Uncle Max," I said, "If Auntie Lucy doesn't want it anymore, do you think I could have...."

"Get your coat!" Mum said loudly, pushing me towards the door.

I hadn't brought a coat but knew what she meant and didn't ask again.

"Uncle Max was crying," Jessica said as we walked home.

Peter looked up from his wheel chair, "So?"

"Grown ups don't cry."

"They do," Peter said, "They cry when they're drunk."

"Why?"

"Because whiskey makes them cry."

"Why do they drink it then?"

"Because they're sad."

"It makes his breath smell," I said, "He stinks."

Mum's hand came down on my bottom, "Don't be rude."

"...Uncle Max was sad and so he drank some whiskey and cried and then he drank some more whiskey and then he cried again then I wanted to ask him for Auntie Lucy's suffragette medal but Mum made us go home and we had some hot milk and I fell asleep as soon as my head hit the pillow."

"Thank you, Georgina," Miss Keppel said.

I closed my 'News' book and sat down.

"Did you really see a dead body?" Gerard Taylor whispered.

"Yes, it looked like this."

I did my impression of a corpse.

"Wow!" he said, "I wish I'd seen one."

We stood on the playground at lunchtime facing one another in two long lines. The boy between the lines raised his hands above his head and shouted, "British Bulldogs Across!"

We charged across the playground trampling over those who fell. The boy in the middle caught seven children, Gerard Taylor among them. I safely reached the other side and we all lined up again.

Eight children stood in the middle with their arms above their heads,

"British Bulldogs Across!"

We charged. Gerard Taylor caught me round the waist. "Can I kiss you?" he said.

"Why?"

"If you let me kiss you, I'll let you go."

"Okay."

He put his arms around my shoulders and kissed my cheek.

Fourteen children stood in the middle with their hands above their heads, "British Bulldogs Across!"

I ran into Gerard Taylor, "Do you want to kiss me again?"

"Yes," he said, "and then I'll let you go."

All lunchtime he kissed me until Mrs. Prout, the dinner lady, hurried across the yard, "Stop that! Stop that now!" she wagged her finger in my face.

The following morning on my table I found a giant, yellow *Refresher* chew and a McGowan's sticky toffee bar.

"Do you want to be my girlfriend?" Gerard Taylor said.

"No," I said and wished that he were James.

Miss Keppel moved between the desks with a fistful of letters in her hand, "Fold them carefully and take them to your parents. Woe betide anybody I see dropping this letter on the yard or forgetting to take it home."

Beverley Winter's hand waved in the air, "Miss Keppel, what does 'Vocation' mean?"

"Is the letter addressed to you?" Miss Keppel said, "Does it say at the top 'Dear Miss Winter'? No it doesn't. It says 'Dear Parents'. Are you in the habit, Beverley Winter, of reading other people's mail?"

"No, Miss Keppel," Beverley said and I smiled at her for solidarity's sake.

"However!" Miss Keppel's voice grew louder by the syllable, "Since the question has been raised, can anyone explain to the class what 'Vocation' means?"

I'd have bet my box of soldiers that Catherine Gould would raise her hand, "It means being a nun or a priest."

"A vocation," said Miss Keppel without acknowledging the answer, "is a calling from God. God calls us all to serve him in different ways. The privileged few are called to the priesthood or religious life but marriage or a life of service can be a vocation too. You have the honour of being invited next week to a Vocations Exhibition in Holy Saviour's hall. Many nuns and priests are coming, for your benefit, so you can learn about their way of life and perhaps one day one of you might hear the call of Jesus to follow him in that particular way."

    I looked at the letter and noted the time and the day: Thursday afternoon! There'd be no knitting. It was a sign! A sign from God that he would rescue me from the devil.

Chapter 4

'*Valiant women, I can be one!*' the girl on the sepia card raised her eyes heavenwards and opened her arms to the skies. A ray of golden light shone on her innocent face, emphasising her radiant smile. I stood in front of the mirror imitating her pose, "Valiant women, I can be one!"

On the back of the card was a list: '*Ten signs of a True Vocation*' which I marked with ticks and crosses according to my experience. To those I didn't understand I gave the benefit of the doubt and marked them with a tick then counted my score: seven out of ten! Valiant women, I can be one!

But I'd have to be one with a habit; I couldn't be valiant without a veil. I hung my rosary beads round my neck and, drawing the curtains, practised by lamplight in front of the crucifix with a towel over my head.

"Good morning, my child, I'm Sister Georgina."

Jessica burst through the door and switched on the light, "What are you doing?"

I shoved the picture under her nose, "Valiant women, I can be one!"

"They wouldn't let you be a nun." she laughed, reading the back of the card, "You don't have '*an ardent desire to spread Christ's kingdom on earth*'!"

"I do."

"You don't even know what it means!"

"I do," I said, and added, "my child," to display my new-found serenity.

I went downstairs and mimed to *The Sound of Music* skipping round the cushions and over the hills.

"Mum," I showed her Julie Andrews' face on the record sleeve, "Can I have my hair cut like this?"

"We'll see," she said.

Mrs. Houghton in the Brakenfield Junior Library knew every book on the thirty non-fiction shelves.

"Hello Georgina," she smiled when I'd tied my bike to the door, "what is it today? Castles or suffragettes?"

"Do you have any books about nuns?"

"Let me see," her little fat fingers flicked over a worn card index, "*The Monastery in Medieval England.* Will that do?"

"Is there anything else?"

She shook her head, "We've a good section on saints."

I followed her over the squeaky tiles and watched as she fingered the books, "Is it for a school project?"

"No it's for me. I'm going to be a nun."

"I see," she said, smiling. "Well, there's a few to choose from. Take your pick!"

She left me browsing through martyrs and mystics in search of a soul mate. The bottom shelf housed four leather-bound volumes of *Butler's Lives of the Fathers, Martyrs and Other Saints*. I bundled them in my arms and took them to the counter.

"The 'R' means 'Reference.' You can't take these out of the library."

I sat at a desk on a hard wooden chair and carefully turned the pages. The brightly-coloured pictures of Founders and Fathers depicted all manner of saints but each had the same impenetrable gaze as they lifted their eyes heavenwards. Some carried palms and instruments of torture revealing the means of their martyrdom. Some wore crowns of thorns and blood dripped from their heads and hands, but the feet of all were visible beneath flowing robes.

When my eyes alighted on the words, *'The devil assaulted her with violent temptations'* I knew I had met a kindred spirit. Apart from the fact that she too had been plagued by the devil, the 'Life' of St. Rose of Lima comprised only two pages and I had to be home for dinner.

"*From her infancy her patience in suffering and her love of mortification were extraordinary, and whilst yet a child, she ate no fruit and fasted three days a week...*'

I read on, overlooking the difficult words and old fashioned language:

'*Whenever she was to go abroad in any public place, she used, the night before, to rub her face and hands with the bark and powder of Indian pepper which is a violent corrosive, in order to disfigure her skin with blotches and swellings.*'

I looked again at her picture and the halo that shone round her head. I could see no disfigurement.

'*Extraordinary fasts, hair cloths, studded iron chains which she wore about her waist, bitter herbs mingled in the sustenance she took, and other austerities were the invention of her spirit of mortification and penance.*'

I cycled home scraping my knuckles on garden walls as a penance and made a vow to eat scrambled egg without complaint.

"What are you doing?" Mum said, finding me in the kitchen sprinkling pepper on my hands.

"Nothing, dear mother," I said, for I knew that my penance must be done in secret.

"Have you been in my wardrobe again?" Jessica said.

I hid behind the curtain in the dining room and pulled her chain belt a little tighter under my T-shirt.

She heard me jingling on the stairs, "I knew you had it!" She pushed me backwards but I didn't retaliate. I raised my eyes in the carefully rehearsed pose,

"How blessed are you when people abuse you and persecute you!"

"Silly baby!" Jessica said and pushed me again.

Nobody saw me carry Our Lady of Lourdes into the garden. I mounted her on three blocks of wood in the shed and knelt on the floor with my arms outstretched like Jesus on the cross.

"Ave Maria, gratia plena," she'd be impressed that I'd learned it in Latin, "Dominus tecum," I didn't know the rest.

At first I thought the tapping on the panels was a sparrow until it was punctuated by snorts of laughter. I crept along the floor beneath the window to the door and pushed it open suddenly. James and Alan dived into the bushes leaving Jessica on the grass.

"Georgie's been reading the Bible in bed at night!" she giggled. "She's going to be a nun."

Alan swung from the roof and kicked the side of my chapel, "She might as well be 'cause nobody will ever want to marry her!"

I yanked his ankle and pulled him to the ground, "Get lost!" I said and ran back into the shed, closing the door behind me.

"It doesn't make her any better behaved, does it?" he shouted.

I locked the door from the inside and shouted through the window, "You'll have all black marks on your soul, and you'll go to hell when you die."

"Oh yeah?" he laughed, "I'm really scared."

"Yeah, because you're a Protestant and Miss Keppel says that Catholics go into heaven through the door and only very good Protestants get in through the window. But they won't let you in at all!"

Alan hammered on the door with his fist, "You're the little witch who stole the candlestick! I'm gonna get you when you come out!"

I curled up in the corner and waited until everything was silent. Peering through the cracks between the slats of wood, I searched for any sign of life. There was no sound but I knew they hadn't gone; my only hope was a sudden charge towards the house.

I stuck the key into the lock and turned it slowly and waited...and waited until I couldn't wait any longer. I pushed open the door with a sudden force but still nobody moved. I put a foot onto the step and thought I heard a movement from behind. As I ran forwards a cane shot from the apple tree so swiftly that I couldn't dodge its flight. It landed with an unexpected pain across my forehead and fell at my feet.

"Spot on!" Alan shrieked and leaped from behind the tree but James and Jessica didn't laugh as they emerged from the bushes. They stopped for a second and stared at me then Jessica ran towards me with a squeal of fear.

"You stupid idiot, Alan!" She put her arm round my shoulder, "Are you alright?"

I was fine until I saw the concerned expression on her face. The momentary pain had gone but now, hearing the terror in her voice, I raised my hand to my head. It felt wet. My hand was covered in blood, like the blood that dripped from the forehead of St. Rose of Lima.

"Lie down," Jessica said, pulling me onto the lawn, "or you might faint."

I feigned a swoon and dropped dramatically to the ground.

Alan dug his toe into my side, "Is she dead?"

"No," James said, "she's still breathing."

"Dead people breathe," Alan said, "and their toe nails grow really long."

"Do they hell!" James knelt down beside me.

I opened my eyes and murmured, "Where am I?" waiting for James to take my head on his knee.

"I'll get your Mum," he said.

Mum was in her usual fluster, mopping my head as I sat on the kitchen table, "An inch lower and you'd have lost your eye!"

"You should go round and tell Mr. Radcliff," I said, "and he won't let Alan play out again."

The disinfectant stung when she pressed the cotton wool on my wound.

"Wow!" I saw my reflection in the kettle, "Can I have a bandage instead of a plaster?"

She stuck on the plaster, "Why is it always you? We never have all this trouble with Jessica."

I squeezed the skin around my forehead until the blood showed through the plaster,

"Peter," I said, tapping on his bedroom door.

"Shh," he said when I walked in, "listen!"

He lay on his bed with a radio pressed to his ear.

"What are you doing?"

"Listening to police messages. They're following a car round town."

There was crackling and muffled voice said, 'Ten four'.

"They've got him!" Peter sat up, "Juliet Whiskey Lima. That's the registration number."

"Lima?"

It was a sign! It was a sign that St. Rose of Lima would carry my prayer to God and by my penance Peter would be healed.

I sat by his feet and the crackling grew louder then stopped. He fiddled with the dials and turned the radio off.

"Do you want to be in my club?"

"Yeah."

"This is the Operations Room." He reached into his bedside table and pulled out a map of Brakenfield, "I'll listen for the police messages then I'll give you instructions and you can go to the scene on your bike and report back to me."

"What do I have to report?"

"Everything. But you'll need a new identity; I'll make you a card and give you a code name so if anyone stops you, you tell them you're called Mary Smith."

"I don't want to be Mary Smith."

"Okay, you choose a name," he was already busy with scissors and card, cutting out a rectangular passport.

"Emmeline Pankhurst."

"No, that's silly. Choose another."

"Rose Lima,"

"Okay."

"What's yours?"

"Alfred Jones."

"What happens now?"

"Get down behind the window and look out. Tell me if you see any suspicious-looking-characters."

Only one old woman walked by with a shopping trolley.

"Shall I make a list of suspicious-looking-characters that we already know?"

He handed me a pencil and I sat down on the floor:

"ALAN RADCLIFF
MAX WIDDICOME
MISS KEPPEL
JESSICA MEADOWS
ENEMY BLACK"

"Here," Peter gave me my Identity Card, "That's your code number on the top, you'll have to memorise it: 8967524. Have you got that?"

"Yes, Alfred," I said and passed him the list.

"Uncle Max isn't a suspicious-looking-character."

"Okay, I'll cross him off but Alan is Enemy Number One."

"You have to pass a test to prove you're fit to be in the club. There are three things you have to achieve: courage, intelligence and strength."

"Okay."

"Test number one: courage. You've got to go into a Maximum Red Alert Zone. You've got to touch Enemy Black."

"I can't do that!"

"Sorry," Peter sighed and shook his head, "that's the rule. No one can be in the club unless they touch Enemy Black."

"Have you done it?"

"I don't need to; I'm in charge. And anyway you can run away but I can't."

He knew I couldn't resist any reference he made to his wheelchair and he looked at me through wide, expectant eyes.

"Okay, I'll do it."

"Good," he said, "set off now and I'll time you. You've got fifteen minutes."

I skipped along, waving my sword in the air. I could pretend that I had done it. Peter would never ask for proof; but God would know I'd lied and my membership of the club would be invalid. There was no choice; I had to prove that I was brave. As long as the gate was shut I would be safe. He might bound up at the wall or skid across the drive but he couldn't reach me.

There was no sound, no sudden movement in the bushes. I leaned around the lamp post and saw no sign of life but chances were he would be hiding, waiting to pounce. I gripped the post's cold concrete and swung a little further... the gate was shut!

I breathed deeply and moved slowly towards the wall. A sudden jingling from the garden took my breath. The beast was there! I touched the wall and took another step but I was terrified now and he smelt my terror and charged from the bushes in a frenzy. His body clanged against the gate until the whole frame shook beneath him. He barked and my heart beat so quickly that my legs shook and I needed to run.

"Dogs know when you're frightened," Miss Keppel had said, "Stay calm and they won't bother you."

She said the same of the wasps that buzzed around the classroom in September.

I tried to stay calm but the tar beneath my feet began to move. I *knew* he couldn't reach me; he was tethered to his chain, but I saw his teeth when he growled and the purple tongue that hung from his jowls.

I walked more quickly but I didn't run. I put my fingers in my ears to block his bark and walked on until I came to the next garden. The barking stopped and silence made me brave. I turned to see him mooching over the lawn. I cowered by the gatepost, drawing my sword from my belt, and waited for him to come nearer. It didn't take long. He sniffed along the drive, slapping his padded paws on the broken flags. I stuck the cane through the gate and wiggled it about until it pressed against something soft. When the barking started again I dropped the sword and ran. Peter didn't say I had to touch him with my hand. I ran until I'd passed the seventh lamp post. I had done it!

In the kitchen Mum was sitting next to Peter whose pensive eyes were far away in thought.

"I did it!" I said and pulled up a stool beside him. "I touched him with my sword!"

Mum looked at me and put her finger on her lips.

"What's wrong?"

"Go and play," she said quietly, "I'm talking to Peter."

I jumped off the stool and wandered upstairs where I found Jessica lying across her bed sobbing into her pillow.

She looked up, "Have they told you?" Her cheeks were red and blotchy and her eyes puffy with tears, "There's a doctor in London who thinks he can help Peter to walk again."

I knew it! I knew my penance would prevail on God to grant my prayers! I leaped onto Jessica's bed and bounced up and down, "Yippee! Yippee!"

"They're sending us away."

"What?" I bounced on to my knees and came to rest beside her.

"They're sending you and me to stay with Uncle Bernard all summer."

"Why?"

"Because they're going to London with Peter."

"Can't we go with them?"

"No," she said and burst into tears again.

I patted her head as though she were a puppy, "Why can't we stay here with Uncle Max?"

"I don't know;" her voice quivered, "they should let us stay with Mr. Radcliff. James said we could."

She raised her head from the pillow and, opening her fingers in front of her eyes, peeped at me, "Well, he said *I* could, he didn't mention you. They haven't got room for you as well. It's your fault I have to go to Uncle Bernard's."

"But James has got a massive house. There's plenty of room for me too."

"No," she said, "you take too much looking after."

I sat at the top of the stairs and waited for the kitchen door to open and when it did I bounced down the steps on my bottom and landed at Peter's feet. I touched his knees, "Are they going to make you better?"

"No," Mum said firmly, "they haven't said that. They want to look at him and there's just a slight possibility that they may be able to help."

"It's great!" I said to Peter and he smiled hesitantly. "They will make you better. I *know* they will!"

He wheeled himself into the front room and fingered the piano keys.

"Mum, it's my fault that Peter can't walk so can I come with you to watch them make him better?"

She pulled me towards her and sat down beside me on the stairs, "Don't build his hopes up. We don't want him to be disappointed."

"Can I come with you anyway?"

"No. It'll take a long time. Uncle Bernard and the girls are happy for you to stay with them for the holidays. They've got a huge garden and plenty of room for you to play. You'd be better off there than in London."

"I'd love London," I said. "There's a statue of Mrs. Pankhurst in Victoria Tower Gardens and I could go to see the..."

"There won't be time for anything like that. Dad and I will be at the hospital all day with Peter."

"Can't Uncle Max look after us?"

"No," she said without any explanation, "it's all arranged. We'll take you and Jessica to Brigthorpe next Sunday."

Her smile was sad and worry lines had gathered around her eyes. I nodded and wandered out into the garden. Kneeling in the shed I stretched out my arms, "Ave Maria, gratia plena, please make Peter's legs better and I'll be a nun and be good forever and ever."

Chapter 5

My one previous encounter with Uncle Bernard occurred when I was far too young to form an opinion of his character. He was chosen as my godfather solely on account of his being the only available male relation in Brakenfield on the day of my Baptism other than Uncle Max who, having already performed that role for both Peter and Jessica, felt the burden of an extra godchild too great a responsibility. It was fortunate for me, Auntie Philomena often said, that my Christening happened to coincide with the only visit Uncle Bernard ever made to Brakenfield or I might have been left a god-orphan. Personally I could never see the advantage of possessing a godparent who had never sent me a present and believed his duties were complete the minute the ceremony was over.

All I knew of him was his hand writing on picture postcards, 'Greetings from Florence,' 'Greetings from Seville', 'Greetings from Rangoon, Havana, Algiers' and the familiar message, 'Best wishes from Bernard, Marie and the girls.'

The sight of a postcard on the floor in the porch among the junk mail and bills always filled me with excitement. I opened the atlas and sat at the dining room table tracing every river and mountain range in the region, trying to pronounce the enchanted place names while Dad sniffed contemptuously, "He's showing off again. Only time he ever writes is to tell us he's been somewhere else."

Between his travels, Uncle Bernard settled for several years in Paris where he lectured at the

Sorbonne and married a French teacher of English, before returning to England to settle in remotest Brigthorpe.

The car drove on through endless country lanes and I stared out of the window at the trees on either side of the road. They leaned like old ladies, their backs bent by the wind that must have always blown in the same direction across the interminable fields dotted by a few dilapidated cottages.

"I need the toilet," Jessica said.

"It's not far now."

We drove on and on.

Eventually we came to a narrow track winding towards a solitary house high up on the hillside.

"That's it," Dad said.

I looked at Jessica and she at me with fear in her eyes.

"It's not a house," I said, "it's a mansion!"

Her lip quivered, "How does the post man ever find it? There isn't even a road name."

"Bernard wouldn't want a house with a number on an ordinary street," Dad mumbled.

"The house has a name," Mum said, "Brigthorpe Hall. That's how the postman finds it."

The wheels crunched over a gravel courtyard and a woman in a wide-brimmed hat and Wellington boots strode smiling towards us calling foreign phrases whose meanings were immediately apparent by her cheerful wide-eyed expression.

"There's Marie;" Dad said, "she even manages to look glamorous in wellies!"

When I saw how Aunt Marie greeted Jessica with affectionate kisses on both cheeks, I wouldn't get out of the car. I clung to the seat and hoped they might not notice if I stayed for the journey home, but the bright smile of the French woman appeared in front of my eyes.

"Little Georgie," she said in a voice both strange and beautiful, "come, meet your uncle and cousins!"

I loitered around the car as Dad pulled out our cases, "Can't I come back with you?" I whispered.

"You'll love it here," he said in an unconvincing monotone.

Aunt Marie's hand slipped into mine and she led me over the gravel towards the door. She talked of what a wonderful summer it would be, "There's so much to do, so much fun for you to have!"

Dad had never had much to do with his older half-brother - a term that had led me to believe quite wrongly that Uncle Bernard would be a sort of half-man, small in stature like a goblin or a gnome. In fact he was a huge mountain of a man whose straggling curls and shaggy beard gave him the appearance of a lion. He was the first man with a beard that I had ever known and from the moment I saw him I knew he was a suspicious-looking-character and made a note of the fact with the intention of passing the information to Alfred Jones at the first opportunity.

Two girls stood beside him in the doorway with their hands clasped in front of them and their mouths contorted into forced smiles.

"Meet your cousins," Aunt Marie said, "Claudette and Claire."

They stuck out their hands politely for me to shake but as I stepped forwards to greet them I caught their sideways glance at one another and the beginning of a scornful smile across their lips. I postponed my greeting, bent down to pull up my socks as I waited for Jessica to speak.

"We're very happy to be here," she said in a well-rehearsed tone, "aren't we, Georgie?"

"Yes." I crossed my fingers behind my back.

Claudette, the older and taller of the two, looked down her nose through small circular spectacles, "Shall we show them their room?"

"Yes," Aunt Marie tousled my hair and turned my head towards a wide staircase with banisters on either side. The posts at the top and bottom were crowned with giant spherical lamps like huge green goldfish bowls.

"Come this way," Claudette said imperiously as we picked up our cases.

"It's massive!" I whispered.

"I hate it!" Jessica replied.

"We've given you a shared room. Maman thought you'd like that since that's what you're used to." Claudette's high-pitched voice was cold and bore no trace of her mother's beautiful accent.

"Is your Mum French?" I asked, feeling obliged to say something.

Claire swept her hand through her long ginger hair and laughed mockingly, "Of course she is. Do you speak French?"

I shook my head.

"Our other cousin speaks French," she said.

"Ginger hair;" I thought, "Suspicious-looking-character number two."

The top of the stairs opened into a square from which two corridors ran in opposite directions.

Claudette opened her hands like a tour guide, "There's a bathroom here but you won't need to use it as you have your own in your room."

"I need to go now," Jessica said and I looked at her pleadingly begging her not to leave me alone.

Claudette nodded, "We'll wait for you."

I dropped my case and sat on top of it, looking around the square landing. Claudette followed my eyes to a puppet theatre from which three grotesque marionettes stared at me.

"We play here sometimes," she said but she looked too tall and serious to play.

Wooden toys peeped out from a chest in the corner where a blackboard stood on an easel, and two small desks - far too small for the long-legged cousins - bore an ominous reminder of Miss Keppel's classroom. Across the walls stuffed foxes in fish tanks climbed on branches and bared their teeth.

"Does your father hunt?" Claire said.

"Sometimes," I lied but she threw her sister a knowing glance.

Claudette extended a finger and pushed her spectacles higher up the bridge of her nose, "I didn't think there was a hunt in Brakencourt."

"Brakenfield," I said quietly.

"Brakencourt, Brakenfield, wherever," she shrugged.

When Jessica returned we picked up our cases and followed the cousins down the corridor to the right. We passed through two sets of doors before arriving at our room which was bright in the light of the midday sun but the furniture was dark like Auntie Lucy's.

"Decide between yourselves who has which bed," Claudette said, throwing open a door at the far end of the room. "This is your bathroom. You'll probably want to freshen up before lunch, so when you're ready come back the way we came and take the first door on the right at the bottom of the stairs and you'll find the dining room."

"Wow!" I said to Jessica when the cousins had gone, "It's like living in a castle!"

"Curtains round the beds!" she said, throwing herself backward onto the quilt.

We ran around opening doors and drawers, sharing out the furniture for our clothes. Everything smelt musty and damp and Jessica was reluctant to put her freshly ironed dresses in the ancient wardrobe.

She sat down on the mat beside her bed, "I don't like it here. I want to go home."

"Me too," I snuggled up to her and when she began to cry I felt tears sting my eyes, too. "At least we're together," I said and let her tears fall onto my cheek.

"Come on," she shook my shoulders, "we can't let them know we're sad. It'll upset Mum."

We went into the bathroom and washed our faces with the flannel gloves left for us on the basin. Jessica put her face to the mirror and stretched her eyes, "Can you tell I've been crying?"

Mum and Dad didn't stay for lunch. Making some excuse about not wanting to leave Peter with Uncle Max, Dad couldn't get out of

Brigthorpe quickly enough. Mum seemed more reluctant to leave us and returned three times to the doorstep to kiss us goodbye.

"Be good girls," she said the first time in a firm voice.

"We'll write to you," she said the second time more quietly.

On the third occasional her voice almost broke, "We'll pick you up as soon as we can." Then, calling her thanks to Uncle Bernard and Aunt Marie, she hurried to the car and disappeared down the hillside.

Jessica's forehead wrinkled into a deep frown, "If you frown as hard as you can," she whispered, "it stops you from crying."

We stood together frowning on the doorstep.

"Oh dear," Aunt Marie said in her beautiful voice. She crouched to our height and looked at us through deep and gentle blue eyes, "You'll feel better when you've had something to eat."

We sat on carved wooden chairs at the dining table in a room with huge French windows opening onto the courtyard. Uncle Bernard spoke to us but his words, muffled by his beard, were incomprehensible.

Aunt Marie came in carrying a big glass dish of something strangely pink.

"Do you like prawns?" she said.

"Yes thank you," Jessica smiled.

Of course we had never eaten them before. Huge pink prawns still in their shells. The cousins dived into the bowl and scattered them over their plates. Even the grown ups joined in, cracking them with their teeth and spitting out the shells. I gnawed a piece of bread and tried to be invisible. A pile of shells collected in the middle of the white tablecloth. I looked at the whiskers and thought I might be sick. I pulled my forehead into a frown hoping it might have the same effect on my stomach as it had on Jessica's tears.

"Georgie," Aunt Marie said, "you're not eating. Aren't you hungry?"

"She always picks at her food," Jessica said and immediately turned to me apologetically, "she's only got a small stomach."

I managed to swallow a prawn and waited for the next course. A single poached egg on each of our plates and another huge bowl in the middle of the table filled with a green slimy mass.

"What is it?" I said.

"Spinach," Claudette said authoritatively. "It's very good for you. It makes you grow."

Aunt Marie laughed like a melody and Uncle Bernard made an indistinguishable sound through the green slimy spinach in his beard.

"Shall we take them round the gardens after lunch?" Claudette asked as though we weren't there.

"That's a good idea."

"We'll take Boston with us."

"Boston?" Jessica said.

"Our dog."

A dog! My heart began to race.

"Jessica's afraid of dogs," I said.

"Oh he's not a big dog. He's only a pup!"

But it wasn't its size that bothered me; it was knowing that it was there; the suspense, the fear of fear; the anticipation of a sudden bark and the speed with which it would charge towards me.

Sometimes at night I terrorised Jessica by crawling from my bed across the darkened room. She heard the floorboards creak and my knees brush over the carpet, coming closer and closer. She knew I wouldn't hurt her but she lay petrified, waiting for me to pounce.

"I know you're there," she'd say and I would hear her stop breathing to listen for my approach. I could almost smell the terror on her skin; her fear of being startled; the fear of fear.

The moment the back door opened the beast ran in so quickly that I felt its weight against my legs even before I saw its shape or form. It bounded round the kitchen and into the hall then back again with even greater speed.

It *was* a big dog: a German Shepherd pup, bouncing and brimming with energy. It knew the second it saw me that I was afraid. In its wild, yellow eyes I could read its sense of its own omnipotence. I wanted to run but I stood as still as a stone, muted by the panic in my heart.

"Are you coming?" Claire said carelessly walking into the garden.

"Your dog," I mumbled, trying to sound unafraid, "is it alright?"

She glanced at the brute, "Yes, he's fine."

It ran around me in the kitchen, barking and slapping its padded feet on the marble floor, then stopped, crouching on its back legs, baring its teeth and growling at my intrusion. I backed away and almost climbed onto the cooker but the further I moved the more ferocious the dog became. It raced around in circles, jumping up, yelping and panting and putting its paws on my legs.

"He doesn't like me," I said but the cousins didn't reply. When I looked to Claire for mercy I saw pleasure on her face. She stepped back into the kitchen and leaned against the cabinet prolonging the torture for what seemed like an hour before her sister tired of the game and shouted above the yelping,

"Boston! Va t'en!"

The dog was slow to obey the command. Its thin tongue hung from its jowls and its breath came in rapid bursts.

Almost sitting on the hot plate now, I tried to form sensible thoughts.

"Dogs know when you're frightened," I recalled.

It was too late to pretend I wasn't afraid. I was paralysed with fear.

"Jessica please!" I almost screamed, "Help me!"

Claire knelt down on the floor and rubbed her hand vigorously over the dog's shiny coat as though to congratulate my tormentor, "Come on, Boston," she said, "Georgie doesn't like you."

She slipped her hand down Boston's collar and pulled him away. His paws skidded on the floor as she slid a leash into his collar and offered him a biscuit.

My heart beat slowed and pounded against my ribs in a heavy, rhythmic motion that shook the whole of my body and pulled my stomach into my chest.

"Are you alright?" Claire smiled with sham concern, "You look pale."

"I'm tired," I said, "I'm always tired when I've been in the car for a long time. Can I have a rest instead of coming round the garden?"

"No," Jessica said urgently, "you know that fresh air makes you feel better."

Claudette sighed, "If he upsets you so much, we'll leave Boston here."

Her sister pouted and whined, "Maman said we could bring him with us."

"Put him in the enclosure," Claudette said. "You can see she's unused to animals."

Claire sulkily dragged the beast from the kitchen but turned when she reached the door and stared at me callously, "Don't think we're keeping poor Boston locked up for the whole of the time you're here. Our other cousin loved you, didn't he, Boston?"

Their garden wasn't a garden; it was a park filled with separate sections from flowerbeds and herb gardens to wild, untamed meadows. We walked for miles and I thought Mum and Dad would be home by now and wondered if they missed us as I missed them.

"We'll collect the eggs since we're passing," Claudette said when we reached a series of wire-fronted hen houses. She undid a latch and directed me inside, "You get those," she pointed to a fat white hen perched on three small eggs. She frowned at my reticence, "Millie is docile, she won't hurt you."

The hen looked at me with a sideways tilt of its neck. I put my hand towards the eggs and the hen put its beak near my fingers. I jumped back. I tried again and it moved again.

"I told you get the eggs," Claudette said but I didn't answer.

"What's the matter?" Claire pushed passed me, impatiently snatching the eggs and storing them in her pockets, "Have you never seen a hen before?"

Millie was suspicious-looking-character number three.

I slept well the first night and awoke to the sound of a thousand birds singing outside. Jessica was asleep when I tiptoed into the bathroom and pushed open the long window. The air, so clear and fresh, rushed into my face and throwing back my head I saw the sky was bluer than I had ever seen it. The unkempt sun was splashed a faded yellow as though someone had taken a pot of paint and swished it across the horizon until it spilled over and dripped across the green fields sparkling with dew.

Leaning out of the window I realised, from the semicircular wall below me, that the bathroom was in a kind of turret and I was a princess awakening in a castle. Sheep grazed in the unfenced fields and some wandered up to the wall beneath the window. I watched them for a while and stretching out my arms greeted them as my loyal subjects.

I splashed water on my face and hurried back to Jessica, bounced on her bed and called, "Wake up, wake up!"

She pushed her arm out of the quilt and felt for the clock, "It's only half past four! Go back to sleep."

She rolled over and pulled the quilt across her face. I put on my shorts and set off in search of adventure.

The house was quiet and the creaking of the floorboards echoed on the walls where the black-eyed foxes stood motionless. I came to the square at the top of the stairs and fingered the marionettes, tugging their strings to make their arms wave.

"Good morning, Mr. Ugly!" I said and the puppet replied, "Good morning, Your Royal Highness."

The stairs were in darkness but sunlight shone through the windows of the hall below, throwing the shadow of their frames across the carpetless floor. I slid down the banister and followed the light. On a wide window seat overlooking a dark green shrubbery stood a large golden cage inside which sat the ugliest bird in the world. The silky blackness of its wings gave it a sombre funereal appearance like the ribboned hats of Victorian mourners. Its clawed feet clung to a thick wooden perch and it stood so still I thought it was another stuffed monument to Uncle Bernard's prowess as a hunter. When I stuck my fingers through the bars the bird let out a loud squawk.

Some doors led to rooms I had not yet explored. I wandered through them all and found them filled with curious objects: strange carvings and ornaments, vases and lamps gathered by Uncle Bernard on his travels. When I reached a small door at the end of a passage I was certain it led to a room filled with treasure. The door wasn't oblong like the ones at home. It was arched in dark wood with a big iron handle into which I slipped my hand and lifted the latch. The moment it opened I heard a scurrying of feet and a loud bark followed by a ferocious growl.

Boston flew out from the darkness and I fled in terror, too desperate to escape to take time to close the doors behind me. He was hot on my heels as I bounded up the stairs leaping to avoid his yapping jaws. He panted and barked at the same time and I heard myself calling out in a voice that seemed separate from me. I jumped over the top of the banister and the dog leaped up, catching his nose on the spherical lamp that fell to the floor with a loud crash.

On the landing I ran into the arms of Aunt Marie who held me and calmed me and called something in French that silenced the beast and sent him crawling downstairs.

"Naughty Boston," she said, "he knows he shouldn't come upstairs. Did he frighten you?"

I snuggled my face into the warmth of her stomach and felt her arms around me like a blanket. By now Uncle Bernard and the girls were standing bleary-eyed in their night-clothes in front of the puppet theatre.

"What's the matter?" whined Claire.

"Georgie's let Boston out," Claudette peered at me, trying to see without her spectacles.

Aunt Marie crouched to my height and took my face in her hands, "What were you doing?" she said softly.

I had to think quickly of an excuse, "I needed the toilet."

"Didn't Claudette tell you there's a bathroom next to your room?"

I didn't answer. Uncle Bernard drew a hand across his brow and walked slowly down the stairs, "I'll find Boston and bring a brush to sweep up the glass."

"Go back to bed," Aunt Marie told the cousins and taking my hand led me to our room.

"You're dressed very early," her voice, deepened by sleep, was even more beautiful, "but you must rest a little longer or you'll be too tired to enjoy the day."

She looked at Jessica sleeping peacefully like a good child, and opened the door to the bathroom, "When you've finished," she whispered, "go back to bed for a little while. Claudette will call you for breakfast."

She kissed the top of my head and I thought she was beautiful.

Within a week Jessica had sufficiently endeared herself to the cousins to be invited to join their games. They sat in the square on the landing and played schools with Claudette as the teacher, or wandered through the garden making perfumes in jam jars. I hung around them and sometimes they gave me a role: the audience who had to clap when the puppets performed a show, or the monitor in the classroom who was sent to bring paper and pencils, but they weren't exciting and I soon grew tired of their company.

"Our other cousin is a boy," Claudette said. "He's older than me. He goes to Boarding School not far from where you live."

"He's very handsome," Claire giggled, "Claudette wants to marry him when she grows up."

Claudette responded angrily in French then turned to Jessica, "Do you know any boys?"

"Yes," Jessica said and told them all about James.

"He's very brave;" she said, "his mother died when he was small but he never cries about it."

"Our other cousin is an orphan now," Claudette said, "both his parents are dead."

Claire listened intently to every word then looked at me with a superior smile, "I don't suppose Georgie has a boyfriend."

"She's too little," Jessica said.

I looked out of the window and thought what adventures we might have if James were to arrive with swords and bows and arrows, but the cousins in pretty ribbons and white sandals never wanted to get dirty and Claudette was too old to know how to play Crusades.

No visitors ever came to Brigthorpe Hall except the aged Madame Buisson who arrived in a thick herring bone coat three times a week to clean and tidy the place. She shuffled in and out of rooms with a duster and a gloomy expression.

"Does she never speak?" Jessica whispered to the cousins.

"She's from Paris," Claudette said carelessly, "she misses home."

"Why doesn't she go back?"

"She used to be Maman's nanny when she was a child. She doesn't know anyone else so she followed us here."

Claire put her fingers in the corner of her mouth and stretched her lips down to pull a face like Madame Buisson's. It was a good impression but I didn't laugh; I felt sorry for the strange lonely woman.

"She looks very sad," I said.

Claudette frowned at me, "It's very kind of Maman to let her work for us. She pays her far more than she's worth and she's much too old to be of any use."

I followed the old woman into the kitchen where she stood swishing the plates about in a bowl of soapy water. I gathered the breakfast cups and saucers from the table and took them to the sink.

"Hello," I said, "I'm Georgie."

She replied with a nod, took the crockery from my hands and stood in silence as I volunteered to dry up. Her hair was so tightly drawn back into a topknot it pulled with it the skin of her cheeks and temples until the bones of her face were visible like a skeleton covered in cellophane. Over a huge pink floral dress she wore a white apron like a story book grandmother.

I picked up a tea towel and on tiptoes reached for a plate from the draining board. She looked at me without saying a word and the silence was embarrassing.

"I like your pinafore," I said.

She didn't answer.

I tried again, "Do you like washing up?"

Not a word.

I asked if she liked Boston, if she'd been a suffragette, if she knew any nuns or had ever visited London. Still no reply until suddenly she dropped the dish she had been scrubbing and, wiping her hands on her apron, moved her head towards me with a disagreeable frown.

"Eh?" she said loudly as though I were deaf.

I didn't know what to say so I asked again if she'd been a suffragette and the frown deepened. She raised both her arms in the air and gesticulated wildly, gabbling away in a language I had never heard before. She plunged her hands back into the water and in something like a cross between a growl and a burp said something else. I nodded and said, 'Yes,' several times.

She didn't speak again although I followed her round all morning, dusty room after dusty room and the day dragged slowly by. At lunchtime when all her tasks were completed, she took off her apron and dug her hand into the pocket of her huge floral dress.

"Pour toi!" she said scowling, and handed me a small plastic bag of sugared almonds. She almost smiled then nodded and mimed the action of eating.

"Thank you!" I shouted because she was old and French, but she waved her hand as though she could not bear my gratitude. Any moment, I thought, she would force me into the wire-fronted chicken runs where she would feed me on sugared almonds fattening me up for a feast like the witch in *Hansel and Gretel*.

I found Aunt Marie in the garden, "Are there any jobs I can do?"

"Ah, ma petite," she put her beautiful face close to mine until I felt her breath on my cheek, "there are always jobs to do in a garden."

She talked of herbs and flowers and shrubs and I weeded small patches of soil, passed her the clippers and gathered petals and fruits in a basket.

"Will you teach me French?" I said.

She laughed like a brook and chattered in a language whose meanings I grasped by the smile in her eye.

"My Dad says that dandelions are weeds," I said, "but I think they're beautiful."

She crouched down beside me and looked at the yellow petals, "Mais oui. Comme le soleil!"

She gathered me in her arms like a bouquet of flowers and lifted me up to the sky, "There is beauty in everything," she said, "if we take time to look for it!"

Her eyes were bluer than the delphiniums that she fingered as she wandered over the lawns.

I sat alone in the summerhouse with a little pad and pencil and wrote a poem entitled, 'Com Le Solay.' If only the cousins would keep their distance and Boston would run away, I thought I might learn to be happy in this sunny world of flowers.

Uncle Bernard put his head around the door, "Ah, Jessica, there you are!"

I slipped my note pad into my pocket, "I'm Georgie."

"So you are!" he smiled vaguely. "Where are your cousins?"

"I don't know."

"It's time for their riding lesson. Aunt Marie's given me instructions to find them. Do you want to help me look?"

He held out a giant hand in which I buried my own and I skipped along beside him until we came to a wooden frame where blackcurrants grew. He picked a few from the bush and licked his lips in satisfaction, mumbling something to himself.

"Yes," I said and he gave me a handful of blackcurrants. I ate the first but it left a bitter taste that convinced me they were poisonous. When he turned away I stuffed the others into my pocket and as we walked a big red stain spread over my shorts.

"Oh! What has happened to you?" Aunt Marie ran from the doorstep.

I put my hand into my pocket and pulled out the soggy fruit. Uncle Bernard began to laugh like a volcano and his shoulders shook like an earthquake. Aunt Marie put her arm around his waist and they rocked together laughing like children.

"I love you, Aunt Marie," I said.

Claudette pulled on her riding boots and glanced at Jessica and me standing on the step, "Are they coming with us?"

"Can you ride?" Claire said.

A real horse! The excitement started in my toes and worked its way to my arms, "Yes! I can."

"She can't," Jessica said. "She's never been on a horse."

"I've been on a donkey in Scarborough."

"That's hardly riding," Claire adjusted her jodhpurs and slapped her crop on her thigh.

Jessica chose to stay with Uncle Bernard. She had, she said, never been fond of animals and was frightened of horses.

"I'm not," I said, "I love horses!"

"Non, Maman," Claire spoke in French to her mother and though I didn't understand the words I could tell by her tone that she didn't want me to come.

Aunt Marie half closed her beautiful eyes and shook her head making her ear rings dance, "It is very rude, Claire, to speak French in front of your cousins who don't understand."

"She hasn't got a hat or any clothes," Claire sulked.

Uncle Bernard fingered his beard, "We've bought dozens of hats and jodhpurs. I'm sure you'll find something to fit her."

"My niece hasn't ridden before, Mrs. Jarvis," Aunt Marie explained to the grey haired old lady who wandered in and out of the stables with buckets of water, "Do you have something for her?"

The old lady looked me up and down as though I were an exhibit in the science museum, "She's very small. Peggy would probably be best."

Aunt Marie let go of my hand and drifted away to watch the cousins jumping low fences in a sandy arena.

"Come on little 'un," Mrs. Jarvis said. "Come and meet Peggy. She's only a small pony, not skittish and she's used to beginners."

I followed her into a barn that stank of sweat and apples and manure but I didn't mind the smell; I thought of knights and battlefields.

Peggy was enjoying champing the straw and refused to come when called.

"Come on, girl," the old lady said, "there's work to be done."

She lifted a saddle from a hook on the wall and strapped it round Peggy's girth. The closer I got, the bigger Peggy grew until I thought I might walk underneath her without banging my head on her belly.

"Right, little 'un," Mrs. Jarvis dragged the horse from her stall, "climb up here on this fence and I'll sort out your stirrups."

I tried to mount like a cowboy, swinging my leg high behind me but it took a shove from the old lady to get me seated. As Mrs. Jarvis played with the buckle and adjusted the leathers, I held tightly to the reins, but the horse hadn't satisfied her hunger and insisted on lowering her head to champ at the straw on the ground. I yanked the reins to regain my balance and the pony made a loud whinnying noise.

"No! No! No!" Mrs. Jarvis said sternly, "Don't pull on the reins like that, you'll hurt her. She has a very delicate mouth and she feels the slightest tug of the bit. Speak to her, she responds to that."

"Hello, Peggy," I said.

Mrs. Jarvis led me into the yard, tied a guiding rope to the pony and handed the end to a young boy who stood in the middle of a field for half an hour as Peggy and I walked round and round in circles.

"Oh, James," I whispered on the breeze, "I wish you could see me!"

From the height of the horse I looked over the fields where the cousins were cantering and jumping over tree trunks and bars.

"Do you want to trot?" the boy said.

I nodded.

"Trot on!"

For the rest of the lesson I bounced up and down until my bottom felt sore and the chinstrap grazed my neck. Whatever I did made no difference to the pony. If I shook the reins she didn't go faster, if I dug in my heels she never stepped out of line. Just round and round and round the endless circle until I grew dizzy. I patted her neck and stroked her mane but she didn't respond at all.

"You ride well," Aunt Marie said, lifting me from the pony. "You kept your heels down and your back straight. That's good."

Claudette and Claire didn't speak to me but gushed to their mother about the boys on the other horses and how well they had jumped today.

I wriggled around in the back of the car, trying to keep the weight from my saddle-sore bottom and planned to write a letter to James to tell him I'd been riding.

"Your mother phoned while you were out," Uncle Bernard said as we pulled off our boots on the doorstep. "Peter's going for surgery tomorrow."

A sudden fear gripped my heart, "Is he alright?"

"Yes, he's fine," Uncle Bernard nodded, "but it's a big operation. They think he'll be in theatre for several hours."

I went upstairs and rummaged under my pillow for my rosary beads, "Please God make him better and I'll always be good. I'll never complain about anything ever again."

I waited for an answer. God had to tell me Peter would be alright.

"Please God, make him better. Let him walk again."

I *needed* an answer but God was silent. I uncovered my pocket Bible and opened it at random for a message. My finger came down in the Gospel of John:

"*Martha said to Jesus, 'If you had been here my brother would not have died.'*"

It was a sign, a message from God. Peter needed me. I had to go to London.

Chapter 6

Aunt Marie floated serenely into the garden and pruned the dead leaves from her plants. For all my explanations she couldn't grasp the urgency with which I needed to go to London.

"Her head is filled with flowers," I thought. "She's too beautiful to understand. Only ugly people take time to consider important things."

I thought about important things and I would grow wise and ugly like Auntie Philomena. Jessica with her perfumes and parasol would grow up to look like Aunt Marie; her face unmarked by the wrinkles of contemplation.

Aunt Marie handed me a bluebell and offered to let me flatten it in her press, stick it onto a card and send it to Peter.

"I need to be there," I insisted, "I have to go."

"I understand how you feel about your brother," she said softly. "My brother and I were also very close."

"Does your brother live in France?"

"No," she looked across the roses and gently stroked their petals, "he lived in England until he died last year."

Poor beautiful Aunt Marie. She was too beautiful to suffer.

"Was he very old?" I said.

She shook her head, "He had an accident."

"Did he fall off a roof?"

"No. It was a road accident. He and his wife were both killed."

I put my hand into hers, "That's sad."

"Yes. But I know he's happy now in heaven."

"Heaven," I whispered and explained the Bible message and told her the whole story of the stolen candlestick.

"What sort of God," she said, widening her beautiful blue eyes, "would punish one child for another's mistake? What sort of God would punish anyone for a mistake?"

"It wasn't God. It was the devil. But God's stronger than the devil so if God lets Peter walk again, I've promised to be a nun."

She smiled as though to repress laughter, "Being a nun may be a very good way of life," she said, "but I don't think God expects you to make him such promises when you're so young."

"Saint Rose of Lima," I explained, "dedicated her whole life to God when she was only a child. She made herself ugly so people wouldn't like her and she never ate any fruit."

Aunt Marie put her hands on my face in the gesture I loved, "God doesn't need another Rose of Lima. He wants you to be Georgie, just as you are."

Poor, beautiful Aunt Marie, she had no concept of my theology. Nothing I might say would help her understand. I should have to find my own way to London.

"Jess," I said when we climbed into bed, "do you want to come with me to visit Peter tomorrow?"

"Don't be daft, London's miles away."

"I have to see him. "

"You can't."

"With the money that Dad gave us, we could get a train ticket."

"Go to sleep," she said.

But I couldn't sleep. There was too much to think about. I had seen Brigthorpe Station on the way to the stables and though it was some distance from the Hall, I knew it was light before four-thirty and I was certain I could walk it in an hour.

When Jessica's breath flowed in a deep regular motion, I crawled out of bed, packed some clothes in my rucksack and counted the pound notes in my purse. Dad, afraid to be outdone by Uncle Bernard, had given us plenty of money for our stay.

"If they take you out," he said, "make sure you offer to pay your own way."

With the pocket Bible and rosary beads carefully tucked into the side pocket, I dragged my rucksack into the bathroom, hid it beneath the basin and crept back to bed.

"Four o'clock, four o'clock, four o'clock," I said.

It was something Peter had told me, "Say the time you want to wake up three times before you fall asleep and you wake up at exactly that time."

A muddy pathway led from the kitchen to the series of huge wire cages inside which the hens were asleep. Beyond was an apple orchard and beyond that endless fields as far as the eye could see. The place wasn't wild and exciting, it was quiet and gloomy and I wondered how I'd come to find myself alone in the grounds of a mansion a million miles from anywhere.

The road into Brigthorpe went on forever, punctuated occasionally by yet another ancient milestone half buried by long grass. No one was working in the fields; no vehicles passed as I trudged until my feet stumbled over each other. Loneliness clung like a fog and the deeper I delved into it the darker it became. I ate some of the bread and jam I'd packed into the rucksack but it only increased my thirst and I'd not thought to bring a drink. On and on and on, field after field and still no life, no movement in the dew-drenched ferns, only the sound of the wind hissing through the trees.

 At quarter to six by the station clock I reached the village and, fearing that a milk man or farmer might become suspicious of a child alone at that time in the morning, I hid behind a dustbin and waited for the ticket office to open.

 Trains came and went without stopping while I ate another slice of bread and jam. I caught a spider in my hand and watched it crawl over my fingers until people began to gather on the platform. I shook the dust from my clothes and mingled with the passengers; men with brief cases and women in smart suits. Nobody asked for a ticket and nobody seemed to notice a little girl travelling alone.

 I looked out of the window and watched the fields rushing by.

 'If you had been here, my brother would not have died.'

 I slipped my hand into the side pocket of the rucksack and gripped the crucifix dangling from my rosary beads.

 "Please God, let me reach him in time."

 I counted seven country stations like a condemned prisoner counting the hours until dawn. At every station I sighed and with every sigh came a deeper longing to get off the train and run away to the days before Peter broke his back.

If Peter wasn't healed I could see my whole life stretching in front of me; tomorrow and the next day and the day after and all the days ahead going on and on like the stations or the Stations of the Cross.

At last the countryside vanished into a mass of blackened buildings, white towers and high rise flats. The passengers gathered their belongings and moved into the aisle. I stood among them looking out of the window for a sign that said 'LONDON.' Busy commuters rushed across the platform between guards and porters. An oily-black pigeon alighted on the sign: 'LEEDS'.

My heart sank. London was a million miles away.

Carried by the tide of travellers down steps and under tunnels, I reached the exit where uniformed rail men collected tickets. I slipped through the barrier in a mass of bigger bodies and found myself in front of the ticket office.

"A child's ticket to London, please."

"Are you travelling on your own?"

I pointed into the crowd, "My Dad's waiting for me. He's already got his ticket."

I gave the woman all my money and she handed me a little change.

"What time does it go?"

She looked at her watch, "Twenty minutes."

I wandered aimlessly dragging my rucksack behind me. The blank faces of strangers were hard and unapproachable and I was afraid to ask directions to the train. Upstairs, downstairs, Platform 6, Platform 9, Platform 12 and trains speeding in and out to everywhere but London.

"My Dad says where do we get the train to London?" I asked a guard.

He waved his hands in the opposite direction and I dragged the rucksack over the dusty floor. More stairs, more and more bodies and an increasing loneliness in my heart. I wanted to be back in bed, waking up and seeing Jessica wiping sleep from her face. I wanted to hear Aunt Marie laugh like a brook and see the sunlight dancing in her eyes.

"Which train is it to London?" I asked a porter who pushed a trolley across the platform.

"Can't you read?" he said aggressively, pointing to a train that said 'KING'S CROSS.'

"No, I need to get to London."

"London King's Cross," he stamped away across the platform.

I climbed into the train and went to sleep.

'KING'S CROSS.' London was enormous and exciting! I smiled at my freedom and my courage; when Aunt Marie heard what I'd done she'd wonder at my bravery and James would give me a medal. But I was hot after the journey and afraid I might die of thirst. I bought a hot dog from a vendor and a bottle of milk from a newsagent's.

"Can you tell me where the hospital is?" I asked the woman behind the counter.

She shuffled the newspapers in front of her, "Which hospital?"

"The one in London."

"Which one?" she said in a strange southern accent, "St. Thomas's, the Royal Free, St. Bartholomew's, Guy's. Which do you want?"

Brakenfield had only one small Cottage Hospital and I had thought that London would be the same.

"Are you hurt?" she said, looking up from her papers.

"No. I've come to see my brother. He's having an operation on his back."

She came around the counter and walked to the door, leaning out of the shop and pointing up the street, "If you go up there you'll get to University College Hospital. Is that what you want?"

"Yes, thank you," I said.

"Hang about," she caught my shoulder as I turned to walk away, "aren't you a bit young to be wandering round on your own?"

"I'm with my Dad," I said, "he's waiting for me over there," I waved my arm in front of me.

I followed the direction she had indicated but I saw no sign of a hospital. I turned back and wandered through a dozen streets, round in circles and up and down the same pavements. The high buildings that surrounded me grew taller and I walked more quickly, going nowhere and realising that I was tired and hot and hungry and alone in a massive city. I came to a gate that led to a small park where the air was cool and refreshing after the smog of the station and the streets. A drinking fountain sprayed clear sparkling water and I splashed it eagerly over my face and hands. I pulled off my shoes and cupped my hands to sprinkle water onto my toes. I had no idea what time it was but my stomach told me I needed to eat. I sat down on a bench, shaded by a tall tree and took the last remaining slice of jam and bread. Although cars and buses growled on the road behind me, the park was peaceful. I half-closed my eyes against the sun and lay down on the bench.

"Hello," a man's face appeared over my head, "can I join you?"

I sat up and wriggled along the bench.

"What's your name?"

I bent down to pick up my shoes and remembered my new identity, "Rose," I said, "Rose Lima."

"What are you doing here?"

He pulled out a packet of fruit Polos and offered me one but I shook my head.

"I'm visiting my brother. He's in hospital."

"Is he?" his voice was gentle and quiet. "Which one?"

"I can't remember the name."

"Perhaps I can help you," he smiled and unbuttoned the cuffs of his turquoise shirt, "I'm a doctor. What's he in hospital for?"

"He's having an operation on his back to make him walk again."

"Right," said the man knowledgeably, "I know where he'll be then. What's his name?"

"Peter."

"Ah yes, Peter. I know him well. He looks a bit like you, doesn't he, Rose?"

"Does he?"

"Spitting image of you. I've been looking after Peter."

"Wow!" I said.

Now I knew for certain God had answered all my prayers. He had brought me here to the park to find the doctor who would cure Peter.

"Is he going to be alright? Will he walk again?"

"He's going to be fine!" The doctor smiled and put his arm around my shoulder, "Do you want to go and see him?"

Everything was going to be alright. I put on my socks and shoes and tied my laces while the doctor looked over my head and around the deserted park. He put out a hand for me to hold and led me back through the gate.

"My name's Sam," he said, "and if you like you can call me Uncle Sam."

"Okay," I said but I didn't call him anything.

We walked back through busy streets and over crossings. His long legs strode quickly until I couldn't keep pace and he dragged me behind him.

"It's a long way," I said when we had been walking forever.

He stopped and looked at his watch, then digging his hand into his pocket, pulled out a wallet.

"It's too early to go to the hospital," he said, "they won't let you in until visiting time. Do you fancy some chips while we're waiting?"

I didn't want to wait any longer. But he was a doctor who knew the hospital rules and I was hungry.

Sam didn't say much when we sat in the snack bar, faced with a plate of pale French fries. He took hold of the plastic tomato and squeezed ketchup like blood all over his chips and stared at me as I ate. When he reached for the salt I thought it quite odd that a doctor's nails should be so encrusted in grime. His fat stubby fingers were out of proportion to the rest of his small hand and when he rolled back his sleeve I saw a mermaid tattooed on his forearm.

"What time is visiting time?" I said.

"Later. Eat your chips." He continued to stare and I began to feel uncomfortable.

I ate more slowly, wondering what would happen when I'd finished. When I looked at his face he smiled at me and, pushing his plate across the table, came out from his seat to sit beside me.

He put his arm around my shoulder again, "Are you enjoying your chips, Rosie?"

I nodded and tried to smile when his fingers ran over my neck. I was jammed in my place between him and the wall and the growing anxiety that urged me to leave was heightened when he moved closer and whispered, "It's a long time until visiting time. Why don't we go back to my house for a while?"

I looked at the woman who was wiping the tables but she paid no attention to me.

"Is something wrong, Rosie?" His fingers were twisting my hair into curls and his face was so close to my own I could smell the stale odour of his breath.

"I need the toilet."

His eyes narrowed in an instant of annoyance but he blinked away the expression and smiled, "Okay, but don't be long."

He stood up and let me pass and I hurried into the toilets praying that some kindly lady might walk in. Nobody came for a long time then the woman who had been wiping the tables stuck her head around the door.

"It's okay, she's here," she called to Sam whose face appeared over her shoulder. "Your Uncle was worried about you when you were such a long time,"

I tried to explain, "He isn't...."

"Come on, Rosie, Peter will be waiting," Sam said loudly, taking my hand and dragging me from the door. "Her brother's in hospital," he told the woman as he pushed me out of the cafe, "and we're off to see him."

We were back on the street before I could say anything and Sam's hand gripped me more tightly than when he first led me from the park. I slipped my other hand into the side pocket of my rucksack and felt for my rosary beads.

"Where are we going?"

Sam walked faster and faster.

"Is the hospital this way?"

I knew for certain now that he wasn't a doctor; for all I knew he wasn't really called Sam, and I sensed as an animal senses a kind of danger though I didn't know what he planned to do to me. I was safe as long as we stayed in the crowd and instinct suggested I should be quiet. The tightness with which he gripped my hand displayed his strength and I doubted he'd fall as easily as the boys in judo lessons in the basement gym. I clung to the crucifix in my rucksack until it dug into my skin.

He took me down a stairway, which led underground and without letting go of my hand bought two tickets for the tube. Down, down wooden escalators into what might have been hell. I inhaled the smoky air and diesel fumes, breathlessly struggling to keep pace with him.

"Does this go to the hospital?" I said hopelessly as we stood on the crowded platform.

"Yes." He didn't look at me.

When a train arrived and the door flew open he pushed me ahead of him into the crowded aisle. Strangers clung like monkeys to the handles that hung from the ceiling. Sam reached up to take hold while resting his other hand like a vice on my shoulder. More people piled in and I saw my chance. I wriggled from his grasp and slithered between the bodies, leaping between the doors as they started to close. Sam scowled at me through the glass then the train disappeared into a tunnel and I stood breathless on the platform, the crucifix digging into my palm.

Afraid that like some monster from a film Sam might emerge from the tunnel, I ran back to the escalator and followed the exit signs until I came to a barrier which I couldn't pass for want of a ticket to slip into the slot. Desperate to escape from the claustrophobic station air, I crawled on my knees beneath the barrier and was halfway through when my eyes met with a pair of black shiny shoes and the long legs of a man in uniform.

"What do you think you're doing?" his hand came down and pulled me to my feet.

"I want to get out."

"Where's your ticket?"

"I haven't got one."

"There's no free rides here," he said, leading me out of the stream of travellers, "If you ride on the train you have to pay for a ticket."

"I've not been on the train."

"Oh no? So what are you doing here then?"

"Going to see my brother. He's in hospital and I have to be there."

The man smiled, "Do you think I was born yesterday?" and he called to a policeman standing by the ticket booth, "Excuse me, Officer," his voice was dramatic and obviously intended to frighten me but he winked at the policeman as he spoke, "we seem to have a fare dodger here."

The policeman slowly came over and took a notebook from his pocket.

"I caught her trying to crawl through the barrier," the man said. "Can I leave it with you?"

The policeman nodded and I thought he was going to arrest me. He and the railway man began to talk.

"Travelling without a ticket is tantamount to theft. Children have to learn..."

I didn't wait to hear what I should learn. Arrest would mean prison and forcible feeding. I slipped between their legs and lost myself in the crowd. Tripping over bags and feet and banging into elbows, I scurried here and there, backwards and forwards until the sunlight met my eyes and I could breathe again.

Policemen stood on every corner while suspicious looking characters like Sam walked through the streets. I hid in doorways, peeping round lamp posts, searching for signs to the hospital. I couldn't ask directions now. There was probably a warrant for my arrest and soon my picture would appear on posters in shop windows:

'WANTED ! HAVE YOU SEEN THIS FARE DODGER?'

London wasn't exciting. It was cruel and ugly and unwelcoming. While I cowered behind shop displays and sat behind trees the hours passed until the shops began to close. The sun sank and the sounds of the city changed. The rush of the traffic and the bustle of the daytime faded into sounds of celebration. Music from bars, chattering in restaurants and I walked on, frightened of every footstep in the street. Every man looked like Sam whose grimy fingers might at any moment reach out from the crowd and seize me by the throat.

I found myself in a coach station and wandered around for a while, spending what was left of my money in a drinks machine. I would never find the hospital now; I might as well go home. I read the destinations on all the coaches. None said Brakenfield or Brigthorpe; they were going to distant cities: Newcastle, Birmingham, Bristol. People in groups piled on; families, parents and children. I wanted to be with my family. I sat between the drinks machine and the wall and cried.

The crowds thinned and I was alone amid the diesel and exhaust fumes. A man came from an office and, calling 'Good night' to his mates, locked the Waiting Room. His mates disappeared into the darkness and the man with the keys came towards me. He didn't see me but stopped by one of the coaches. He pressed a button and the door opened and he walked up and down inside for a while then re-appeared to lock the station office. I watched him go.

I was cold and tired and more frightened than ever. Rats would come out at night and if I fell asleep they would gnaw through my skin to the bone. If my eyes closed, Sam would find me and carry me off to his den to devour me like an owl devours a mouse. I could feel the pain of my intestines splattered over my body and see the blood oozing from my wounds.

"Please, please, please God, look after me!" I clung more tightly to my crucifix. Then an idea came to me! I'd seen the button that the man had pressed to board the coach; it would be safer inside than out. I walked along the line and pressed the buttons at every door but none of them opened until I came to the fourth.

A whooshing sound like a thousand vampire bats made me jump back in terror. I threw my arms over my head and waited for their attack. Nothing happened. I peeped through my fingers and saw the door had opened. I climbed aboard and made my way to the back seat where, closing my eyes, I curled up in a ball and fell asleep.

Scratching noises like the sound of a rat scurrying over wood made me sit upright. The dim reflection of the lamps in the coach station had gone and now the light of morning made everything clear. I peeped between the headrests and looked down the aisle. A tall black man was singing to himself as he swept between the seats with a wiry brush. He was moving closer and closer and I tried to cower beneath the seat but, sliding to the floor, found my hideout blocked by metal heaters. There was nowhere to go.

The singing stopped mid-bar with a sudden gasp, "What the…"

Two huge brown eyes stared down at me.

"Hello," I said.

All I saw was the enormity of his smile. Each tooth was white and straight but not one touching its neighbour so that when he smiled his mouth looked like a zebra crossing. He started to laugh, to shake and giggle like a little boy and he leaned the brush against a seat and sat down beside me. His smile took a long time to fade shrinking so slowly that I couldn't tell when it ended

"How did you get in here?" he said.

"Through the door."

He was talking to himself not to me when he said in a West Indian accent, "Never in my life! I've heard of babies in telephone boxes but this!"

"I'm sorry," I said and he laughed again.

"Where do you live?"

"Brakenfield."

He shook his head. He'd never heard of it.

"Come on," he gesticulated with a huge pink palm, "come with me."

Not another Sam, I prayed, but I had no choice but to follow. I dragged my bag from the seat and walked behind him towards the office where he showed me to a chair and went to talk with the men behind a desk. The clock above them showed quarter to six. I yawned and wiped the sleep from my eyes.

The men came round the desk and asked me lots of questions; all of them staring at me as though I were in the freak show.

"Must be a runaway," one of them said at last and moved away to the telephone, "I'm phoning the police."

I wondered if a runaway was the same as an outlaw; they'd probably seen the WANTED posters with pictures of my face.

"What's your name, love?" a bald man said.

I thought it safer to stick with my new identity, "Rose Lima."

"Well you wait there," he said, "and we'll sort you out."

I sat on the chair debating whether it was worth another escape but I was tired of running. The man came back with a smile and a plate of toast, "There you are, breakfast!"

I mumbled a 'thank you' and nibbled the crust until a policewoman appeared.

"Hello, Rose," she said, crouching to my height, "what have you been up to?"

I should probably go to prison for twenty years and no one would know where I was or come to visit me. Peter might be dead and I'd never see my family again.

I frowned to stop the tears that were welling in my eyes, "My brother's in hospital. I came to London to see him but I don't know where the hospital is."

"I see," her face was kind as though she believed my story. "What's your brother's name?"

I ran my fist across my eye to wipe away a tear. I couldn't remember his alias, "Peter Meadows."

"Meadows? And you must be Georgie?"

The sound of my name made me feel less afraid. I belonged; I was real again.

"We've been looking all over for you." Her radio crackled with the sounds of police messages I'd heard in Peter's room. She spoke into it but I didn't listen. I was too weary to care what happened now.

"The police in Brigthorpe contacted us yesterday when your aunt found you were missing. Everyone's been searching for you."

"Does my Mum know?" I said.

"Come on," she led me outside, "we'll take you to the hospital."

Chapter 7

Peter couldn't walk. He pushed himself onto his legs and balanced for five seconds but he couldn't take a step.

"There are other doctors," Mum said, "and they're making new breakthroughs all the time. We just have to be patient."

"Don't give up," Dad said, "maybe with more physiotherapy it'll happen."

But it didn't happen and Peter gave up trying. I went to church and stood in front of the altar, "You cured all those lepers and people with horrible diseases. Why won't you cure Peter?"

The Good Shepherd smiled and never said a word.

"You're not kind," I said, "you don't care about us!" And I walked from the church without genuflecting but that night as I lay in bed afraid of the dark, I felt for my rosary beads, "I'm sorry," I said, "I didn't mean it. *Please* make Peter walk again."

I built a hermitage behind the shed and resolved to become a Contemplative Carmelite like Theresa of Lisieux. I borrowed her *Story of a Soul* from Auntie Philomena's bookcase,

'I had seen earth's beauties, now I had no eyes but for the beauties of heaven; and if it would help other souls to share these with me I was ready to shut myself away in a prison.'

If it would help Peter to walk again I was ready to shut myself away in my hermitage but when it rained the roof leaked so I gathered my books and holy pictures and joined the others sitting in the dining room.

"When we grow up," James said, "I'm going to buy a restaurant with a wine bar like my Dad's. I'll serve the drinks and you can be in charge of entertainment."

"Yeah," Peter said and drew a ground plan, "we'll have a stage here and tables all round the front."

"I'll be a waitress," Jessica said, "and when we make a lot of money I'll buy an apartment in Poppy Field Court."

"My Dad could buy ten apartments in Poppy Field Court tomorrow if he wanted," Alan said.

I knelt up on a chair and looked at the plan, "Can I be part of it?"

"They don't have nuns in wine bars."

But already I doubted my vocation. God hadn't cured Peter yet and I wondered if he ever would.

"What shall we call it?" Peter said.

"*The Music Room?*"

Jessica entwined her hair around a finger, "How about *James's Bar*? Or *Jessica's*?"

"*Georgie's* sounds better."

"You won't be there," Alan said. "You'll be locked in a convent with all your hair shaved off."

I took a piece of paper from Peter's file pad and drew a ground plan of a convent, counting the number of cells along the corridor, "If I had a wine bar," I said, "I'd call it *The Counting House.*"

"Yeah," James squeezed my arm, "*The Counting House*. I like that. Well done, Georgie!"

At Easter, James and Alan went to America with their Dad whose brother was a millionaire in Rio. Throughout their three-week absence Jessica sat at the window, threading beads onto a string and looking at the aeroplanes flying overhead.

"He's been gone so long," she sighed dramatically raising her hand to her forehead, "I'm so lonely."

She thought she was Ingrid Bergman in a Sunday afternoon film.

"Don't be so mawkish," I said, "he'll be back in thirteen days."

I knew because I ticked them off each evening in my diary.

"Silly baby," she huffed, "you're too young to understand."

Peter sat in his room trying to make up tunes on his guitar.

"Shall we write an opera?" I said.

"Okay. You do the words and I'll do the music."

"It's about a beautiful French woman who meets a Russian soldier in a garden filled with flowers. They dance and she decides to run away with him but in London she gets kidnapped by a wicked count called Sam."

Peter looked surprised but said, "Okay."

I had never told anyone about Sam.

In two hours we created three lines:

'The guests are coming down the path, Marie.

    'Yes I can see.

'Pray look again, Marie.'

"That's a good start," Peter said.

I sang it for Jessica.

"It's boring," she said, "really boring."

"It's not as boring as you."

She looked at me and yawned dramatically.

The doorbell rang with a loud commotion downstairs.

"Max," I heard Mum's voice, and hung over the banister to listen, "whatever is it?"

"It's Auntie Philie. She's had a do."

"A do?" Mum said.

Jessica and I stared at one another for a moment then hurried down to the kitchen to hear the news.

"One minute she was fine," Uncle Max was saying, "and the next she just flopped."

I wriggled towards him. His breath smelt of whiskey and his eyes were as red as his nose.

"Is she dead?" I said.

Mum pushed me aside, "Have you called the doctor?"

Uncle Max danced from one leg to the other, huffing and squashing his cheeks with his fingertips, "I didn't know what to do so I came round here."

"Don't worry, Max," Mum said gently, "I'll go round."

Dad was out at work so we had to go too.

Auntie Philomena hung over the side of her chair. Mum helped Uncle Max to straighten her up but she flopped again. Her mouth curled down at the corner and a thin stream of dribble dripped down her chin and onto the carpet.

"What's up with her?" I said as we waited for the doctor.

"Looks like a stroke."

A stroke? God had struck her down!

"Is she going to die?"

"Make yourself useful," Mum said, "go upstairs and pack some of the clothes from her wardrobe."

It seemed insensitive.

"She might not die," I said, "shouldn't we wait and see what the doctor says before we get rid of her clothes?"

"Clothes for the hospital, stupid," Jessica said, "Nighties and things."

"Come and help me," I said.

I didn't want to go upstairs on my own; it meant passing the spooky bathroom where a mirror threw reflections of statues across the landing. Auntie Philomena collected saints like other people collect dolls; they stood in huge glass globes and each had a different coloured candle, which she lit on their feast days.

"It's a wonder the house doesn't burn down!" Dad said on the Feast of All Saints.

Keeping close to Jessica, I climbed the stairs and peeped under the bath. It stood on little legs that opened into claws; perhaps she was so wary of the devil that she had to be sure he hadn't come disguised as a bath.

Jessica threw open the bedroom door and I saw his face.

I let out a scream of panic, "It's the devil! It's the devil from the haunted lodge! He's struck her down! She'll probably die tonight."

Jessica held my arm as I tried to escape down the stairs, "It's only a picture," she said, "it's the Sacred Heart."

I wriggled to break free, "Don't go in there. The last time he saw me Peter fell off the roof."

She hesitated a moment then closed the door, "We'll say we couldn't find any clothes."

It was suppertime on Ward 2 when we arrived on Sunday evening. Auntie Philomena was sitting on a plastic chair with a plate of dinner pushed up to her chest. Liver, green beans and potatoes. She was recovering well, the doctor said, but something about her had changed. I noticed as soon as I saw her; there was something strange about the way that she smiled. Auntie Philomena never smiled; she didn't know how. Yet here she was toothlessly grinning at everyone who passed and sometimes at no one at all.

We walked to her bedside and dutifully kissed her but she'd forgotten our names.

"It's time I was going," she said, "I've things to do."

Dad looked embarrassed and whispered to Mum who sat down on the edge of the bed.

"How are you feeling?" she said.

Auntie Philomena smiled and nodded.

I leaned towards her ear, "Are you better?"

"Are you?" Auntie Philomena said.

Jessica pulled a face.

Mum prodded the liver with the bent prongs of the fork, "Are you hungry?"

"Yes," Auntie Philomena said, "you have that."

They had taken out her dentures and left them in a pot on the locker beside her glasses. She looked old and frail without them; tiny in the vast hospital ward.

"Georgie," Mum said, "go to that sink and rinse her teeth."

Jessica's lip curled in disgust.

"You do it," I said to her.

"She told you."

"Go with her, Jessica," Mum said.

I took the dentures to the sink and, holding them in my fingertips, rinsed them under the tap. They were slimy and grinned up at me like the smile of a skeleton. I closed my eyes and held them at arm's length.

"That's a good girl," said a passing nurse, "you are helpful aren't you!"

She spoke to me like the nurses spoke to Peter when he was in hospital. Jessica laughed when she'd gone, "You are helpful aren't you!"

I moved the teeth up and down near Jessica's face.

"Stop it!" she said so I chattered the teeth together and chased her up the ward trying to bite her bottom. I dropped the grin into the pot and held it out to Auntie Philomena.

"Put your teeth in," Mum said, "then you can have your tea."

Auntie Philomena took the pot and pushed it towards me, "Do you want one?"

Jessica laughed.

"It's your teeth," Mum said, "your *teeth*!"

"No I've not had my tea."

Mum shook her head and fished around in the pot picking out the top set and trying to stick them into Auntie Philomena's mouth but she swung her arm defensively in front of her face, "Get off," she cried, "you're hurting me. Leave me alone. You're wicked, you are, wicked!"

Mum moved back quickly as a nurse passed with a sympathetic smile.

Auntie Philomena shoved the plate away, "When does the bus go?"

"Do you know where you are?" Mum said into her ear.

"Yes."

"You're in hospital."

Auntie Philomena's brow furrowed into a confused frown, "I'd better be off. I've to get to Mass."

"You're in hospital," Mum said again, taking her hand and squeezing it gently. "You've been poorly, but you're getting better now."

Auntie Philomena hummed to herself until her eyes began to close and she dozed in the chair.

The ward smelt of liver, old dinners and commodes. I looked around at the faces of the other patients. Some were sitting up, chatting with relations as they ate their tea, but one woman lay in bed, shaking and crying out as though in pain. A nurse went to her bedside and ran a hand across her cheek but her cries continued. Slowly the clattering of knives on plastic plates subsided and those who had no visitors slept in their chairs, their heads slumped like Auntie Philomena's over their chests, their mouths open or clenched as they chewed their gums.

"Excuse me," Mum said to a passing nurse, "could I have a word about my aunt?"

The nurse leaned backwards against Auntie Philomena's chair, "She's doing well. She'll probably be home in a day or two."

Mum looked horrified, "After a stroke?"

"No," the nurse said calmly, "it wasn't a stroke. The doctors think it was a T.I.A.. It has similar symptoms to a stroke but it's not so severe and the effects are usually short term."

"Right," Mum nodded but I knew that she didn't understand.

"Are you the carer?" the nurse said.

Mum shook her head quickly, "She's normally independent. She goes out, shopping and to church,"

The nurse nodded.

"She seems so..." Mum hesitated as though she didn't dare say the word, "confused today. She's not normally like this."

"It's probably being in hospital," the nurse said reassuringly. "A change of environment often has this effect on elderly people. Once she settles, she'll start to pick up."

"I like Auntie Philomena more now she's bonkers," I said as we left the ward.

"Georgie," Mum snapped, "that's an awful thing to say!"

"I know what you mean," Jessica whispered, "she's not so scary."

"I didn't have much faith in what that nurse said," Mum told Dad as we drove home.

"Brakenfield Hospital's rubbish," Peter said, "they never make anybody better."

"I know," I said, "there aren't any good doctors here. They can't do anything. If I were a doctor..."

Then it came to me: the answer to everything! If those doctors couldn't do it, I'd do it myself! I'd become a doctor and cure Peter's legs.

I climbed onto my bike and sped to the library where I found a book called *How My Body Works*.

Mrs. Houghton looked surprised when she stamped it, "No saints or suffragettes today?"

"No. I'm going to be a doctor."

I bought an exercise book from Mr. Fitton's Paper Shop and copied down the names of all our bones.

Jessica came in and looked over my shoulder, "What's that?"

She picked up the book and turned to the chapter on babies. She held it in front of her face for a long time and her eyes were wide open as she read.

"I'm telling of you," she said as she closed the book and put it down on my bed, "I'm telling Mum you're reading rude books."

She went downstairs and I turned over the pages to see what she'd read. There was a picture of a woman with an upside down baby inside her but it wasn't as interesting as bones.

"Mum," Jessica said at teatime, "how do you have a baby?"

Mum clattered the plates together and became suddenly very busy, "You have to pray very hard."

I wondered if I'd overdone the praying and hoped an upside down baby wasn't lying inside me.

Jessica knelt in front of the bookcase and pulled out the books she'd outgrown.

"Do you want these," she said, "they're too babyish for me?"

She only read boring books now: *Debby Lane, Student Nurse; Sally Brown, Air Hostess*.

I looked at her *Famous Five* collection but I didn't want them. I'd read *Bluebeard* from the library and it had scared me so much I'd had to hide it in the bottom of my sock drawer so the evil man couldn't escape and murder me along with his wives. *The Famous Five* was dull in comparison.

"No," I said and Jessica dropped the books into the bin.

"Someone might want them;" I said, "you could sell them."

It was a good idea. There were so many things round the house that no one used. We could put them together and sell them at the gate.

"Who'd want your old rubbish?" Jessica said.

"People buy things at jumble sales. We could go round and collect things from people and sell them for Brakenfield Hospital. They could buy some new doctors and Peter won't have to go to London again."

Peter liked the idea and we elected him to broach the subject with Mum.

"We'll see," she said which was as good as a 'yes'.

For a week we visited neighbours and relations, gathering all the junk that nobody wanted. We bought some little white stickers and priced each item carefully. Jessica made a sign to hang on the gatepost:

"SALE TODAY for BRAKENFIELD COTTAGE HOSPITAL."

"What are you putting in the sale?" she said.

I'd been through all my toys but could find nothing I didn't need.

"Peter's given his jigsaws and I've given my books. You've not given anything," she said.

I went through my toys again and came downstairs with my violin.

"You can't sell that!" Dad said.

"I can't play it. There isn't a bow."

"Well you're not selling it. It cost a lot of money."

Dad had funny notions about things that were unimportant.

We stood behind a pasting table at the gate and waited for the customers to arrive. Hoagey came first and bought a pile of old plates that Uncle Max had donated. They were chipped and cracked.

"She'll use them for baking apple pies!" I whispered to Peter and he laughed but we saw them later on her lawn filled with bacon rind and breadcrumbs for the birds.

People came in groups. For a long time there was no one, then everybody arrived at once, fingering the objects and examining the price tags. Old people and people with children bought the most. One woman came by and bought the complete set of *The Famous Five*. As she watched the woman stuff the books into a shopping bag, a pained expression spread over Jessica's brow. She'd changed her mind and didn't want to sell.

"Never mind," I said, "it's all for a good cause."

"Yeah, well why don't you give something then?" she snapped.

I peeped around the gate but no one was coming.

"We should have advertised it better," Peter said.

I hurried down the drive for a stick and the dustbin lid then climbed onto the wall. BANG! BANG! BANG! It made an amazing noise.

"Roll up! Roll up!" I shouted, "Best sale in town!"

But a banging on the window drowned the sound of my makeshift drum. Mum was gesticulating frantically, "Stop it! Stop it!" she mouthed through the glass.

"Silly baby," Jessica said, "you'll drive everyone away."

I stood up on the wall and looked down the road, "Someone's coming!"

It was a family group. A fat little boy and a long older girl running ahead of their parents towards us. As the boy came closer I recognised the tight curls and rosy cheeks of Gerard Taylor. I didn't want him to see me in my Saturday clothes.

"I won't be long," I leaped off the wall and hurried to the back garden to hide until he'd gone.

I peeped up the drive and saw the family talking at the gate. Jessica was laughing and then she disappeared through the front door. The family didn't go away. They picked up this and that and hung around until Jessica returned carrying something green in her hands. It couldn't be...she couldn't have what I thought she had.

Peter held up our wares: a saucepan, his jigsaws, and packet of tea...the green shoebox that Jessica had brought from the house. She took off the lid and Gerard Taylor peered inside. His Dad dug into his pocket and pulled out some coins.

"NO!" I ran up the drive but I was too late. Gerard had the box in his hands and the family shouted, "Good bye!"

Jessica was dropping the coins into the tin.

"What was that?" I said.

"We all gave something except you," she said, "and it wasn't fair."

I ran inside and upstairs to the bedroom. The wardrobe door was open - all my brave battalions gone!

I screamed and flew downstairs.

"I hate you! I HATE YOU!" I cried, dragging Jessica backwards onto the ground. She screamed and Peter shouted, "STOP IT!"

I squeezed Jessica's arm so tightly I hoped it would fall off but Mum came out and dragged me indoors, "For heaven's sake! Can't you do anything nicely!"

"She's sold my soldiers," I sobbed, "she's sold them *all* to Gerard Taylor!"

Mum relented for a moment but I screamed all the louder, "I hate her!"

"Be quiet!" Mum said firmly but I wouldn't and she shook me and swung me to the bottom of the stairs, "Go to your room until you've calmed down."

"No."

She slapped my legs, "UPSTAIRS!" she said and I stamped on every step.

I pulled open Jessica's wardrobe and threw her clothes all over the floor, screwing them up and trampling on them. I opened her secret diary, where she wrote descriptions of James, and scribbled on every page in coloured pencils. I opened her jigsaw boxes and mixed up all the pieces then stuffed them back onto the shelves bending the cardboard.

I lay down on my bed and bit the pillow, "I hate you! I hate you, God! I hate everything!"

Auntie Philomena got worse. She didn't believe she was in hospital. Someone was trying to break in to kill her and a baby was lying asleep on the floor.

"She may have an infection," the nurse said, "we'll send off a urine sample."

Antibiotics made Auntie Philomena sick but they didn't halt the confusion. She refused to stand up and her joints began to stiffen.

"We can't force her to move if she doesn't want to," the physiotherapists said.

"I never thought I'd see her like this," Mum sighed, "they've suggested she move into a Nursing Home."

Dad shrugged, "Well she can't go home in this state."

"She'd hate to live in a Nursing Home, she's always been so independent."

"She could go for a while until she bucks up a bit."

Mum smiled sadly. She knew Auntie Philomena would never buck up. She visited the hospital three or four times a week and on Sundays we all had to go.

Auntie Philomena sat in her chair talking nonsense or praying the rosary. Sometimes she looked as though she was asleep then the Hail Mary would start up again. Each 'Hail' like a groan of agony.

"How many decades are there?" Jessica said.

"Fifteen."

All those prayers, I thought, all those hundreds of prayers and still she didn't get better.

"She must have said at least thirty."

"She forgets," Mum said.

Auntie Philomena forgot everything. She forgot we were there and she forgot to get dressed and sometimes when she was dressed forgot that she should be and took off all her clothes. We gaped at her nakedness; wrinkled skin like an elephant's and floppy bosoms that stuck to her ribs and got caught under her arms.

Mum turned our faces away and pulled the curtains round the bed.

"It's alright," I said, "I'm not embarrassed. I'm going to be a doctor."

I wasn't embarrassed when she picked through her food with her fingers. I watched her carefully, trying to work out which bones she was using but it made me sad to watch her. Even when we laughed it made me sad.

"It isn't fair," I thought, "all those saints in her house, all those Masses and benedictions and look at her now."

Maybe God didn't exist. Maybe she'd have been better off with the devil.

Chapter 8

When they came back from America, James and Alan invited us to see their holiday slides; tedious scenes of a city that might be anywhere in the world but I sat on the floor in front of James and leaned back on his legs.

"It's so exciting," Jessica said, "were there cowboys and Indians?"

"It's South America," Peter yawned at the fourteenth slide, "cowboys lived in the north."

"Have you never been abroad?" Alan sneered.

James hardly said a word but when he did his voice was strangely deep and masculine. I asked him lots of questions to hear this new, exciting sound and when he answered I looked at Jessica and giggled.

"Grow up!" she whispered.

James looked tired and his jet-black hair was matted on his head. I wriggled backwards snuggling into his feet and looked at his framed school photograph on the wall; all smart in his Brakenfield blazer with a cricket bat in his hand.

"Jessica's taking her 11+ soon," I told him, "and if she passes she can go to Grammar School."

"Of course I'll pass it. It's easy," Jessica said and Peter stuck his fist into her ribs. She looked at him and he shook his head quickly and frowned.

James blushed and ran his hand through his hair, "Exams are a waste of time. They don't prove anything about intelligence."

"Did you know," I said, "that there are over two hundred bones in the human body?"

As we walked home Peter looked up at Jessica, "You shouldn't have said that in front of James. He failed his 11+."

Jessica's lip quivered, "He can't have done. He goes to Grammar School."

"His Dad pays for him to go."

There were tears in Jessica's eyes, "I didn't know."

"They do fencing and archery at James's school," I said. "Will they do that at St. Agnes's."

"Don't be stupid, it's a girls' school!" she said.

"Now you're getting bigger," Dad said to Peter, "it might be better if you have a room downstairs."

The record player was moved into our bedroom and Peter's bed was lowered over the banister.

"Can Georgie move into Peter's old room?" Jessica said.

"You move into it," I said.

"It's too small for me and you're younger."

But neither of us had it. Dad filled it with boxes and papers and Peter's clothes. Peter still came upstairs sometimes, pulling himself backwards on his hands, and his arms grew stronger but his legs were useless and his hips grew bigger until he couldn't fit comfortably into his wheelchair. The new one was bright and shiny with a funny shaped cushion with little foam bits that moulded to his shape; there were more spokes in the wheels but the hubs jutted out and caught on the walls.

"It's no good," Dad said as Peter tried to turn the corner into the front room, "it's not going to go through."

Peter rammed the chair backwards and forwards with a mounting frustration. He turned round and tried to go in backwards but the hubs tore the wallpaper and scratched the doorposts and still the chair was jammed.

"It's useless," he slammed his hands on the arms, "this new chair's useless."

Dad looked at Mum who raised her eyebrows and rubbed her finger over the marks on the door.

"We'll have to take it back," Peter said, slipping from the cushion onto the floor and shuffling on his bottom across the carpet. Dad folded the chair and pushed it into the room.

"There's no point in changing it. As you get older you're going to need an even bigger one."

Mum and Dad spent a lot of time whispering together. When we walked into the room they burst into silence.

"Something's going on," I told Jessica and spent the rest of the week spying through curtains and listening behind doors but I didn't understand what they were saying - something about mortgages and estate agents.

"It must be something exciting," Jessica said, "because estate agents organise holidays!"

"They might be planning to take us on a surprise holiday this summer! We might go to America like James did."

Summer arrived and no one mentioned holidays. At breakfast time Mum stared directly at me, "I want your room to be spotless this morning. Not one sock, not one book, not one crumb on the floor."

"Why?"

"Someone's coming to look at the house."

"What for?"

"Someone from the estate agents. We're putting it up for sale."

Jessica squeezed her eyes until tears appeared.

"Don't start that," Dad said, "we've enough to worry about without your tears."

"Are we moving?" Peter asked.

"It would be better for all of us if we found somewhere else. A bungalow, perhaps, or a place with a downstairs bathroom."

Peter munched his toast thoughtfully.

"It'll be great to move house," I said, "if I can have my own bedroom."

"Don't count on it," Dad mumbled into his corn flakes.

"I'm going to tidy up really well and then I'm going to start packing."

Mum shook her head, "It takes a long time to sell a house and we haven't found a new place yet. We don't know what we can afford until we find out how much we'll get for this."

Jessica sobbed in front of the mirror in the bedroom.

"I don't know what's the matter with you," I said, sorting my clothes into neat piles, "we won't have to share a room anymore."

"You don't understand," she squealed, "we might move miles away from here and then we'll never see James. We might never see him again!"

"We're not moving out of Brakenfield. We'll just go to a bigger house. It might even be nearer to James's."

"They want a brand new house or a bungalow and there aren't any bungalows in Brakenfield. We'll probably go miles away."

"Why does it have to be a bungalow?"

"For Peter, stupid! It'd be easier for Peter."

"I hope it's tidy up there," Mum called, "he'll be here in a minute."

I went into the garden to think which was better: having a room of my own or living close to James. It didn't take long to decide and the sight of the shed, the apple tree and rhododendron bushes made me sad. I didn't want to move away; I suddenly loved living next door to Hoagey. The forbidden fruit on her tree was as tempting as the apples of Eden. I sat on the shed floor, spying through the slats of wood, unwilling to face the intruder who had come to invade our world.

They couldn't sell *home*, they couldn't! Strangers would wander through our rooms, trample over my shrine and sully our garden. Peter wheeled himself onto the grass. Would he be happier in a bungalow? Would he feel less strange if we all slept downstairs as he did?

"Peter," I whispered through the keyhole, "do you want to live in a bungalow?"

"No. I want to stay here."

"Tell Mum and Dad, then we won't have to move."

"It's not up to me," he sounded grumpy. "They just want to move. It's nothing to do with me."

"Don't worry," Mum said when the estate agent had gone, "we won't move to a new place without letting you see it first."

I didn't want 'a new place.' I wanted home.

An ugly sign sprouted in the garden: "FOR SALE"

I walked into it and leaned against it, hoping it would fall down. Maybe the wind would blow it over, maybe the leaves would disguise the words; but the wind that stripped the branches in October left them winding their black bones around the post to accentuate the message: 'FOR SALE'.

When people came to view the house I hid in the garden, not wanting to see the faces of the Infidel who would occupy our castle and seize our land.

"It's horrid," I said, "like when you're dead and people pick through your things."

I prayed no one would like it and that Mum and Dad would give up trying to sell.

"Mr. Radcliff says it's a buyers market," Peter said, pretending to be grown-up as he held out the *Money* section of the newspaper. "You'd be better off postponing the sale for a year or two."

"What would he know?" Dad said. "How often has he moved house? Anyway, if we wait for the right time we could be waiting forever."

That was the idea.

Mum said, "We can't have the place looking a mess when people are coming to look round,"

She tutted at my untidiness, following me round with a duster and Hoover, complaining of the bits that fell from my clothes. Each morning she sat at the breakfast table devising new schemes to tempt the buyers.

"Sweep the leaves off the drive," she told Dad, "and the front door could do with a new coat of paint."

She looked at Jessica and me, "I'll leave a little brush at the bottom of the stairs and every time you go up or down you can sweep the edges where the dust gathers."

"Bloody candlestick," I huffed as I poked a cane around trying to fish it out from under the shed. Everything had gone wrong since I brought that candlestick home. I dug a deep hole and buried it under the bushes.

When I came in, Mum was standing on the kitchen step and staring at the shoe rack, "The back porch is a mess. It puts people off."

"If anyone wanted the house," Peter said, "they wouldn't be put off by an untidy porch!"

"One...two...three...four pairs!" Mum frowned at me, "You don't need four pairs of shoes out at the same time. Take some away."

I carried my pumps upstairs and returned to find her crouched in a ball examining the carpet, "Someone's brought soil in."

"It wasn't me," I said, but I knew it was.

"Jessica's bringing her shoes, go and get yours. I want to see where it came from."

"What about me?" Peter said.

Mum blushed, "We know it's not from you."

Peter glared at her, "I still have legs and feet, you know. Just because I don't use them, doesn't mean I don't have them."

I smiled at him but he looked away.

"Why do you want to see our shoes, anyway?" I said.

"Because you don't believe me when I tell you what a mess you've made. I want you to see it for yourself."

I gathered the soil in my hands and threw it out of the back door.

"That was silly," she said, "somebody will walk through it and trail it into the house."

"I won't be me, will it?" Peter growled and wheeled himself away to thump the piano.

"What's the matter with him?" I said.

Mum shook her head, "It's his age."

But it wasn't his age; it was his legs.

"Will he never get better?"

She tousled my hair.

"Aren't there any other doctors in London who can help him?"

She smiled and I took it as a 'No.'

"When I'm a doctor," I said, "I'll make him better."

I collected Our Lady of Lourdes from the shed and brought her indoors for the winter.

"What do you want me to do?" I pleaded, "I'll do anything in the world if you'll make Peter better."

Her smile never flickered but a cobweb hung from her hand. I wrapped it round my fingers and remembered something I'd read; in the olden days old women used cobwebs instead of gauze on wounds. People thought they were witches.

I looked at Our Lady's face, "I wish there were witches today," I said, "they might heal Peter. You never help at all. I'm not going to even talk to you anymore," and I opened my library books to read about bones.

Mum was worn out with all the coming and going to the hospital.

"From now on," Dad said, "you're all going to have to help more round the house."

He drew up a rota for the washing up, and Jessica and I were given dusters to clean the mantelpieces and shelves.

"It's not fair," Jessica moaned, "Peter never has to do anything."

"It's because he's a boy," I said and hummed the *March of the Women*.

"It's easier," Mum said leaning over my shoulder as I swished the dishcloth round the washing up bowl, "if you keep the dirty things on the left and the clean things on the right. That way you won't miss anything."

"Do you know how many bones there are in the human body?" I said.

Mum inspected the forks on the draining board.

"Two hundred and six." I emptied the washing up bowl and dried my hands, "They're all different shapes and..."

"Rinse the dish cloth," Mum said, "or it will smell."

"If you cut a bone in half it isn't empty."

"Stop going on about it," Jessica said, "we're not interested."

"If people would use the spoon rest," Mum said, making a great display of wiping down the surfaces, "there wouldn't be all these marks everywhere."

Peter came into the kitchen, "What do you want me to do?"

"Nothing," Mum smiled, "we've finished."

"You should have asked me," he said, "I can do things too!"

All evening he sat alone humming and writing down tunes in the manuscript book Mum had brought from town. He was learning the accordion and the music sounded like France.

An angel appeared behind the door of the Advent Calendar.

"Mum," I said, "why don't people see angels anymore?"

She didn't answer. She was reading a letter.

"In the olden days," I said, "people saw angels all the time. There's a story in the Bible about an angel called Raphael. He went on a journey with a boy called Tobias and he cured a woman by waving a fish in the air. I think someone made it up. I don't think any of it is true."

Mum looked up from her letter, "Aunt Marie's invited us to Brigthorpe Hall for Christmas."

Dad leaned over her shoulder and read the letter.

"What do you think?" he said.

"I don't know. Supposing someone wants to see the house?"

"At Christmas?"

"What about Auntie Philomena?"

"She can't tell one day from the next. She won't even know it's Christmas."

"Even so…" Mum said.

"You have to think of yourself. You need a break."

"I don't think it's fair to leave Auntie Philomena on her own at Christmas," Jessica said but I knew she was thinking of James.

A fortnight before we broke up for the holidays, Auntie Philomena moved into a Nursing Home. Three bars glowed on the electric fire where she sat with her chin on her chest and her mouth half-open as she slept. The heat hit my face, and Jessica's cheeks glowed like a Halloween pumpkin.

Mum knelt down and gently took the wrinkled hand, "How are you?" she said but Auntie Philomena didn't wake.

"It's sweltering in here," Peter stretched to switch off the fire.

"O God, why won't you take me!" Auntie Philomena moaned in her sleep.

I wondered if she'd live forever: Auntie Philomena the Everlasting.

Dad plonked a bunch of grapes on her bedside table and Peter and I picked through them, secretly spitting the pips into the pillow.

Auntie Philomena stirred and pulled her blanket towards her chin, "It's cold," she shivered before opening her eyes.

Jessica tucked the blanket round her arms.

"Mary?" she said, peering through cataracts.

"No, it's me, Jessica."

"I'm perished."

Mum nodded and switched on the fire again, "Shall I fetch you a cup of tea?"

Like a hamster emerging from a nest, Auntie Philomena stretched her neck and looked around the room, "I'm perished," she said again.

"I'll see if I can find you a warm drink." Mum said.

"What?"

"I'll get you a drink,"

"No. I don't need the toilet."

Jessica looked at me and I started to laugh.

Mum walked onto the corridor to look for a nurse.

"Are you there?" Auntie Philomena called.

"Yes?" Dad said.

"Are you there, Lucy?"

"Who's Lucy?" Jessica said.

"Auntie Lucy. She's forgotten she's dead."

"Has Lucy gone?" Auntie Philomena frowned.

"Yes."

"Oh dear," she fingered the edge of the blanket, feeling her way to the corner. She tugged the fringe and pulled it out from behind her arm, turning it over and fingering back to the opposite edge. "I'm perished. What are we going to do?"

Mum put her head round the door, "I'm getting you a drink."

"Is Lucy there?"

"No, she's gone."

Mum stood in the doorway, ignoring the cries from the bedroom.

"Lucy, are you there?"

A woman in a bright pink overall hurried passed.

"Can I get a cup of tea for my aunt?" Mum said.

"She'll be having supper soon."

"She's cold. I thought a warm drink might..."

"They get a cup of tea with their supper at half-past six."

I glanced at the clock on the locker. It wasn't yet four thirty.

"I'll make it," Mum offered, "if you'll show me..."

"She's been wet twice this afternoon already. We don't want to have to change her again. It makes her bottom sore."

Jessica guffawed then tried to turn her laughter into a cough.

Mum's outraged expression must have made an impact because the woman blushed and, with an irritated shake of her head, said grudgingly, "I'll have to ask Matron, she doesn't allow visitors into the kitchen."

"Thank you."

"Will you help me?" Auntie Philomena's voice grew louder and louder, "Are you there, Lucy?"

Peter stared at her, "What does she want?"

"Is Lucy there?"

"No," Mum said, "but I'll help you."

"I'm perished."

"I know. I'm trying to get you a drink."

Auntie Philomena flinched and her mouth drooped at the corners, "Don't shout at me," she said quietly.

"I'm not shouting."

But Mum *was* shouting.

We sat in silence until the woman came in with a cup of milky tea that had splashed into the saucer, and plonked it on the table in front of Auntie Philomena.

"There you go, Philie," she said.

Philie? I thought how terrible it must be to be old, having your bottom wiped by a woman in pink who called you 'Philie'.

"Don't tell the others," the woman said as she left, "they'll all be wanting them. We haven't time to be making tea every two minutes."

Auntie Philomena sipped the drink and I looked at the sad expression on her face; so lost and wounded like a helpless animal in unfamiliar surroundings.

"Is your tea alright?" Mum said to drown the slurping noise as Auntie Philomena dribbled.

Auntie Philomena moved her head as though looking for something.

"Do you want something?" Dad asked.

"Is it time for '*The Forsyte Saga*'?"

"It's not on anymore."

Auntie Philomena cocked her head like a bird listening for a sound, "Is it time for '*The Forsyte Saga*'?"

"It's not on today."

"Sunday. It's always on Sundays."

"It's finished."

"Sunday. Yes, it's always on Sunday."

Mum shook her head and squeezed the cold red hand, "We'll put it on for you," she said and turned on the television.

"Is this it?"

"Yes."

But it wasn't. It was some old film about a sea monster.

"That's better," Auntie Philomena smiled. She was happy again and Peter smiled too, as he stared at the screen.

A nurse came in to take Auntie Philomena's blood pressure. While she chatted with Mum I looked at the stethoscope hanging from her neck. I wanted to tell her that I knew all about stethoscopes and bones so I stared at her until she looked at me.

She smiled, "What's your name?"

"Georgie."

"Do you want to listen to your heart, Georgie?"

She stuck the ends of the stethoscope in my ears and pressed the flat bit to my chest. I heard the steady boom, boom, boom and a gushing sound like an ocean inside me.

"This is called a stethoscope," she said.

"I know. I'm going to be a doctor when I grow up."

She laughed, "Wouldn't you like to be a nurse?"

In the excitement of having the stethoscope round my neck, I forgot myself, "No, I have to be a doctor so I can cure Peter's legs."

As soon as the words came out I wished I hadn't spoken. Through the corner of my eye I could see Peter staring angrily at me and as soon as the nurse went away he gripped the wheels of his chair and spun round towards the door.

"Idiot," he growled, "what did you say that for?"

"I'm sorry."

His lip curled like an animal's and I was afraid.

"I'm not ill, you know?" His voice was getting louder and Mum tried to calm him, putting her hand on his arm but he shook her away, "I don't need your help. I'm not sick!"

"She didn't mean it like that," Dad said but Peter jerked forward and sped through the door.

I started to go after him, "I didn't mean it, Peter. I'm sorry!"

Dad held me back, "Leave him."

"I'm sorry." I said.

Jessica put her arm around me in an uncharacteristic display of affection, "It's just his age," she said.

Auntie Philomena leaned forwards and peered at the television screen, "Is that Irene or Fleur?"

Mum glanced at the giant sea monster dragging a sailor under a ship, "Irene."

"She's aged," Auntie Philomena said, "and she used to be so pretty."

Peter sat in silence all the way home; a silence that clung to my clothes like the smell of the Nursing Home. It hovered around the dashboard and seeped into the stitching on the seats. It was a horrible cruel silence, more violent than any angry words.

"Did you think Auntie Philomena was a bit better today?" I said to snap the mood.

"Yes," Mum said, "and I'm sure she enjoyed your visit."

Peter's eyes were fixed on the rear lights of the car in front, "She didn't even know who we were."

We sat at the tea table in silence broken only by the sound of cutlery on plates until Peter started ramming his chair to and fro, "Move up," he said to Jessica, "you're taking up too much room."

Jessica shuffled.

"Move!" he said again and this time shoved her plate towards me.

Mum pushed it back, "Leave her alone."

Peter speared a potato with his knife, "Tell her to stop moving about. She's shaking the table."

"I'm not doing anything," Jessica said.

I wriggled further away trying to make more space.

"Georgie's doing it now!"

Mum sighed and Peter moved Jessica's plate again.

"Leave it," Dad said, glaring at Peter but he wouldn't leave it. He started moving things all round the table, pushing everything away from him, tutting and huffing.

"Peter," Dad said firmly, "I won't tell you again."

I wanted Peter to forgive me. I wanted him to be happy. I tried to think of something to say.

"There isn't much room here," I said, "so it'll be better when we get a new house."

"Stupid house!" Peter shoved his plate away. "It's not my fault we have to move. It's not my fault!"

Dad stood up quickly and took the handles of Peter's chair, "Go to your room and calm down."

"Get off!" Peter said, jamming the wheels with his hands. "Don't push me about!"

"Let go!" Dad tugged Peter's fingers.

Mum picked up Dad's plate, clattering it onto her own in a frenetic effort to tidy the table. She whipped my tea from beneath me and dropped the knife and fork noisily into a tureen then hurried around the table noisily clearing things away.

"You wouldn't push me if I could walk!" Peter cried.

"For heaven's sake! Act your age!" Dad was shouting now.

"STOP IT!" Mum banged the plates down heavily onto the table. They looked at her and she frowned at each of them in turn. Her hands were trembling and she bit her lip to stop it quivering, "Stop arguing."

Dad sat down again.

"Georgie," she said, "you and Jessica go and get ready for bed."

Jessica looked at the clock, "It's only..."

"Go!" Mum said and the force of her voice catapulted both of us through the door.

I stood at the top of the stairs in my pyjamas trying to hear what Peter was saying. When the door opened and Mum saw me she wiped the sadness from her face with the back of her hand.

"Are you two washed and undressed?" she smiled like an actress.

I scurried beneath the blankets and hugged Mum when she came upstairs. I wanted to tell her I knew she was hurting but I knew she would only brush it aside. The hug said enough, it said, "I love you," and "I wish that something could change and we could be happy again."

I had slept for a long time when the sound of the front room door opening woke me. I heard the squeaking of Peter's wheelchair and sobbing in the hallway echoing upstairs. Jessica was asleep and, as the landing light was off, I knew that Mum and Dad were already in bed. I crept onto the landing and the sobbing, grew louder and louder, coming from Peter's silhouette in the hall. He went into the kitchen and came out with a glass of milk. I stood at the top of the stairs tugging my hair with my fingers, and then Peter looked up and saw me.

"Come down," he said.

I tip toed through the darkness.

"I've made up some new tunes," he turned his face away so I couldn't see his tears, "do you want to help me write the words?"

Chapter 9

Every bench in the little church was decked with greenery: holly, rhododendron leaves, sprigs of pine and fir gathered from the fields and farms of Brigthorpe. Night-lights in painted jam jars lined the window sills, and candles flickered in the Advent wreath. In the alcove of a side altar three real lambs, guarded by shepherds in sheets and tea towels, curled up in the hay and bleated like babies. Joseph and Mary giggled and the shepherds put their hands over their mouths to hide their laughter.

Uncle Bernard's voice boomed like a torrent,
"O little town of Bethlehem,
How still we see thee lie,
Above thy deep and dreamless sleep
The silent stars go by...'

I wriggled down the bench and whispered to Aunt Marie, "I've never stayed up this late before!"

She put her arm around my shoulder and snuggled against me.

"Will Father Christmas have been when we get back?"

She shook her head, "You have to be asleep first."

I tried not to yawn as I peeped round a pillar to see the crib.

The priest talked of the 'the spirit of family' and prayed that our homes may be blessed by the peace of Christmas,

"God's love for us is so wonderful that for our sake he was willing to share our suffering and become as helpless as we are, as helpless as a tiny defenceless baby…"

I looked at the crib, "Please, Baby Jesus, for Christmas will you make Peter's legs better?"

Baby Jesus didn't answer. He was probably asleep. The whole world would be asleep except for the congregation gathered for Midnight Mass.

"He knew all about suffering," the priest was saying, "He wasn't born in a palace or even a church. He was born in the midst of the squalor and violence of a busy little town; born in a stable attached to an Inn."

My eyes began to close and I dreamed of a wine bar called *The Counting House* to which two strangers came; a man and a woman.

"Is there any room in your wine bar?" the man asked. He had a beard like Uncle Bernard's and he said his name was Joseph. "My wife is having a baby."

His wife was beautiful like Aunt Marie.

"There's plenty of room," I said, "Come in!" and a perfect little baby was born who looked at Peter. By the beauty of his gaze, the baby drew him from his wheelchair until he began to walk and skip and run.

I prised open my eyes with my fingers and when everyone knelt down to pray, Aunt Marie closed her hands across her face in contemplation. I wondered what she prayed for. What did any adults pray for? I wondered if she prayed in French and if she did, I knew that God would listen to every word

I rested my head on her arm and looked along the bench. A sandy-haired boy of about James's age sat between Claudette and Claire. This was their 'other cousin' with whom I had not yet spoken.

Since our arrival in Brigthorpe that afternoon, no one but Claudette and Claire had been allowed anywhere near him. Claudette shielded him with more care than a guard at the gates of a palace. If anyone asked him a question, she answered before he had the chance to open his mouth. I guessed he would be like Claudette and Claire but his skin was clear and his smile more gentle than theirs. He wasn't handsome like James but his blue eyes glistened like Aunt Marie's and when he laughed his whole face radiated joy.

"Gabriel," Jessica had said when we were alone, "that's a funny name for a boy."

"It's an angel's name," I replied.

The priest gave the final blessing and we stood up to sing:
'Once in David's royal city
Stood a lowly cattle shed.'

Mum put out her hand and pulled mine into her sleeve as we began the long trek up the hill towards the Hall. It was colder now and the fields were sparkling with frost. The stars above Brigthorpe dotted the deep night sky like glistening jewels in a dark blue cape and a misty haze covered the face of the moon.

Uncle Bernard looked up at the heavens, "That's a snow moon."

"I hope it snows," Aunt Marie said, "it is so beautiful here when it snows."

"You haven't been here in the snow, have you Gabriel?" Claudette said.

The boy shook his head but didn't look at her. He was watching Dad push Peter over the bumpy road.

"Peter," he said suddenly, "can I push your chair?"

Peter turned and smiled at him.

"He's heavier than he looks," Dad warned but Gabriel only shrugged.

"Shall we go fast?" he said and started to run. They sped up the road ahead of all of us and from way up the hill I heard Peter laughing, "Go on! Go on! Faster!"

Mum let go of my hand and stepped quickly towards Dad. She looked at him with worry in her eyes but Dad held her arm, "Leave them. They're okay."

"What if they bump into something? What if he falls out?"

"So what? He's enjoying himself."

I started to run behind but Mum called me back.

"Can't I go with them?"

"No. You stay with me."

"You don't want her running away again," Claire sniggered, "the police will be far too busy to go looking for her."

We walked for a while in silence, moved by the beauty and stillness of the night, then Aunt Marie starting speaking to Mum.

"He's coped very well with his parents' death."

"Poor lad," Mum said. "It must have been dreadful for him."

Aunt Marie nodded, "But he's like his father. My brother was always independent. I only wish..." she shook her head sadly, "Bernard and I would have been happy to take him but it was his mother's side of the family who became his guardians."

"Didn't he want to stay with them for Christmas?"

Aunt Marie opened her eyes very widely, "They've gone skiing."

Mum nodded knowingly.

"They're good to him," Aunt Marie conceded, "They give him all he needs but they're always so busy. They never seem to have time to spend with him."

"I suppose while he's away at school..." Mum began.

"That's another thing;" Aunt Marie said, "it's too soon after the death of his parents for him to be away at Boarding School. He hasn't settled there at all. He's very unhappy. He needs a family, some stability."

Boarding School? It sounded so exciting: midnight feasts and parties in the dorm. I wanted to tell Aunt Marie how much I'd love it, but it sounded like an adult conversation that I wasn't supposed to hear.

"Brakenfield Grammar has an excellent reputation," Mum said.

Brakenfield Grammar? He went to the same school as James!

"I know," Aunt Marie nodded, "but I can't help thinking that he must be lonely, so far away from everyone he knows."

"You must tell him," Mum said, "he's more than welcome to call in on us anytime. We'd be glad to have him."

Lights shone through the windows of Brigthorpe Hall and a line of little coloured lanterns flickered from the huge tree at the entrance, along the hedges and over branches.

I gazed in wonder and Aunt Marie followed my eyes. The seriousness disappeared from her face and her mouth slipped into her habitual smile, "Lights to guide Père Noel to the chimney!"

"He'll be here soon!" I said excitedly.

Claudette looked at me over her spectacles, "You don't still believe..."

"Claudette!" Aunt Marie said with an unfamiliar sharpness, then she spoke to her sternly in French. Claudette shrugged and turned away.

I looked at the flickering lights and could hardly wait until morning, "Will he know we're here and not at home?"

"I wrote to tell him," Aunt Marie smiled.

Gabriel, who had been charging round the courtyard, bouncing Peter over the cobbles, suddenly stopped in front of us.

"Look," he pointed to the lights, "it's snowing!"

Fine white flakes fell like confetti across the lamp-lit courtyard. We stood as though we had never seen snow before.

Uncle Bernard put his arm around Aunt Marie, "Merry Christmas," he whispered and kissed her.

"Joyeux Noel!" she smiled.

By morning the whole earth was white and the sky as blue as Aunt Marie's eyes. Across the valley, church bells rang and we skipped and danced and ran up and down not knowing which presents to play with first. Uncle Bernard, his shaggy beard streaked with white, 'Ho-hoed' like Father Christmas as he lumbered round the room stepping over wrapping paper, and toys.

We gathered in a circle and opened our gifts in turn while the voices of choristers rang from the record player:

'Yea, Lord we greet thee,
Born this happy morning...''

I wanted the morning to last forever; the excitement and the wonder. Uncle Bernard gave me a thimbleful of sherry and its warmth spread from my throat to my cheeks as he told tales of Christmases in distant lands.

"Let's bring Boston in and give him his present!" Claire said holding up a bone-shaped parcel.

I scrambled across the room and hid behind Dad's legs.

Uncle Bernard watched me move, "Since Georgie doesn't like him," he said, "take the present to him instead of bringing him in here."

"Papa," Claire moaned, "he always comes in on special days."

Uncle Bernard looked at Aunt Marie who looked at me indecisively.

"We could bring him on a lead," Claire said and Uncle Bernard relented.

Lead or not I knew he would reach me. He'd remember me from last time when he chased me up the stairs.

Gabriel leaned towards me, "Don't worry," he winked like a man, "I promise I won't let him hurt you."

The dog came in as bouncy as ever, chewing at the wrapping paper, bounding round the tree. He didn't come near me but I clung to Dad's trouser leg, afraid to come out. Claire encouraged his exuberance. She undid the lead and held the paper in the air to make him jump and every moment she stepped closer and closer towards me till the beast almost landed on my knee.

Gabriel sat down on the floor beside me and quietly summoned Boston. He held out a flat palm and the dog licked his hand then rested its chin on his lap.

"He's not vicious," Gabriel said, "just playful."

He stroked Boston's nose and head and the dog's tail wagged sweeping papers over the floor. Crouched in front of Gabriel, Boston seemed to shrink. He wasn't so scary now he was almost endearing.

I let go of Dad's trousers and knelt up, daring myself to go nearer.

Gabriel said, "Do you want to stroke him? He likes being stroked."

I put out a finger and touched his side. The dog didn't flinch. I tried two fingers, then three, then my whole hand, running over the silky coat that felt so warm and soft. Boston made a purring sound.

"He likes you," Gabriel smiled, "that's his happy noise."

"Look, Peter, I'm stroking him!" I said.

Claudette sat down on the floor and edged herself between Gabriel and me, "Hello, Boston," she said turning the dog's head away, "you love Gabriel don't you?"

Sated with turkey and Christmas pudding, Aunt Marie suggested we make the most of the snow. Uncle Bernard disappeared into the outhouses and returned with two wooden sledges.

"Jump on!" he told Peter, then he and Dad dragged the sledges up the slopes beyond the Hall where, wrapped in waterproofs and scarves, we whizzed through the trees, throwing snowballs and zooming down the hills.

People from the village began to gather and, lining up on the brow of a hill, they organised sledge races and snow fights. Below us, on a frozen lake, ducks skated and slipped on the ice while the village children threw bread and the crusts of mince pies.

Jessica, like the Snow Queen, sat on a sledge and ordered Gabriel to pull her over the hills. Claudette and Claire climbed on the back and I ran towards them so quickly that the snow ran over my wellies and froze my toes.

"Is there room for me?"

"No," Claudette said as they disappeared into the white horizon.

"Here," Peter called, "drag this to the top then you can come on it with me."

We whooshed downhill and met the others at the bottom. Peter rolled off and turned over and over in the snow, sucking at it like a puppy and throwing it over his legs.

Gabriel watched him, intrigued, "Do your legs ever hurt?" he said suddenly.

I couldn't believe it. He shouldn't have asked. No one ever mentioned Peter's legs. I waited for his fists to slam on the snow, his eyes to narrow and the anger rise in his voice but he simply put out his hand and, letting Gabriel drag him back onto the sledge, said, "No, I can't feel them at all."

I started to laugh with relief and Peter laughed too as he shook the snow from his cap. Claudette and Jessica came over, dragging Claire on the sledge.

"Come on, Gabriel," Claudette shouted, "drag us back up the hill."

I lifted the rope from Peter's sledge and began the ascent but had only taken a couple of steps when the rope grew slack in my hands and the weight stopped pulling on my shoulders. I turned and saw Gabriel crouched behind pushing the frame up the hill.

"Gabriel," Claudette called, "come on, we need you over here!"

"No you don't," he laughed, "you can manage it between three of you."

"You'd better keep an eye on Georgie," Claire shouted, "or she might run away and we'll have to call the police again."

I didn't care what she said now. Gabriel had chosen Peter and me and she was jealous.

"What happened to your legs?" Gabriel said.

"I had an accident. I fell off a roof."

There was neither sympathy nor self-pity in Gabriel's voice when he replied, "My parents had an accident. They both died."

"Yes," Peter said, "I heard. It must be awful for you."

"It is," Gabriel answered candidly and I was embarrassed.

"Do you go to Brakenfield Grammar School?" I said.

"Yes."

"We live in Brakenfield."

"I know. Aunt Marie told me."

"We know someone who goes to your school."

Gabriel didn't answer.

"He's called James Radcliff. Do you know him?"

He nodded, "He's in my year. He's not a boarder. He's a day boy."

I turned round again, "Is he your friend?"

"No."

"Do you like him?"

Gabriel wrinkled his nose, "He's okay," he said but I thought he didn't mean it.

"I'm going to Grammar School when I'm eleven," I said.

Gabriel's shoulders squirmed a little, "It's Christmas. Let's not talk about school."

When we reached the top of the slope, Mum and Aunt Marie appeared carrying huge flasks and a packet of plastic cups.

"Hot soup!" Aunt Marie called like a dinner lady and handed out the steaming broth to all the villagers.

I held the warm cup in my wet gloves and sat in the snow. Gabriel's face was glowing like a beacon, his bright pink nose peeping out from his hood. He stood on the sledge, balancing as though it were a surfboard. With his arms outstretched and his knees bent he kicked himself off from the top of the slope. Claudette and Claire cheered and ran beside him hurling snowballs, willing him to fall but he stayed upright until the sledge crashed into a tree, catapulting him headlong into the snow.

"I'm really glad we came to Brigthorpe," Peter smiled.

Aunt Marie sat toasting chestnuts on the fire, "Peter, will you play something for us on the guitar?"

He blushed, "I've not brought it with me."

"We've got one," Uncle Bernard said, refilling Mum's glass with red wine as he made his way to the door.

"You play the guitar?" Gabriel said.

"Not very well."

"He does," I said, "he's really good at it. He plays the accordion too."

"I play the piano," Jessica said.

Gabriel sat forwards holding his lemonade glass in both hands, "I want to learn the guitar. Will you teach me?"

"I'm not that good."

"Just a few chords or something?"

With a bottle in one hand and a guitar in the other, Uncle Bernard returned, "Here we are! I think it's in tune."

Peter ran his fingers over the strings, "What shall I play?"

"Something we can all join in," Mum said and I noticed how flushed she had become. Two tumblers full of wine were more than she normally drank in a year. A dry sherry at Christmas and the occasional shandy was all she was used to. I wondered if she was drunk and I hoped she wouldn't cry.

Mellowed by the firelight and wine, Dad leaned back in his chair and smiled contentedly, "A folk song," he said, "one we all know."

Peter strummed a few cords thoughtfully and began to sing,

"Fare thee well to Prince's landing stage,
River Mersey fare thee well,
I am bound for California,
A place I know right well."

I had heard him singing the same song in his room. I didn't know the words but I recognised the tune and when Uncle Bernard boomed into the chorus I hummed along.

'*So fare thee well, my own true love,*

When I return united we will be,
It's not the leaving of Liverpool that grieves me
But my darling when I think of thee.'

We started to clap and even the miserable cousins were smiling. Mum sang loudest of all and swayed to and fro in her chair as though she were on a boat. Everyone laughed together and the laughter was so beautiful it almost made me sad.

"Play something else," Mum slurred as she spoke.

Uncle Bernard was still singing the chorus of the song that had ended so Peter played it again. I looked across the room to where Gabriel was sitting. His face was flushed and his mouth contorted. I thought he was laughing and I laughed loudly then I saw that he wasn't laughing at all. There were huge tears on his cheeks. Aunt Marie saw them too and she moved to his side. She put her hands round his head and, without a word, buried his face in her bosom.

There were ropes and beams in the outhouses and Gabriel made a swing, spreading straw on the floor to make a soft landing if we fell. Peter sat picking the pieces of mud from his wheels as we took it in turns to climb on the ropes and move to and fro on the swing.

"My turn!" Claudette said, sticking out her bottom as she tried to climb the rope. She slid up and down and hinted that someone should help her or give her a shove but nobody volunteered.

"Am I next?" I said.

Gabriel nodded and I shinned to the top and crawled along the wooden beams in the roof.

"If we got a really long rope," Gabriel said, "we could fix one end up there and slide down it. We did it in the scouts when we went to camp."

I didn't know what he meant but it sounded like fun.

"Do you mind staying up there for a few minutes, Georgie?" he said.

Did I mind? What a strange thing to say. James never said 'do you mind?' He said, "Georgie, do this,' or, 'you can do that' but then, he was more of a man, I supposed; I'd never seen James cry.

Uncle Bernard and Dad came out to help. They secured the rope round the beam and fastened the other end to the ground at the far side of the barn. Since I was still up at the top I was offered first go.

"Hold on to the wood with both hands," Dad said, "then just push yourself off."

With a noise like a zip I flew down the rope and landed in the straw at the bottom.

"My go!" said Claudette but she couldn't climb up. Uncle Bernard tried to hoist her but she squealed and wriggled and said she was falling. Claire tried next but she only made it half way up the rope when her fingers gave way and she landed in a heap on the straw. It couldn't have hurt her; she didn't fall far and the landing was soft but she pouted and started to cry. While Uncle Bernard comforted her, Gabriel turned to Jessica,

"Do you want a go?"

She looked at Claire then shook her head, "No, thanks."

"Your turn then, Peter," Gabriel said.

Peter looked at him with a mixture of embarrassment and confusion on his face. At first I thought it was some cruel joke but Gabriel's eyes were wide open with innocence.

"How?" Peter said quietly.

Gabriel bit his lip thoughtfully, "Your arms are okay, aren't they?"

Peter nodded and his face became red.

Gabriel moved the wheelchair to the end of the rope then he sat down by Peter's feet, "Get on my shoulders and hold onto my head. That'll give you a start so you can pull yourself up on the rope."

I slipped my hand into Dad's and tried not to think of the thud...slam...thud and a body falling onto concrete. The straw was thick on the ground; it hadn't hurt Claire at all. Dad squeezed my fingers and smiled at me then let go of my hand to steady Peter as he slithered onto Gabriel's shoulders.

"Geronimo!" he cried as he whooshed through the air and landed in Uncle Bernard's arms.

Claudette and Claire said it was too cold in the barn. They tried to persuade Gabriel to return to the Hall but he had go after go and they tired of waiting.

"Come on, Jessica," Peter said, "if I can do it, you can."

"My arms aren't as strong as yours," she said and followed the others inside.

When Uncle Bernard and Dad had gone, I kicked around the barn while the boys started chatting. I buried myself in the straw, pretending that I was a spy hiding from the Germans who, if they found me, would arrest me and shoot me at dawn.

"Will you teach me the guitar before you go home?" Gabriel said.

"It takes a while to learn it," Peter said.

I stuck my head out, "You can come round to our house. We don't live far from your school."

"Yeah," Peter said, "but we're supposed to be moving soon."

"We're not allowed out of school very often. I hate it there. I wish I didn't have to go back."

"Is that why you cried last night?" I said.

It was a reasonable question but Peter stared at me in horror.

"No," Gabriel said without the least sign of embarrassment, "that's not why I cried."

Chapter 10

Someone was coming to see the house; someone who'd been before.

"Sounds hopeful," Mum said, "nobody else has been twice."

It sounded ominous.

"They won't be coming into our room, will they?" I said.

"Of course they will, so I hope it's tidy."

I went into the garden but it was raining and Mum hammered on the window for me to come in, "I don't want you trailing mud in when people are coming."

She stood in the doorway, spreading newspapers over the plastic mat that covered the kitchen floor. It was the usual rainy-day routine.

"Take your shoes off on the step," she said.

I hopped inside.

"If they're wet put them on the rack in the porch."

I obeyed but a drop of rain dripped onto the unprotected carpet.

She thrust a newspaper into my hand, "You're dripping all over!"

Visitors weren't exempt from this rainy-day-routine. Where politeness prevented her asking them to take off their shoes, she dropped subtle hints and walked before them, spreading newspapers as though she were laying a red carpet before a queen.

"It's like living in a mosque," Dad said.

"What's a mosque?" I said but he told me to go and tidy my room.

"If you were God," I told Mum, "you'd have given people wings so we could hover about and never stand anywhere."

"That's probably why he made angels," Peter said, "to keep heaven's carpets clean."

"James," I said, "we know a boy with an angel's name and he goes to your school."

James didn't look at me. He was watching Jessica rummage through the drawers and pull out a note pad.

"He's called Gabriel," I said.

James turned round and began to laugh, "Gabriel Deroux?"

I nodded.

"Little weasel-face!" James said and puckered his lips.

Peter frowned, "Is that what you call him?"

"Yeah," James laughed, "because he looks like a weasel."

I didn't know what a weasel was but I was proud to have made James laugh, "Yeah," I laughed very loudly, "he *does* look like a weasel."

Peter shook his head.

"He's a wimp," James said, following Jessica out of the kitchen, "what can you expect with a name like Gabriel?"

"Yeah," I jumped about excitedly, glad to be part of the joke, "he is a wimp; he's always crying."

As Peter wheeled himself past me he looked up at me with the same expression that Jesus had when St. Peter denied that he knew him. I winced but I didn't stop smiling,

"Well," I said, "he *did* cry."

"You'd cry if our Mum and Dad had died," Peter said.

I squirmed, feeling cruel and guilty.

"Georgie," Mum called, "I told you to tidy your room."

I stuffed the dirty clothes with papers and books beneath my bed. I didn't like the people who were coming; no matter who they were I didn't like them.

Jessica peeped round the door, "Come down to Peter's room," she whispered, "we're making plans."

James, with a pen and note pad in his hand, sat on Peter's bed.

"Now we're all here," he said, "we can put the plan into action. Georgie," he looked at me seriously, "we've got a special job for you."

I began to feel proud.

"Can you whoo?" he said.

"Can I what?"

"Whoo like a ghost."

I lifted my arms in the air and flapped around the room, "WHOO...WHOO."

"Hush," Jessica said urgently, "we don't want Mum and Dad to hear."

"That's fine," James said. "Now then, you need a hiding place."

"Under the stairs," Peter suggested, "they won't want to look in there."

"Right, what time are they coming?"

"Two o'clock."

"That gives you time to get ready."

"Get ready for what?" I said.

"Nobody wants to live in a haunted house, so when these people come to look round we want them to think there's a ghost."

"She doesn't need to whoo," Alan said, "she can just look at them. That'll scare them away."

James silenced him with a glance then turned to me, "You have to hide under the stairs and when they get here make that noise, only don't overdo it."

"No," Jessica said, "don't do it too loudly."

"Just loud enough for them to hear."

"Some ghosts make other noises," Alan said, "they throw things around and make banging noises."

"Poltergeists," Peter said.

Jessica, sitting so close to James she was almost on his lap, nodded, "If you want to you can tap on the wall or take my chain belt and shake it. But don't overdo it and don't break it."

"What will you be doing?" I said.

"We'll talk to them and try to put them off."

"Can't I do that?"

There was no window and no light under the stairs; the ghostly noises might scare me more than the prospective buyers.

"No," Jessica said, "you're not very good at that sort of thing."

"Will you come with me and be a ghost as well?"

"Don't be silly. Two ghosts would be overdoing it."

"Next plan;" James said, "what else don't people want to find in houses?"

"Rats," I said.

James nodded but Peter shook his head, "Where would we get rats from?"

"The pet shop."

Jessica clung to James's arm, "We're not getting real rats?"

"We could get some hamsters instead."

Alan snorted, "They'll know the difference between rats and hamsters. Anyway there isn't time to go to the pet shop."

"Someone could hide in the cupboard under the sink and scratch on the door like rats do."

"That's a good idea," Peter said and James wrote it down.

"Who's going to do it?"

Nobody answered.

"Well I can't do it," Peter said, "I'd never get down there."

"I'm too tall," James said, "I wouldn't fit in."

"You need me to do the talking," Jessica said and they all looked at me.

"You do it, Alan," I said, "you like scaring people."

"Get lost! I'm not getting in a cupboard."

"You'll have to do it, Georgie," James said. "Go under the stairs and make the ghost noises, then when they go into the dining room, sneak into the kitchen cupboard. Make sure you close the door properly and when you hear them in the kitchen start the noises."

"That's not fair. I have to do all the hard things!"

James chewed the pen, "You've got the easy part. It's Jessica who's got the really hard job. She's going to tell them all about the noisy neighbours and the all-night parties they have next door."

Jessica smiled at him.

"What all night parties?" I said but James looked at Peter's alarm clock, "You'd better go and hide, Georgie, and don't come out until they arrive or your Mum and Dad might suspect something."

"It's only half past one. They're not coming for another half an hour."

James opened the door and looked up and down the hall, "They might come early and we have to be ready."

He bundled me into the dark room whispering, "Don't overdo it," as he closed the door behind me. While I waited I heard laughter from Peter's bedroom. They were having fun while I sat in the dark. I played with my hands and worked my way up my arms trying to count all my bones. I pushed my fingers between each rib until I felt sick and my legs began to ache, curled up beneath me. I wondered if that was how Peter felt, sitting in a chair all day.

"Where's Georgie?" I heard Mum say.

"She's probably in the garden," Jessica said.

"They'll be here soon. She'd better not come in all covered in mud."

The back door opened and Mum called my name.

"I saw her go upstairs," Peter said, "she wasn't muddy."

There was a lot of coming and going outside the door.

"Georgie! Come down, I want a word with you."

I opened the door an inch and peeped out but a swift hand caught it, "Get in! We don't want them to know you're there," James said irritably and slammed it shut,

I sat in the darkness hearing the annoyance rising in Mum's voice, "She'd better not have wandered off."

"She's probably asleep," Jessica said, "I'll go and look."

Her dainty little footsteps pattered above me like the sound of rain on glass.

"It's okay," she called cheerily over the banister, "she's fast asleep up here."

It was ridiculous. Mum would never believe that, but the doorbell rang and distracted her.

A family arrived. Three voices in the hallway: booming masculine tones drowning the whimpering of a nervous little croak and the drawl of a younger person.

"Have you a place to sell?" Mum asked.

The man answered, "We've had several offers."

"You're lucky," Peter said, "there hasn't been much interest in this place."

Mum faked a little laugh.

They were outside the door. It was a good time to start, "Whoo.... Whoo...whoo..."

The man's voice was so loud I doubted he'd hear me.

"Whoo...WHOO...WHOO!"

No one responded or said, "What's that?"

It was time to summon the poltergeist. I scratched the door then banged on the wood with the back of my hand. A sudden thump then "Whoo," again. That was convincing. I frightened myself.

Light burst into my eyes as Dad pushed open the door, "Georgie? What are you doing?"

I crawled out to be met by eight pairs of feet. James raised his eyes to heaven and turned away as Jessica glared at me.

I stood up, feeling foolish, "I lost a book. I was looking for it," I said but nobody took any notice.

Mum shoved me towards the dining room behind a large and noisy man whose belly hung over the belt of his trousers.

"We told you not to overdo it," Jessica whispered angrily as she followed me into the room.

"We're hoping for a quick sale," the man said as he sat down and the chair groaned beneath him.

A tiny, mousy haired wife and a gawky teenage girl sat down on the settee where Mum served them tea in the china cups she saved for Christmas and Easter.

The mousy wife nodded a lot, "We've been lucky," she said, moving a ring from one finger to the next, "a lot of our neighbours have had an awful time trying to sell."

She spoke very quickly as though the words ran uncontrollably from her tongue and her lips couldn't keep up with them.

"Nobody wants to come to Wycaster," the man said.

"Wycaster," Mum said, pretending she hadn't noticed that the wife's tea had slopped into the saucer and dripped onto the carpet each time she raised her cup, "it's a nice place. Why do you want to move?"

The gawky teenager peered out from behind a fringe, "Wycaster's a dump."

"It used to be lovely," the man said, "but it's gone down these past few years. Vandals, graffiti, yobs coming home from the pub..."

I waited for Jessica to seize her chance: the noisy neighbours, the parties. I nodded to her but she refused to look at me. We couldn't let the chance go by, "It's the same round here," I said, "wild parties, noisy neighbours."

The woman dropped her cup into the saucer with a great splash. Tea dripped down her fingers and she wiped them secretively on her skirt.

Mum pretended to laugh again but she threw me a look that said I'd be in trouble later, "It's a quiet neighbourhood. We have an elderly lady living on this side and..."

The mousy wife nodded again and again, "It seems very pleasant."

It wasn't working. They liked the place.

"Of course," the man said, his face puffing out like a bullfrog's, "we'd need to negotiate with you about the price. This place obviously needs a lot doing."

Mum stuffed a Bourbon biscuit into her mouth and shoved the plate across the table towards the wife whose anxiety seemed to be increasing by the second. She snatched a biscuit and gnawed at it like a gerbil.

"We had the roof done two years ago and the whole place was rewired last summer," Dad said.

"It's very spacious," the wife nodded, "and a lovely garden where we could sit out in the summer."

Her husband stared at her with an expression that said she should be quiet. She shuffled a little and raising her cup to her lips made an involuntary slurping noise that made me laugh out loud.

Mum spoke loudly, "We have had other offers."

"I understood," the man frowned, "that you wanted to sell quickly. We're not part of a chain so we could be ready as soon as you like if you're willing to come down a bit."

"We've already knocked nearly a thousand off the original estimate," Dad said.

Mum was sitting on the edge of her chair moving her head one way then the other as though she were watching a tennis match.

The man's cheeks puffed out again until his eyes almost disappeared beneath them, "Take it down another five hundred and we might settle."

"We'd need to think very carefully," Dad said.

Mum, no longer able to ignore the tea stain that was spreading across the carpet stood up and peeped into the woman's cup.

"Shall I take that from you?" she said.

The woman poured the dregs from the saucer into her cup before handing it to Mum, "We would like another look around."

"Of course," Mum said brightly.

The man stood up and stuffed his belly into his trousers.

Peter nudged me and moved his eyes to the door. I slipped out of the room and hurried to the kitchen cupboard but it was filled with buckets and bottles of disinfectant and bleach. I tried to climb between them but there was no room so I piled the bottles into the bucket and put the whole lot under the table.

Climbing in legs first, I caught my ankle in the U-bend and was still trying to release it when the party arrived in the doorway.

Everyone ignored me, half-in, half-out of the cupboard as Mum pointed out the fittings and curtains. The gawky teenager, whose hair covered her eyes, slopped over the tiles and stared down at me. Her nostrils quivered then she looked away. She could never move in to our house; I would go on hunger strike first and chain myself to the gates.

They mumbled and snuffled around then walked out. Only James was left in the kitchen as I finally dislodged my foot from the pipe.

"I did well telling them about the parties," I said hopefully, "do you think I deserve a medal?"

He sniffed in disgust.

"You were useless," he said, "completely useless."

Everything was stacked in boxes and I moved among them filled with a sadness that said a whole world was passing away. It wasn't far across town to the new house, only a ten-minute bus journey, but the distance by road was irrelevant. It was too far to walk to James's and we weren't allowed on buses on our own.

In the hustle and bustle of moving, Mum and Dad were in a bad mood. They couldn't find things they needed because the boxes weren't properly labelled. They blamed each other and shouted when I tried to help.

"Don't undo that! I've just fastened it up."

"You're in the way. Go and find something to do."

But there was nothing to do. Everything had been packed.

I sat on the floor in Peter's room and played with my shoelaces. I had grown to love that room; it smelt of Peter and his belongings. It made me think of castles and Crusades.

"When I grow up," I told him, "I'm going to buy a really big house."

I closed my eyes and imagined what it would be like. It was a huge place in the country with spacious rooms: rooms with meaning; a music room, a library, a place where children could run and feel at home; a place like Brigthorpe Hall where I could wander around the garden with wide, beautiful eyes like Aunt Marie's.

"Make yourself at home!" I'd say and that would mean open drawers, go through the cupboards, take off your shoes, have a bath, do what you like.

There'd be a garden with bushes and tall trees to lose myself; dark places and a pond with frogs and insects whose names I didn't know; perhaps a lawn surrounded by flowers, but more the wildness and no one caring what I did, or where I went, and I could say, "Make yourself at home."

Strangers carried away the furniture.

"Can I go with them in the lorry?" I said.

"No," Dad shoved me into the back of the car, "there's isn't room. Sit there until we're ready to go."

I thought of the devil's candlestick buried beneath the bush. I hoped it would grow into a curse tree to drive the new people away. Then we could move back and everything would be as it was.

The new house was horrid. It stood in the middle of a row of identical houses in a new estate that looked like Toy Town. Failing to find a bungalow large enough, Mum and Dad negotiated with the builders to have a bathroom fitted downstairs and doorways wide enough to let a wheelchair pass. There was the same number of rooms as in the old house but each of them was small and square; no alcoves now to sneak into, no cubby-holes to play in. The spare bedroom was filled with all the furniture there wasn't room for downstairs so Jessica and I had to stay together in a bedroom two thirds of the size of the one at *home*.

We squabbled over space.

"I'm bigger than you," she said, "I need more room."

I had a new bed with drawers underneath where Mum stored blankets. There was nowhere to shove my rubbish when she came to inspect the room.

The garden was a neat square of lawn with a patio, a flowerbed and two saplings. There was nowhere to hide; nowhere to climb or fire arrows. The shed was filled with plant pots, spades and Dad's petrol-driven lawn mower; nowhere to build a chapel or an operating theatre.

Jessica lay on her bed with a thermometer in her mouth. I took her pulse and felt her brow.

"You have a fever," I said, digging my hands into the pockets of Mum's white dressing gown. "You'll have to stay in hospital for three weeks and you'll need a sling."

I opened the First Aid box and bandaged her arm.

"This afternoon," I told her in an official voice, "I'm going to take your tonsils out. Open your mouth."

She did as she was told.

"Very nasty," I said, "I'd better take them out right away."

I took the scissors from the box and put them on her tongue but she jumped away.

"I'm not really going to do it," I said, "lie still."

"I don't trust you," she pulled off the bandage, "and anyway this is boring."

"Everything's boring since we moved here." I said.

Sometimes on Saturdays Dad dropped us off at James's house and every Sunday afternoon he and Alan came to visit while their Dad played golf. They stayed for tea and sat talking in Peter's room.

Everyone grew up too quickly and in the space once filled with castles, conversation grew. I felt lost and ill at ease, never knowing what to say, fidgeting with the elastic in my socks, wishing we were in the old house, wishing they would play Crusades.

"It's squashed in here," Alan said, staring up at the ceiling, "I'll bet I could change a light bulb without standing on anything."

"It's a horrible house," Jessica said, "I hate living here."

"It's not my fault!" Peter rammed his hands against the arms of his chair, "I didn't want to move either."

"I know," Jessica said.

"Well stop blaming me!"

No one had blamed him.

"It's his legs," I thought, but didn't say a word.

James dug his hand into his pocket and pulled out some coins, "Are there any shops round here?"

"There's one on the corner."

He looked at Jessica, "I'm going to buy some chocolate. Do you want to come with me?"

She jumped up eagerly.

"I'll come, too," Peter said.

James looked at the wheels on Peter's chair, "It's okay, tell us what you want and we'll get it. We'll be there and back in two minutes."

They were gone for over half an hour.

"It's Friday, it's five to five and it's *CRACKERJACK!*"

Jessica stuck her tongue into a Walnut Whip and watched T.V. as she waited for Dad to come home. She couldn't wait to tell him the news; every time there was a noise from the kitchen, she jumped from the chair.

"You'd better not tell him;" she warned me, "it's my news, not yours."

The back door opened and she bounded out of the room, "I've passed my 11+! I can go to St. Agnes's in September."

She had a list of things they needed to buy: a tie, a blazer, a tennis racket.

"I wish I could go to St. Agnes's," I told Mum, "they learn French and science."

"You'll have to work hard then you can go too."

"We do French and science at our school," Peter said.

Jessica was running around excitedly, "Can I go to see James on Saturday? I want to tell him I'm going to Grammar School."

"Can we all go?" I said.

Peter's lips flickered into a half-smile, "I don't want to go to James's anymore."

"Why not?"

"It's boring and..." he shook his head and spoke more quietly, "I always feel I'm in the way."

"That's daft!" I said.

"I don't think he really likes me."

"Of course he does!" I said, "James likes everyone."

Saturday was such a disappointment. James and Jessica went for a walk and wouldn't let me go with them. Alan was doing his homework and Peter had stayed at home.

I sat in the Radcliffs' front room and looked out of the window, wishing that Auntie Lucy still lived next door. Uncle Max came into the front garden with a pair of shears. He stood on a stool and began to clip the hedge unevenly.

"Hello little 'un!" he said when I went outside, "What are you up to?"

"Jessica passed her 11+."

"Jolly good. Where are your playmates?"

"They don't want to play. They think they're too old."

"Come round," he said, "you can play in the stage coach."

I didn't want to go; it wasn't fun anymore, sitting on a stool in the shed while he cracked a cane on his thigh and shouted 'Giddy up!' Every time he leaned towards me I smelt whiskey on his breath. He was dirty and unshaven and when he took me inside for a cup of milk I thought how different it was since Auntie Lucy had died. She'd never have the left the sink piled high with greasy plates or let the rubbish bin overflow till eggshells fell onto the sticky floor.

"Uncle Max," I said, looking at the empty bottles in the corner of the room, "did you drink all that whiskey?"

He put his hand to his mouth and squashed his cheeks.

"Why do grown ups get drunk?"

He sat down and put his chin on his hand, "To forget."

"Forget what?"

"Forget how hard life is."

"Do you want me to help you tidy up?" I said.

"There's no point. No one else ever sees it and it doesn't bother me."

"You'll get germs. They make you ill and you'll die."

" 'Appen I will," he said hopefully, "it can't be any harder than living."

He reminded me of Auntie Philomena praying that God would take her.

"I don't want to die," I said.

"Of course you don't. You're young," he ran his finger nails over the bristle on his chin. "Make the most of your childhood, Georgie. Happiest days of your life."

"I don't think so. It's horrid being a child. People always tell you what to do and no one ever listens to you."

He poured himself a 'little tot of whiskey to keep out the cold.'

"Do you want one?"

I thought I should say 'yes' to be polite.

He took an eggcup from the draining board and poured some into that. I thought it looked like the specimen jars at the hospital but I dipped my tongue in and felt it burn me. When I raised the cup to my lips it stank like Uncle Max but I made a channel of my tongue and poured it down my throat.

"It was different when your Auntie Lucy were alive," he said, "she knew what was what."

"I know. I loved Auntie Lucy."

He frowned and sniffed then started to laugh to himself, "Did I ever tell you about the time when..."

He had another tot and so did I. He told me a million stories that I'd heard many times before. He did the actions, rolling up his sleeves as Auntie Lucy used to do. The whiskey that burned my tongue numbed my mouth. I poured a little drop more into the eggcup and soon his stories began to make me laugh. It was strange because they'd never been funny before. The more he talked, the closer his nose got to the table.

"Can you still wriggle your ears?" I said but the words didn't come out properly and he laughed until his forehead banged on the table.

I started to hiccup and I couldn't laugh anymore and suddenly Dad was in the kitchen.

"Max!" he said, dragging him back from the table, "What the hell do you think you're doing?"

Uncle Max made a strange noise.

"She's only a child, for God's sake!"

Dad pulled me from the table. My legs were very wobbly and I thought I might be sick. James and Alan came to look at me through the car window.

"I've been drinking whiskey," I said to James. I thought he'd be impressed.

"Why?" he said.

"To forget."

"Idiot." he said.

Jessica climbed in beside me, "You look a funny colour."

"Children who drink whiskey die," Alan said.

Dad, fuming and angry with everyone, switched on the engine and drove off without saying good bye.

My breath came in rapid bursts and my cheeks felt floppy.

"Are you okay?" Jessica said.

"I feel sick."

"We're nearly there," Dad said, desperately opening the window, "just hang on a bit."

But it was too late. I heaved a couple of times and was sick across the floor of the car.

"Take a deep breath," Dad said, "you'll feel better," but I thought my stomach was going to explode.

Jessica complained of the stench of whiskey and sick. Dad cursed Uncle Max.

"It's the last time you're going round there on your own. He wants locking up."

"It would be better," Jessica said, "if Georgie doesn't come with me to see James anymore."

Chapter 11

Jessica sat at the tea table with a smug expression designed to make us ask why she was smiling. I deliberately didn't notice and talked a lot about anything that came into my head.

"When you go to Grammar School you'll learn chemistry. You have to learn chemistry if you want to be a doctor. When I'm a doctor I'll..."

"You'll never be a doctor if you don't eat your tea," Mum said.

Jessica's smile grew until her teeth showed and still nobody asked her why.

"They make things in test tubes," I said, "and they have gas taps and Bunsen burners. I know what a Bunsen burner is."

"Mum," Jessica said, "next weekend there's an Open Day at Brakenfield Grammar and James has asked me to go as his guest."

"That's nice," Mum nodded.

"They're doing all kinds of sports and things and there's a concert in the Hall."

"A concert?" Peter looked up, "I'd like to go."

Jessica stopped smiling for a second then shook her head casually, "You'll have to ask James."

"I'm sure he'll want Peter to be there," Mum said.

"Can I come?" I said.

Jessica's smile had disappeared, "We can't all go," she huffed, "he only asked me as his guest. He won't want you there. You're too little."

"I don't care," I said, "I don't want to see some boring school. I've seen it. It's a dump."

Once a week in the last term of school Sister Margaret took our class swimming in the pool at Brakenfield Grammar where the changing rooms stank of sweat and urine and the sticky floor was slimy under bare feet. There were no cubicles, just lockers and hooks on white tiled walls where I stripped in corners, ashamed of my nakedness and the huge green knickers Mum always made us wear.

I was too ashamed of those knickers to join the other girls doing handstands on the playground. Everyone else did handstands; four girls in a line; one, two, three, four straight up against the wall. Their summer dresses billowed like umbrellas then fluttered like a parachute displaying bare tummies upside down beneath white knickers. Some had little flowers on or bows, all dainty and pristine, and the boys laughed and the girls pretended to be cross but they carried on flipping themselves up and down against the wall.

"Your go, Georgie," Beverley said.

I pretended I hadn't heard.

"What's up? Can't you do it?"

I shook my head.

"There's nothing to be scared of. It's easy!" she lunged herself forwards again.

I knew it was easy. I didn't even need the wall; I could do it in the air with nothing to balance against. I'd done it ten thousand times in the garden...but that was different; I wore my shorts and nobody would see my thick green knickers.

On Sunday afternoon James brought Jessica's programme, "You can watch me in the cricket match," he smiled, "and they'll be serving strawberries to the spectators."

Peter sat forwards in his chair to look at the programme, "What's this Folk Band?"

"It's just something the boarders do."

"Are they good?"

"I don't know. I've never heard them."

"I'd like to hear them," Peter hinted.

James wouldn't look at him, "It's just a group of boys from my year. They practise in the evenings when the day boys have gone home."

Peter nodded hopefully but James refused to be led.

I looked at the programme; a medieval pageant; archery and fencing displays, "Can me and Peter come?" I said.

James ran his hand through his hair and his cheeks flushed, "It's a bit awkward. There are two flights of stairs up to the Hall. I don't know how you'd manage with your wheelchair."

When he said the word 'wheelchair' he flushed more deeply as though the word embarrassed him. Peter blushed too and nodded resignedly but I stared at James trying to think of a solution,

"Couldn't some boys carry him up?"

Peter frowned at me irritably.

"Sorry," James sighed, "we're only allowed three tickets each and I have to invite Alan and my Dad."

Sister Margaret, obsessed with hygiene and economy, forced us into the showers two at a time. I threw my thick green knickers out of the curtain and wrapped my embarrassment in a towel, cowering beneath the jet to avoid the shower spray. Only one excuse exempted us from swimming: veruccas. But Sister Margaret examined our feet,

"Dry skin," she said, "that's all."

She patrolled the side of the pool in whitened plimsolls, holding a long wooden pole in front of my nose, "Come on! Come on! Have you no stamina?"

I gasped for breath at the end of my final length, clinging to the side and blinking chlorine from my eyes. I slithered up the ladder and my bones turned to jelly but I'd won my award and anticipated the glory of having it presented in assembly.

We stood in the courtyard waiting for the bus to take us back to school, when a group of boys in cricket whites came strolling from the field towards the gatehouse.

Sister Margaret struggled to keep our line in order, "Don't get in the way of the big boys," she said pressing sharp fingers into our shoulders, "remember we're guests here."

I looked up and saw a glowing face. James, tanned by the sun, took long manly strides across the gravel path, carrying a bat beneath his arm and pulling off his gloves finger by finger.

"I know him!" I said proudly.

"Do you?" Beverley said, "Go and talk to him!"

I stepped out of line that he might see me but he kept on walking. He turned his face away to avoid my eyes.

"Hiya, James!" I shouted.

He stopped for a moment as though he recognised my voice but he didn't look round until the boy beside him prodded his elbow and pointed to me. He half turned his head and his profile shone in the afternoon sun like the head of a Roman god on an ancient coin.

"Hello, Georgie," he said quietly, raising his hand in a salutary wave.

"I've just won an award for swimming," I stepped towards him but he moved quickly away.

A sandy-haired boy walking some yards behind looked back and smiled a genuine smile. I didn't recognise him until he came towards me nodding cheerfully, "Well done, Georgie!"

"Gabriel!" I said and my classmates began to huddle around me.

He didn't seem to notice them or care, "How are you?"

"I've won a swimming award."

"That's great!" he said.

"I had to swim five lengths."

He nodded, impressed, then asked, "How's Peter?"

"He still can't walk."

"Does he still play the guitar?"

"Yeah, he's really good at it now."

Gabriel smiled, "I've been having music lessons. I've joined the boarders' band."

"That's nice," I said wrapping the end of my school tie round my finger.

Gabriel smiled again. He looked much taller than the last time I'd seen him, much taller and much broader; nearly as broad as James.

"We're playing at the Open Day on Saturday," he said, "do you think Peter would like to come?"

"Yeah," I said, "but James said we'd never get the wheelchair up the stairs."

Gabriel frowned and shielded his eyes from the sun, "He could use the Masters' lift. The boys aren't allowed to use it, but I'm sure they'd make an exception for Peter."

"A lift!" I said and wondered if I could go too.

Gabriel shuffled from one foot to the other scraping his shoes on the gravel, "Do you think your Mum and Dad would like to come? My uncle can't make it so I was thinking I'd have no guests."

Mum, Dad and Peter…his three tickets gone.

"I'll ask them," I said, "but there'd be nobody to look after me."

He started to laugh, "Of course I meant you as well."

I was embarrassed and I tugged at my tie until the knot became so tight my cheeks began to burn.

"You've only got three tickets," I said.

He shook his head and wrinkled his nose in confusion, "There aren't any tickets. Anyone can come."

"You're not going to show Gabriel up," Mum said firmly, "Jessica's dressed up, Peter's dressed up, why do you have to be different?"

She spread the horrible dress across my bed, "You've got two minutes to put it on or we're going without you."

I hated that dress. More than I hated egg or cold rice pudding, I hated that dress. Red, it was, deep red - Mum called it burgundy - corduroy with a little lace collar that fastened, or had to be fastened, with a stiff hook and eye, and once it was fastened it couldn't be unfastened. It caught in my hair, it choked me, strangled me, and stifled me.

I stuffed my hands through the armholes and dragged the stiff, unyielding corduroy over my thick green knickers.

"Georgie, get a move on!" Jessica shouted upstairs, "Everybody's waiting for you!"

She was still in a huff because she was supposed to be going in Mr. Radcliff's car with James and Alan but Dad had said it was better if she came with us.

"I'm not going round with you when we're there," she said, "I'm James's guest, your Gabriel's."

"Why did James lie about the tickets?" Peter asked.

"He didn't lie. The day boys were only given three tickets each but the boarders were given more."

Dad looked at Mum and raised his eyebrows. He didn't believe a word of it.

"Why didn't he tell us about the lift?" Peter said.

"The boys aren't supposed to use it, it's just for the Masters," I said.

I liked that word: *Masters*. I wondered if Jessica would have *masters* at St. Agnes's.

"It's part of the original Brakenfield Hall," a Master explained, leading us along the corridor. The stone floor sparkled and smelt of polish and the walls' varnished panelling felt sticky under my fingers.

"When the last Squire died a hundred and eighty years ago, he left instructions in his will that it should be used to educate the sons of the local traders and so a school was created."

Mum peeped into classrooms and put on her telephone voice to make comments about the building to the Master who walked on ahead, his gown flapping behind him like a bat. I moved closer to Gabriel who looked like a man in his Grammar School blazer and black tie detailed with a tiny gold crest.

"It's like a castle," I whispered pointing at the high Gothic arches and towers.

"Or a prison," Gabriel said and his eyes drifted to the window.

There were alcoves, stained glass windows and separate houses with old-fashioned fireplaces, chimneys and disused servants' bells.

"Do all the Masters wear gowns?" I said but nobody answered.

A corridor, forming a bridge across the playground linked two incongruous buildings: the 'old school' and the 'new block' - a giant glass rectangle, run down and lacking in character. It smelt of paper and rubber and the sickly odour of the varnished floor of the gym where some big boys in shorts and white T-shirts performed a display on the beams.

"What time does the cricket match start?" I said.

Gabriel shrugged, "It's already started."

"Jessica said she'd come and find us to let us know."

Gabriel didn't answer.

"Shouldn't we go and watch James?" I said.

Gabriel pulled his collar from his throat and coughed, "Cricket's boring. Wouldn't you rather see the Medieval Pageant? There are knights and horses and the Sixth Form and Masters are jousting."

"I'd rather see that than watch James play cricket," Peter said.

We walked beyond the gatehouse and over the fields to a crowded arena where the smell of horses mingled with the scent of newly mown lawns. Bunting fluttered from tree to tree and flags on poles flapped in the breeze.

"I love history," I said, "and I love castles."

Gabriel turned round suddenly, "Have you seen the Chateaux of the Loire?"

Peter sniffed and pulled a white handkerchief from his pocket, "Where's that?"

"In France."

"We've never been abroad," I said.

"You'd love them," Gabriel smiled, "they're amazing! In the evenings everything is lit up; the whole castle shining like a fairy tale palace. I remember one night a boat, lit with torches, came down the river carrying Marie Antoinette or some other queen. Everything was jewelled and shining."

"Wow!" I said, "I wish we could go to France."

Dad put his hands into his jacket pockets pulling his shoulders into a stoop, "You'd probably be sick on the ferry."

Gabriel's eyes were glistening and far away, "A minstrel on the deck played a mandolin and sang an old French madrigal," his brow furrowed thoughtfully as he tried to recapture the tune, "It was so beautiful, like listening to an angel sing!"

"Do you believe in angels?" I said but he didn't seem to hear me.

The sound of a trumpet heralded the appearance of the knights. The crowd surged towards the barrier where William of Brakenfield, mounted on a snow-white mare, raised a lance and charged from a huge marquee.

"Anthony de Graveley," a voice came through the loud speaker, "won his spurs at Agincourt at the age of seventeen. He demonstrated his courage in tournaments across the land and jousted with some of the noblest knights in the realm. Today he challenges William of Brakenfield who remains, as yet, unconquered in the lists!"

Arrayed in bright purple, the challenger threw off his cloak, displaying bronze armour. The squire, who guided his horse, held up a helmet plumed with black feathers, which the knight put on. He pulled down the visor and stretched out his arm for the lance.

"Are they really going to do it?" Mum said.

"Oh yes," Gabriel leaned over the rope that divided the knights from the spectators.

"Isn't it dangerous?"

"They've been practising for months."

"Are they real knights?" I said, and Gabriel smiled,

"Anthony de Graveley is our French Master and William of Brakenfield is the Head Boy."

"There might be French masters when I go to Grammar School," I said.

"There won't," Peter said, "It's a Convent School. They're all nuns."

To the thunder of galloping hooves, a mass of colour kaleidoscoped in the cloud of dust before my eyes. The purple and scarlet cloths that draped the horses billowed and flapped as the opponents charged to the barrier, lowering their lances for the strike. The crowd was silent anticipating of the clash of armour, but William of Brakenfield was yards from the barrier and the lances didn't meet. The knights rode on to opposite ends of the lists and prepared to charge again.

"Have you ever seen such beautiful horses?" Gabriel said.

Peter pulled out his handkerchief and sneezed again. He wrinkled his nose and wiped his watering eyes.

Without looking away from the animals, Gabriel shook his shoulder, "Can you ride, Peter?"

Peter sniffed, "In a wheelchair?"

"Why not? They have a hoist, to lift you on."

"I went riding in Brigthorpe," I said, "and Aunt Marie said I was good at it."

"You should come up here. They open the stables to the public at weekends."

I looked up at Mum, hopefully.

"What do you think, Peter?" Gabriel said, "Do you want to come riding sometime?"

"I think I'm allergic to animals," he sniffed and wheeled himself back from the rope.

Beyond the arena the grassland was filled with stalls selling Victorian biscuits, candyfloss and toffee apples.

"Aren't you hot?" Mum asked Gabriel who looked quite flushed as he pushed Peter's chair.

"A bit," he nodded, "but we're not allowed to take off our blazers."

"Why not?" Peter said.

"School rule. They don't want us to look scruffy."

"That's daft," Peter said but Mum prodded his shoulder,

"They have to keep up standards," she said.

"I'm too hot," I said tugging at the silly lace collar, "I wish I had my shorts on."

"Is there somewhere we could buy a drink?" Mum asked.

"James said they'd be selling strawberries at the cricket match," I said, "I'd like some strawberries."

Gabriel frowned, "Wouldn't you rather have a go at archery?"

"Archery!"

Here was a place I knew I could excel; all those battles in the garden were not fought in vain.

The target was bigger than I had anticipated; the bright gold centre shining like a medal waiting to be won. Gabriel pulled back the string and let fly five arrows. His aim was accurate; all five hit their mark.

"There you go," he said, handing Peter the bow, "close your left eye and look along the arrow. Pull back the string as far as you can."

Peter's arms were strong but the back of his chair stopped his elbow, "It's no good," he said, "I can't do it from here."

"Yes you can," Gabriel insisted, fidgeting with the bolts behind the wheels, "if the back comes off?"

"No," Peter said, "leave it. It doesn't matter."

"What about the arms," Gabriel said, "they come off, surely?"

Peter leaned to one side and Gabriel lowered both arms, "Turn side ways," he said, twisting

Peter around, "That's better. You can pull it back full stretch now."

Peter smiled and pulled back the string. The arrow overshot the target and flew into the white tarpaulin beyond. Peter laughed and took another arrow. This time he hit the mark and the arrow twanged and quivered in the outer circle. Four more, and though he never hit the gold, each one landed on the board.

"Your go," Peter said, handing me the bow.

It was nothing like the canes and string we'd used in the garden. It was curved and shaped with an arrow rest and little markers to show where the arrow should be. The string was tight and I couldn't draw it back more than a couple of inches. I let it go and the arrow fell at my feet.

Gabriel put his arm round my shoulder directing my shot.

"Draw back with your shoulder not your elbow."

I leaned against him and felt his strength pulling the string. The second and third arrows flew through the air and landed in front of the target. The fourth, like the first, fell at my feet but the fifth landed in the centre of the gold.

I waved the bow triumphantly and Gabriel, picking up the arrows at my feet, handed them to me, "Have another go,"

He put his arm around me again and I pressed myself against him. This time two out of five hit their mark, one in the centre of the gold.

"Beat that!" I said, handing him the bow.

He fired five arrows one after another hitting the gold every time.

"You've done this before!" Peter laughed.

He shrugged and smiled to himself.

"You have, haven't you?"

He lowered his eyes humbly, "I won the gold medal in the school archery championship last term."

"Wow," I said, "can I see it?"

He looked away, "I lost it."

"Did James win any medals for archery?" I said.

He shook his head and looked at his watch, "I have to get ready for the concert. It starts soon."

"What sort of music is it?" Peter said.

"I'm in the Folk Band,"

"Playing the guitar?"

"Yeah, but I'm not very good at it. I'm better at singing."

"Does James sing, too?" I said.

"No."

"Shall I go and find Jessica and bring her to the hall?"

"No," Dad said, "you go on ahead with Mum, I'll find her," and he walked off, following Gabriel across the fields.

"Gabriel doesn't like James, does he?" Peter said.

"Everybody likes James," I said.

Music burst like thunder through the speakers; joyful, rousing music; music that made me want to dance. Their voices were clear and strong and within a couple of verses everyone was singing, clapping and stamping feet. It grew louder and louder until, reaching a frenzy, the song ended with a triumphant shout.

They sang '*Seth Davy*' and '*Whiskey in the Jar*' and a tall thin boy, like a centaur with his curls falling over his shoulders and his bandy legs skipping in tight black trousers, stepped forwards to the microphone and tugged his chin.

"Are you all happy?"

"Yes!" we shouted.

He put his hand to his ear, "I didn't hear you!"

"YES!"

"Are you going to sing with us?"

"Yes!"

We cheered like a congregation roused to peaks of fanaticism by a charismatic preacher.

"Come on then, Gabriel," he called over his shoulder, "it's your turn!"

The stage was thrown into darkness but for a light that shone on Gabriel's face. He strummed a few bars on his guitar then moved his mouth to the microphone as though about to kiss it.

'Fare thee well my bonny lassie,
A thousand times adieu,"

His voice was deep and strong.

'I am going away from the Holy Ground
And the ones I love so true,''

He sang slowly at first but gradually picked up speed until he reached the chorus where he stopped abruptly and laughed,

"This is where you join in! You shout 'FINE GIRL YOU ARE!' "

Everyone laughed with him and he started again, faster this time,

''Fare thee well my bonny lassie,
A thousand times adieu....'

I looked at Peter who looked at me in surprise, "He's good isn't he?"

"And still I live in hope I'll see,
The Holy Ground once more,'

"FINE GIRL YOU ARE!" the audience had caught his meaning.

*"And still I live in hope I'll see
The Holy Ground once more...."*

The lights came on and the centaur, tooting the tune on his pipes, skipped across the stage. Another boy was rounder and more subdued, looking so lost in his music he seemed barely aware of his audience. He leaned his head towards the strings of the mandolin as though to listen to his own sound beneath the cheering of the guests. Nobody was silent. Those who weren't cheering were clapping and singing and the whole audience seemed to share one enormous smile.

"I wish I could join them," Peter said without taking his eyes from the stage.

Jessica swayed a little to the music but she wouldn't smile.

"Didn't James want to come and listen?" I said.

"He had to go for a shower after the cricket match."

"Did he win?"

"I don't know. I didn't understand it."

"Is he going to come and meet us here?"

She shook her head and stared at the stage, "He doesn't want to sit in a stuffy hall on a hot day." She was quoting him word for word.

"Mum," Peter said, "can Gabriel come and stay with us for the holidays?"

"He might not want to."

"He does. I asked him. His uncle's going to Germany and Gabriel doesn't want to go with him. He said he'd rather stay with Aunt Marie or us. Can he come?"

Mum looked at Dad, "We'll see," she said.

That evening, a sniffling came from Jessica's bed. I lifted my head from the pillow to listen: a regular sniff and little gasps of breath.

"What's up?"

"Nothing," she said but her voice wobbled.

"Are you crying?"

"No."

I wriggled out of the blankets and shuffled across the room to sit on the side of her bed.

"What's up?" I said again.

The evening sun shone through the drawn curtains and birds were singing in the gardens.

I tugged the top of the sheet and pulled it back from Jessica's face.

"What's the matter?"

"I hated today. It was awful."

"Why? I loved it."

She sniffed loudly and pulled the sheet up to her face, "I was really looking forward to it and it was horrible."

"I wish we could have come and watched James play cricket," I said and she let out a loud sob.

"It was awful. I didn't understand it so I asked him what was happening and who was winning and he told me sit down and watch. He didn't speak to me at all after that and at the end of the game he walked off with his friends and he didn't even look at me."

"Maybe they lost and he was a bit embarrassed."

"He didn't look embarrassed. He walked off laughing with all his friends." She choked and coughed, "I think he didn't want me to be there."

"He invited you," I said, putting my hand on her cheek and trying to understand.

"Yes, but he didn't think you were all coming too. You showed me up."

I pulled my hand away, "I didn't even see James!"

"If you hadn't come with Mum and Dad, I wouldn't have had to go and watch that stupid concert. I could have gone for a walk with James and his friends."

My pity evaporated in an instant. I caught my fingers in her hair and tugged it sharply, "It's not my fault he didn't want to talk to you," I said, stomping back across the bedroom, "and I'm glad we didn't come to see some boring cricket match. We had much more fun with Gabriel."

"Silly baby," she said.

"Anyway," I stuffed my legs under the sheet, "I know something you don't know. Gabriel's coming to stay with us for the holidays."

She sat up, "Why?"

"Peter wants him to and Mum phoned his uncle tonight and asked if he could, so there!"

Chapter 12

Auntie Philomena sat on a chair rocking, mindlessly rocking, like me on the little red rocking horse, and Jessica in the tiny wicker chair when we took it in turns at singing. We rocked and sang a song and I rocked so hard that I pulled the handles over my head and landed flat on my bottom.

Auntie Philomena wasn't singing; she was just rocking to and fro with her lower jaw protruding and her top lip sucked into her mouth. She didn't speak to any of us; she didn't know we were there. She hadn't known us in the Nursing Home and she didn't know they'd sent her back to hospital.

"Infected ulcers on her legs," they said, "and a pressure sore at the side of her toe."

I looked at her legs expecting to see the little white mouth ulcers that came from eating too many sherbet lemons, but they were covered from knee to toe in thick crepe bandages. She rocked on the hospital ward among the old folks sitting like the ruins of an ancient monastery.

"When Gabriel comes to stay," Peter said, "we're going to write some songs."

Jessica folded her arms, "I hope he's not staying all holiday."

"What difference does it make to you? He'll be sleeping in my room. You'll hardly see him."

"James won't want to come round if Gabriel's there."

"Why not?"

"He doesn't like him. He says he's a wimp."

I remembered Gabriel's tears at Christmas in Brigthorpe Hall.

"Only because he doesn't like boring cricket," Peter said.

"It's not boring, you just don't understand it."

"Stop bickering," Mum said, "there are poorly people here."

"Jessica," I said, "what's a weasel?"

"It's like a water rat kind of thing."

"Gabriel doesn't look like a water rat."

"Hush," Mum said.

Auntie Philomena rocked and rocked and I wondered if she'd rock herself out of the chair. She had slipped down and her bottom was close to the edge.

She smelt. She smelt of stale clothes and old people and there was a stronger smell; a thick and stifling stench coming from her foot where a black damp stain spread over the bandage round her toe.

"Mum, what's a pressure sore?" I said but she didn't answer. She leaned across the table and lifted a feeder cup to Auntie Philomena's lips.

"Gabriel can stay all holiday if he wants, can't he, Mum?" Peter said.

She didn't answer.

A bag filled with an orange-yellow liquid hung from a stand at the side of Auntie Philomena's chair. A tube came from the top and wound its way over the bandage and up her nightdress.

I tugged Mum's skirt, "What's in that bag?"

"Be quiet," she said, "people are trying to sleep."

"It's wee," Jessica whispered.

I put my mouth to her ear, "How does she get it into the bag?"

She shrugged and her lips turned down at the corners, "It's disgusting," she said.

Two nurses came by and asked us to move so they could put her on the bed to 'do her dressings'.

We shuffled about and got in each other's way as they drew the curtains round her.

"Shall we go?" Jessica said.

"We've only just arrived," Mum said. It seemed we had been there for a hundred years.

I leaned against the wall between the locker and the next bed and through a gap in the curtains I watched as the nurses cut the bandage from Auntie Philomena's leg. Her foot was black and where her toe should be there was nothing but a mesh of flesh and nail. There was no blood - just blackness, a bluish blackness and I couldn't tell the dressing from the skin. A foot like the devil's black cleft foot; a hoof, perhaps, not a human foot. A foul stench came from the bed, filing my nostrils and spreading through the ward. Later in the car I would smell the same smell; it clung to my hair, my clothes, everything. Even in the bath it wouldn't go away: the thick oppressive odour of decaying flesh; the evil stench of Satan.

Auntie Philomena didn't stir as the nurse pulled away the old dressing and bathed the wound with water. Trying not to breathe, I watched the gauze swabs stained with black and yellow gunge drop heavily into an open bag.

"Georgie," Mum called in a loud and angry whisper, "come away from there!"

I was glad to come away. I wanted to go away from the hospital and never come back. I wished Auntie Philomena would die in the night and we'd never have to see her again.

"Did you see her foot?" I whispered to Jessica.

She shook her head.

"It's horrible. It stinks. She's disgusting."

"That's an awful thing to say," Peter said, "she can't help it. She's poorly."

"Do all poorly people smell like that?"

"Yes."

I looked at Peter's wheelchair. I felt sick and disgusted; how could I ever be a doctor? How could I ever learn to cure him?

The house was full with Gabriel in it. We were squashed around the table at teatime and I had to give up my chair. I sat on a stool piled with cushions and my knees pressed against the table leg. We ate tinned peaches, and the cake stand was piled three tiers high with fruit cakes, butterfly buns and shortbread from a tartan tin.

"These are delicious," Gabriel said, "did you make them?"

Mum nodded, "I'm glad you like them."

Mum liked having Gabriel around; she smiled more than usual and didn't complain about the mess. But Jessica wasn't happy. For the first three days she resented the presence of a stranger in the house. It wasn't that Gabriel was difficult to please and apart from at meal times we rarely saw him as he spent all day writing songs with Peter, but he was *there* and Jessica didn't like it.

"I don't like him to see me first thing in the morning," she moaned, peeping out through the bedroom door, her eyes like slits, her hair a tangled mop, her feet tripping over the dressing gown that wouldn't fasten.

"He talks when I'm trying to watch T.V." she said when he'd offered her a sweet during the adverts.

Three days into the holiday and James hadn't visited at all.

Gabriel settled like one of the family. He sang in the bath and left the door unlocked. He came out of the bathroom draped only in a towel. He dunked ginger biscuits into his tea and walked round the garden with no shoes on.

I was sitting on the floor in the bedroom destroying the hard backed books where I'd written long lists of bones when a knock at the door surprised me. No one ever knocked; they just walked in or called me. I didn't answer; I waited until Gabriel's face appeared,

"Georgie," he said, popping his head round the door, "your Mum says we can walk to Bransden Wood this afternoon. Do you want to come?"

"Me?"

"Your Mum says it's okay if you stay with us."

"Is Jessica going?"

"I haven't asked her yet."

I left the piles of paper on the floor and hurried past him down the stairs, "I'll ask her!"

She pretended she wasn't bothered and as I spoke she never turned her head from the music on the piano.

"I might do," she said casually but I could tell by the way she started to play more slowly that she was thinking about it carefully.

"Why don't you ring James," I said, "and see if he wants to come with us?"

"I suppose," she raised her right hand and turned a page of the music, "his Dad could drop him off here after dinner,"

"Shall I ring him?" I said.

"No," she closed the piano lid, "I'll do it."

The scent of pine trees and newly sawn logs mingled in the afternoon sun. We walked beyond the miniature farm and through the Edwardian gardens where three wooden bridges spanned the river and, crossing over, climbed the slope through the woods. Gabriel, a huge holdall slung over his shoulder, bounced Peter's chair over the roots that crawled across the sun-parched ground like veins on a rotting carcass. I walked beside them as Jessica and James sauntered behind until we came to a clearing where we pulled the blanket from the back of Peter's chair and spread it over the wood chipping and ferns. Peter unzipped the bag on his knee and pulled out the bottle of lemonade and cans of orange Mum had packed for us.

"They're warm," he said wrinkling his nose.

Gabriel seized the bag, "I know what to do; we did this at scout camp."

He hurried down the slope to the edge of the river and, selecting four or five large stones, placed the cans in the water beneath them.

I scrambled down the slope beside him, "What if they float away?"

"The stones will keep them still and the river will cool them."

James appeared beside us, and, brushing past me, lifted a can from the water, "It'll take hours," he said, flicking his finger into the ring pull, "I'm thirsty now."

Gabriel winced but never said a word and instinctively I felt a strange kind of pity for him so I smiled, "I'm not thirsty yet. I'll leave mine in the water."

Peter lay on the blanket and looked up through the branches at the sky, "It's years since I've been here," he said.

Birds were singing in the tall trees and crickets whistled in the undergrowth. Above us, on a gentle slope, the black crag towered like a giant demon reaching for the sun.

Jessica sipped the warm orange juice from James's can, "We used to come fishing here," she said.

I snapped a twig between my fingers, "Can we go fishing now?"

"We haven't brought the nets."

"We could go swimming," Gabriel suggested.

I moved towards the blanket, "We haven't got our things."

Gabriel smiled and dug his hand into the bottom of the hold all, pulling out a pair of trunks, "Be prepared!" he laughed.

James raised his hand in a mock-salute, "Dib, dib, dib," he said sarcastically.

Gabriel didn't answer but looked at me, "Do you want to come swimming?"

I was hot and the river looked refreshing and cool, I stared at the water then whispered to Gabriel, "What about Peter?"

"What about him?"

"He can't swim."

"You can't play the guitar," he said, "but it doesn't stop him from playing."

He jumped up and disappeared through the trees and I started to follow.

"Are you going with him?" Jessica called after me.

"Yes."

"You've not brought your things."

"I don't care!"

I pushed my way through low-lying branches down a narrow, muddy pathway to a rocky bay where I took off my shoes and dipped my foot into the water, "It's like ice!"

"You'll get used to it!" Gabriel laughed and dived into the bushes.

I pulled my shorts higher up my thighs and waded further in; balancing on the stones that wobbled and slipped beneath my feet.

Jessica appeared on the bank and I called to her, "Come on in!"

She sat on a tree trunk undoing her buckles, "Is it cold?"

"Freezing!"

Gabriel charged out from the bushes like a copper flame as the golden sunlight burnished his bronzed skin. Jessica stared at him and then at me. She paddled through the water towards me, wincing at every step, "He's very tanned, isn't he?"

He plunged into the river, the copper flame extinguished by the ripples. Jessica gazed at him as he rose up through the surface with water shining on his body. Waist deep in the river, droplets sparkled on his shoulders and his chest. His hair was darker now and with the palms of his hands he swept it from his face.

"Come on in," he beamed, "it's wonderful!"

I couldn't take my eyes off him; he was so free, so wild and uninhibited. He was so *beautiful*.

Jessica leaned against my arm to balance on the stones.

"Let's go right in," I said.

"We haven't got our costumes,"

"I don't care!"

The slimy water plants slapped against my legs as I tiptoed back towards the bank where I pulled off my shorts and T-shirt and hurried back to the water for the river to hide my green knickers.

The shock of the icy water caused every muscle in my body to contract but the pain was momentary and soon a warm glow swept across my skin.

"Come on," Gabriel called, "you're supposed to be good at swimming!"

I swam away from the rocks and beyond the shallower bank. The deeper it was the warmer the water became, rippling round me, pouring over my body.

Jessica was now thigh-deep in the river, the hem of her dress soaking up the water as she waded from the bank, "Aren't you cold?" she called.

I waved my arms about splashing her face, "It's warm when you get used to it!"

"Come on in!" Gabriel said.

"I've not brought my things."

"You'll dry in the sun."

She laughed and Gabriel looked at me with mischief in his smile. I knew what he planned to do and shook my head, "No," I said, "you can't."

He smiled more brightly and Jessica looked at his face. She laughed but there was terror in her eyes. She shook her head, "No," she backed away from him, unsteady on the stones, "NO! DON'T!"

It was too late, his hands grasped her ankles and he wouldn't let her go. She squealed as she fell backwards, fully clothed, into the water. After a moment's shock she caught her breath and stood up, laughing and shouting.

"This means war!" she hurled herself at Gabriel forcing his head beneath the surface. He came up, coughing and gasping, shaking the river from his face. He inhaled sharply and dived underwater. Jessica, waist deep, looked around waiting for him to emerge. He was gone for some seconds before Jessica screamed with excitement and vanished beneath the surface. Gabriel rose up triumphantly, laughing and pulling her back towards the stones.

James stood on the bank like the statue of a Roman god. He smiled but his smile wasn't real and when I swam towards him, calling, "James, come on in!" he shook his head.

"Look at him splashing about in the water like a weasel."

When Gabriel was dry and dressed, I hid in the bushes, taking off my knickers and putting on my shorts and T-shirt. Jessica shivered on the muddy path wringing water from her dress.

"Look what he's done!" she moaned to James but there was laughter in her voice.

Gabriel laughed too and undid his hold all, "Here," he pulled out a shirt and a dry pair of jeans, "you can wear these."

James stared at the hold all, "What else have you got in there?"

"All sorts!" Gabriel pulled out a ball, a rope and a jumper.

"Be prepared!" James said raising his hand again in another mock-salute.

The drinks tasted more refreshing, cooled by the river's icy water and as we passed the cans around Peter and Gabriel started to sing folk songs:

"We have bread and fishes,
And a jug of red wine,
To share on our journey,
With all of mankind."

Jessica's fingers crawled over the blanket towards James' hand. I tried not to notice and started to sing different songs but the others grew weary of singing and sprawled lazily on the blanket, staring up at the sky.

"What are you going to do when you grow up?" Gabriel said to Peter.

"I'm going to be a folk singer and sing in a wine bar."

Jessica whispered to James and he smiled at her warmly.

"James is going to buy a wine bar like his Dad's," I said.

Jessica threaded daisies into a chain and bound them round her head.

"He's going to call it *The Counting House*," I said, "and Peter's going to sing there. You could sing there too, Gabriel."

"Mm," Gabriel said, thoughtfully and stared at the distant rocks, "let's go up to the crag."

Peter's wheelchair bounced over the stones as Gabriel pushed him up the slope talking of music and songs. James walked behind with Jessica, now clad in a lumberjack shirt and jeans turned up at her ankles, carrying Peter's rucksack over which she'd spread her clothes to dry in the sun. I gathered pine cones and skipped through the trees, running ahead of them and behind them, leaping out from the bushes like Robin Hood surprising the Sheriff of Nottingham.

From his chair at the foot of the crag, Peter tilted his neck to watch Gabriel shinning his way up the smooth grey surface of the rock. With a rope slung over his shoulder he moved like a spider, pressing his feet into crevices, his fingers carefully probing the plane for a grip. Inch by inch he pulled himself up and having secured his foothold on the highest peak, threw the rope down into Peter's lap, "Tie it around your legs and under your arms!"

I dropped the pinecones and ran towards him, "What are you doing!"

"Here, pull this through!" Peter smiled, "Gabriel's going to pull me up."

"No!" I caught the end of the rope and tried to take it from him.

"It's all right," Peter said calmly.

"Stop it! It's a stupid idea."

"What's up?" Gabriel called from the top of the crag.

"He's not coming!"

"It's okay," Gabriel said, "I've got this end secure."

Peter was fighting me now, tugging the rope from my hands. I gripped it tightly but his arms were stronger than mine. He yanked the end and freed it from my grasp.

"Please!" I lowered myself to my knees and looked into his face, "Don't do it, Peter!"

He pretended he hadn't heard.

"Jessica, tell him!"

Jessica looked up to the peak of the crag, shielding her eyes from the sun, "It's not that high," she said.

"Gabriel, you can't! You don't understand!" my voice echoed on the rocky walls, "Please!"

"Push me so I can touch the rock," Peter said, barging his chair into the obstinate rocks that barred his way.

"No!"

He frowned at me and pulled the wheels backwards and forwards forcing them over the fallen stones.

I held the back of his chair to prevent him reaching the crag but he turned to me with determination in his eyes, "Let go!"

I thought I might cry and I frowned to hold back my tears, "Please don't do it, Peter!"

"Don't worry," Jessica said, "Gabriel's strong enough to hold him."

At every inch of his ascent I heard the calm assuring voice of Gabriel calling instructions from the top. Peter's arms were strong and he pulled himself with ease from ledge to ledge, his legs dangling beneath him, limp and lifeless against the crag.

I looked away and tried not to think of the thud...slam...thud....the basement gym and the sound of a body falling onto concrete far below.

A cheer came from the peak, "He's done it!" Jessica laughed and squeezed my arm, "I told you he'd be okay!"

"It's not the going up, it's the coming down," I said.

I wouldn't cheer or watch them but I heard excited voices, "Come on up, you can see for miles!"

The end of the rope landed at my feet.

"Go on," Jessica urged.

I stepped over the rope and wandered away to the other side of the crag.

"What's the matter with her?" James asked as I walked away.

"I don't know," Jessica said, "she's probably just trying to attract attention to herself."

I didn't talk to the others as we walked back through the woods and Edwardian Gardens. I wandered ahead feeling little and silly. Behind me James and Jessica laughed and chattered, and Peter and Gabriel enthused about the climb. I walked more quickly, kicking the stones on the path and wishing I'd stayed in my bedroom with long lists of bones.

I thought about *The Counting House* and imagined Jessica and James being married, and Peter and Gabriel singing in the bar. I could see myself, in my shorts and green knickers, hovering about not knowing what to say, looking as small and scruffy as ever while they all grew up handsome and beautiful.

"Georgie," Peter shouted, "we're going in here!"

I had walked some distance ahead of them and looking back down the slope saw Gabriel turning Peter's chair towards the little farm. I waited until they had disappeared through the gate then followed them to the pig pens where the four-day-old piglets slept under a heat lamp while the old sow sprawled beside them on the wet barn floor. I leaned on the fence and, reaching my arm through the slats, tried to touch the piglets but they were too far away and my arm wasn't long enough so I wandered out to watch the geese slapping their huge black feet over the cobbles. They waddled towards me, encircling me and squawking for me to give them something to eat. I tried to get away but they followed me and I began to run. Some of them gave up the chase but one was more persistent. His long beak looked like plastic as he pecked at my pocket, and a black eye like a bead stared proudly up at me.

"Go away!" I said flapping my arms and dancing away from his feet. I scampered into a barn and hid until he lost interest. The stalls were empty and a sign said the sheep were out in the fields but an old goose sat as still as a stone on the wall. Its feathers were grimy and worn and when it turned its head suddenly, I jumped back in disgust. Where its eye should be was nothing but a mass of green gunge.

It was ugly and repulsive and it turned my stomach. It was me in *The Counting House*: the ugly duckling, the old scrawny goose among the proud beautiful creatures.

"Georgie," Gabriel stepped into the barn, "we were looking for you."

"Look," I pointed to the goose, "it's only got one eye."

Gabriel, showing no sign of repugnance, moved slowly towards it and examined it closely, "Poor thing. I wonder what happened to her."

"It's horrible," I said, clutching my stomach.

Gabriel hitched himself up onto the wall beside it, "There's a horse with one eye at school," he said, "a beautiful white mare; they call her 'a grey.' Someone shot her eye out with an air gun."

"Does it look horrible?" I said.

He shook his head, "The skin's grown over now. The first time I saw her I thought it was disgusting but now when I look at her, it makes me sad. She's such a beautiful horse, I can't think why anyone would shoot her."

He looked at the one-eyed goose with a strange kind of pity on his face. I felt less disgusted now and moved a little closer to the wall.

"Come and sit up here," Gabriel said reaching out his hand to pull me up.

"You see," he said when I had sat down beside him, "it isn't so ugly when you look closely," and his eyes shone like Aunt Marie's when she gathered me like a bouquet of flowers in her arms,

"Mais oui, there is beauty in everything if you take the time to look for it."

"Why didn't you want Peter to come up the crag?" he said suddenly, with his eyes still fixed on the goose.

"That's how he broke his back, climbing down a rope."

Gabriel put out a finger and stroked the goose's head.

"It's my fault that he's in a wheelchair," I said.

"How can something like that be anyone's fault?"

"I dropped the rope."

"It was an accident. You didn't mean to do it."

"No, I didn't mean it," I wondered even as I was speaking why I was telling him this, "I'd do anything to make him walk again. I've made a bargain with God: if he makes Peter walk I'll be a nun."

"And if he doesn't?"

"I'll cure him myself, I'll be a doctor," I said, then remembered Auntie Philomena, "but I couldn't look after people like my auntie. She's disgusting. Her foot's all black like the devil's and she stinks."

He turned to face me and his eyes were filled with understanding, "Isn't it sad how horrid things happen to people?"

His voice was filled with such emotion that it made my eyes water and I frowned so I wouldn't cry.

"It's not your fault about Peter," he said quietly.

I felt my lips begin to quiver, "I wish he could walk again."

"Sometimes," he jumped down from the wall and stared through the barn door, "I look up at the sky and wish I could fly like a bird." He smiled to himself and when he turned back to face me the sadness had gone from his eyes, "but I can't and that's all there is to it."

"People aren't meant to fly," I said.

"Peter's not meant to walk," he shrugged, putting out his hand to help me down from the wall.

I looked again at the goose with its gungy green socket. It seemed more sad than repulsive now. I reached out and touched it and its feathers were soft and warm.

Chapter 13

Auntie Philomena would never come home again and her house had been empty so long that it smelt musty and damp. Mum opened all the windows and stood with her hands on her hips looking around as though she didn't know where to begin. She filled a bucket with hot soapy water and started to scrub the kitchen floor while Jessica floated around the dining room with a duster, trying to look important.

It was an old house with huge dark furniture, a high mahogany mantelpiece and, hanging above the fireplace, a clock that chimed the hour. The square dining table was covered by a thick velvet cloth like a curtain, and an embroidered Last Supper hung over the back of the imitation leather settee. I knelt on the floor, poking through sooty ashes in the cold hearth.

"Do something useful," Jessica said, pushing me out of the way as she dusted the mantelpiece, "you're supposed to be helping."

I blew the soot from my fingers.

"Mum," Jessica called, "tell Georgie, she's getting in the way."

Mum sighed and put her head round the door, "Go upstairs," she said, pointing to the empty suitcases she'd brought with us, "and pack Auntie Philomena's clothes into those. Keep them folded neatly; don't screw them all up."

"I don't want to go upstairs. It's spooky."

"Don't be a baby," Jessica said, thrusting a suitcase into my hand.

The staircase was dark with a door at the bottom covered by a thick brown curtain that caught in the handle when it opened. I gathered it to stop the door from closing behind me as I crept up the creaking stairs on my hands and knees, pushing the suitcase ahead of me to form a barrier between me and whatever monsters may be lurking under the bath. It was a bright morning and the sun streamed through the wobbly windows of the bathroom where tiny specks of dust floated in the beams of light. There was nothing under the bath, only the little clawed feet and the dusty skirting board; and the brightness of the sun spread to the landing illuminating the benign faces of saints holding lilies and roses or nursing the infant Jesus.

 Auntie Philomena's bedroom door was closed but I knew that from the other side a satanic face was waiting to hold me in his stare. I hesitated until the sunlight made me brave and, standing with my hand on the doorknob, I remembered the one-eyed goose in Bransden Wood Farm; the fear I had felt until Gabriel touched its head and looked at it with such pity that all my fears dissolved.

 I opened the door, steeling myself, determined to outstare the demonic eyes until he relented and lifted the curse.

 A gentle face stared back at me; a gentle-eyed Saviour:

Most Sacred Heart of Jesus, I place all my trust in Thee

 It wasn't Satan; it was Jesus wounded by the cruelty of men.

 I thought I had never seen such a sad face and the words of the Good Friday readings ran through my mind:

Without beauty without majesty we saw him,

no looks to attract our eyes; a thing despised and rejected by men...

I couldn't remember the rest but I knew they said the same thing; the man made ugly like the one-eyed horse whose damaged beauty made Gabriel sad.

I pulled out the little chair from Auntie Philomena's dressing table and, climbing up, touched the glass over the splattered heart. Around it a crown of thorns tore into the flesh and I clutched my own heart wondering how much it hurt.

Carefully I ran my finger through the layer of dust across the edge of the frame and blew it until it danced in the sunlight. I lifted the picture from the wall and clambered down from the chair, carrying the image in my arms as I bounced on my bottom down the stairs.

"Mum," I said, "I found this."

She looked up from her bucket, "There'll be all sorts of things like that. I don't know what we're going to do with them all."

"Can I have it?"

Jessica leaned over my shoulder, "It's horrible. What do you want it for?"

"I like it. I'll hang it on the wall."

"Not in our bedroom. It's so ugly."

"Ah, ma petite, there is beauty in everything if we take the time to look for it."

"Silly baby," she huffed.

"On either side the river lie
Long fields of barley and of rye,
That clothe the wold and meet the sky,
And through the field the road runs by
*   To many-towered Camelot."*

"Go on!" I said.

Mum poured the warm water over my head, rinsing the bubbles from my hair. I was the Lady of Shalott, tended by a serving maid who combed my beautiful hair as I waited for Lancelot to gallop beneath my window.

"And up and down the people go
Gazing where the lilies blow,
Round an island there below,
The Island of Shalott."

"Mum, can we go to a castle?"

She rubbed my head so vigorously with the towel that my teeth chattered, "We'll see."

"Can we go to the Chateaux of the Loire?"

She stood up and hung the towel over the radiator.

"Not this year," she said and I wished I hadn't asked. She always seemed embarrassed when we talked about holidays. James and Alan were going to America again and when Mr. Radcliff asked Dad if we were going away, Dad changed the subject.

I squeezed Mum's hand, "I don't really want to go there anyway. I'd be sick on the ferry."

She dragged a comb through my hair and smiled, "There are lots of interesting castles in England. I'll talk to Dad about it."

I went into the bedroom where Jessica was sitting on the floor surrounded by a mass of records.

"Where did you get them from?" I said, picking one up and reading the label.

She snatched it from me, "Let go, you'll scratch it."

"Where did you get them?" I turned my head sideways to read the labels through the hole in the middle of the sleeves.

"James loaned them to me."

"Can I listen?"

She picked one up and blew the dust from the stylus on the record player, "You can listen to them when I'm here but you must *never* touch them. I promised James I'd look after them."

I turned my nose up and pulled a face at her.

The needle bounced over the record and a muffled sound came through the speaker. Jessica lay down on her bed dreamily staring at the ceiling.

"Say goodbye my own true lover,
as we sing a lover's song,
for it breaks my heart to leave you..'

It was a soppy song and Jessica half smiled to attract attention to herself. I leaned over the record player and tried to read the label, "It's rubbish," I said, "put something else on."

"If you don't like it go in another room."

I shuffled the sleeves.

"Don't touch them! I promised James I wouldn't let you touch them."

"Why?"

"Because he said you'll break them or get them all sticky."

"I never break records," I said but she didn't answer.

"Like a drum my heart was beating,
And your kiss was sweet as wine,
But the joys of love are fleeting..."

"Auntie Lucy's records are better," I said. "These are rubbish."

I put on my dressing gown and went downstairs where Peter and Gabriel sat at the kitchen table looking at Dad's *Historic Monuments of Britain*.

"This looks good," Peter said, "Warwick."

"It's too far to drive there and back in one day," Dad said.

Gabriel shuffled on his chair to make room for me, "We're looking for castles, do you want to help us?"

I wriggled up beside him, one buttock on, one buttock off the chair. His shirt hung loosely over the waistband of his jeans and with the tips of my fingers I took hold of the white starched cotton and gripped it tightly. He looked down at my hand and smiled at me but never said a word.

"I'll leave you to look," Dad said going out of the kitchen, "try the North East Coast, there are dozens up there."

Peter and Gabriel peered so closely at the book that their hair touched and I couldn't tell where one head ended and another began.

"Do you think Jessica would like to help us choose?" Gabriel said.

I shook my head, "She doesn't like castles. Anyway she's listening to James's records."

Peter ran his finger down the page, "Dunstanburgh, Bamburgh, Alnwick. There's loads."

"James has got loads of records," I said. "because he gets them from his Dad's wine bar."

Gabriel's hand alighted on a photograph, "Alnwick looks good."

"She won't let me touch them. He says I'll make them sticky."

Peter laughed, "Look at the soldiers on the battlements."

"James has got loads of things. He gets everything he wants. His Dad's really rich."

"What about this one?" Gabriel said, peering more intently at the book.

"That's why they can afford to go to America every year. They can go anywhere they want."

Gabriel looked up and turned to me, "But they won't have as much fun as we'll have in a castle."

"Do you think James might come with us?" I said.

Peter frowned, "No. They have their own holidays. This is just for our family and anyway, there isn't room in the car."

Gabriel leaned back and his shirt slipped from my fingers. He ran his hand through his hair, "Maybe I ought to spend some of the holiday with my uncle."

"I didn't mean you;" Peter said quickly, "you're like part of our family."

Gabriel shuffled about in an embarrassed sort of way, "There might not be room for us all in your car if I'm here."

"Georgie can sit on Mum's knee," Peter said, "Anyway, you can't go back to your uncle, you said he's gone to Germany."

"If I phone him he'll send me the money for a plane ticket."

"On a plane on your own?" I said and Gabriel shrugged and nodded at the same time. He didn't look at either of us and his face was sad.

"Wow!" I said, "I wish I could go on a plane."

Peter frowned at me and shook his head, telling me to be quiet.

"We want you to come with us," he said firmly, "and there's plenty of room for all of us."

Some of the gloom lifted from Gabriel's face, "If you're sure your Mum and Dad don't mind."

"Mum likes you being here," I said, "and Dad does. They both like you."

He looked down at the page, "I like them," he said.

I wanted to hold his hand and I moved my fingers towards it but didn't dare, "Were your Mum and Dad like ours?"

He shrugged.

"Warkworth," Peter said very loudly pointing to the book.

"Did your Dad look like Aunt Marie?" I said.

"A bit," Gabriel stared at the page but I knew he wasn't reading; his eyes never moved.

"Have you got a picture of them? James has got a picture of his Mum. It's in a frame on the table by his bed."

Gabriel pushed back the chair so quickly I tumbled from it, "Sorry," he said putting out his hand to drag me up, "I'm really tired. Do you mind if I go to bed?"

"Georgie," Peter said in a cross whisper when he'd gone, "what did you have to say all that for?"

"I didn't say anything. I was only asking."

Jessica came downstairs still smiling to herself and humming *The Carnival is Over*. I hoped that Gabriel might come back but Peter's bedroom door was closed and there was no sound from the other side so I kissed Mum and Dad good night, and climbed the stairs.

A cardboard box stood in the corner of the room with James's records stacked inside. I peeped over the banister and, seeing no sign of Jessica, closed the bedroom door behind me and rummaged through the sleeves.

There were so many records he could never have played them all; some old, some new, all shiny in their uncreased sleeves. I lifted them out of the box and spread them round the floor, touching them and spinning them on the top of my finger until I heard the kitchen door open and Jessica's footsteps on the stairs. I gathered them together in a pile and tried to force them back into the box but something, something between the cardboard and the flap that was folded inwards, blocked the way. Desperate not to be caught in the act I ran my hand round the inside of the box and pulled out a small plastic bag with something like a giant coin inside. I stuffed it into my dressing gown pocket and rammed the records into place just as Jessica opened the door.

"What are you doing?" she said as I sat on the floor by the box, trying to look innocent.

"Nothing."

"You'd better not be touching those records."

I huffed, "I don't want to touch the stupid records. I'm going to the toilet."

I locked the bathroom door and pulled the shiny object from my pocket. It was a medal; a huge golden medal.

"Wow!" I whispered taking it from the plastic bag and holding it over my heart. I turned it round in my hand and, catching the light, it

threw dazzling reflections onto the tiled walls. I held it to my eyes. In the centre was a bow and arrow with a Latin inscription I didn't understand. On the back, in English, were the words:
BRAKENFIELD GRAMMAR
GOLD MEDAL
FOR ARCHERY

I slipped it into my pocket and shuffled back to the bedroom where, while Jessica undressed, I faffed around pretending to be undoing my dressing gown until she turned her back on me and I dropped the medal onto the top of the box.

"What's this?" I said like an actress, picking it up and reading the inscription out loud.

Jessica, half-in, half-out of her nightie, looked at it over my shoulder and, sliding her hand through the arm hole, took it from me, "It must be James's."

"Gabriel won a gold medal for archery," I said, "but he lost it."

"He should take care of his things."

"I didn't know James did archery."

"He does all kinds of sports. He wins loads of medals."

"Gabriel said James doesn't do archery."

Jessica slipped the medal into the box, "Gabriel's probably jealous because James won a medal and he didn't. If he'd won a medal he wouldn't have lost it, would he?"

"No," I said but something didn't seem right. "Do you like Gabriel?" I said as I climbed into bed.

"He's okay."

"Why doesn't James like him?"

"He's always jealous of everything James does and it gets on James's nerves."

I looked up at the ceiling and felt incredibly sad, "I wish that James liked him," I said, "because I really like him a lot."

The castle stood high on a hillside surrounded by a moat without water. Peter's chair rumbled over the wooden drawbridge like a chariot as, slapping my thigh, I galloped ahead through the stone archway. In front of us a huge tower climbed into the sky, shining mighty and magnificent in the afternoon sun.

I blew a fanfare on a trumpet and sallied forth to take the fortress from the rebels who had swarmed into the keep and hurled pots of boiling oil. I dodged their arrows and swung my sword above my head, kicking their corpses into the cellars and hurling them over the walls into the moat. Their helmets clanged against the walls and their chain mail jingled as they fled from my blows.

"Ha! Ha!" I cried as a rebel sprang at me from behind, "Try that would you!" and I ran him through with my sword.

A bearded highlander struck me with an axe but I fought on, unflinching and heedless of the wound. I raised my shield and my arm was caught by a stronger hand than mine.

"Georgie," Mum said, "don't go wandering off."

I was a prisoner being led to the tower.

A broad wooden staircase led into the keep and, running ahead, I found myself in a dark chamber with rooms leading off on all sides. Worn stone steps led into passageways with dark tunnels and anterooms where I fired arrows through the slits in the walls, hid in fireplaces and leaped out from behind doors.

"For England and Saint George!" echoed around the castle.

Swift black stallions charged into the field and knights in brightly coloured panoplies clashed in mortal combat.

I forgot the others; they no longer existed. There were enemies to slay, battles to be won, the old world had vanished, the real world was here in my head.

In a dark tunnel I peeped through the slit in the wall. A river, as blue as the sky, flowed between trees through a village; peaceful, serene, beautiful:

> *"On either side the river lie*
> *Long fields of barley and of rye,*
> *That clothe the wold and meet the sky,*
> *And through the field the road runs by*
>   *To many-towered Camelot."*

The fields were filled with Crusaders charging with triumphant flags and banners. I edged my way through the tunnel when a whooshing startled me. A pigeon, desperately flapping its wings, brushed past my face and disappeared through the roofless tower and out into the sky. I had wings, I could fly; I could soar above the battlements and rest on the wind.

A strong arm seized me from behind.

"Got you!" a voice cried.

I wriggled free, "No you haven't!" I scurried away from Gabriel to dart into doorways and find other hiding places.

"Georgie," Jessica called, "come out!"

Leaning over a barrier I saw her standing beside Gabriel in the Great Hall.

"You can't catch me!" I taunted.

"Come here," she said, "we want to play hide and seek."

I skipped down the steps, "I'll seek!"

Gabriel led me to a room like a prison cell, "Count to forty," he said and closed a heavy door behind him. I stretched out my arms against the walls, a prisoner chained in a dungeon, and every number between one and forty was a day I had spent confined by an evil usurper.

"Coming ready or not!"

I crept up and down passages and backed along walls to add surprise to my attack. Round and round the same circuit, the same passages, the same chambers, following stairways that led to the places I'd already searched. Upstairs and downstairs and into the entrance where I looked out from the keep and saw, at the bottom of the wooden staircase, Peter sitting in his chair licking an ice cream.

The enchantment vanished.

Mum and Dad sat beside him on the grass; stayed and unexciting. Guilt overwhelmed me; I'd forgotten him. I'd forgotten he couldn't play, forgotten he was stuck at the bottom with no way to enter the enchanted world.

I walked slowly down the steps, "Hiya!" I said, trying to hide my shame.

Mum smiled, "Where are the others?"

I sat down on the grass, "They're hiding."

Peter calmly licked his ice cream and Mum stared down at the valley.

"Are you supposed to be looking for them?" Dad said.

I nodded.

"Go on then, don't spoil the game."

"It's no fun if Peter can't play."

Peter sucked at the ice cream and took a bite of the cone.

I looked at him, "Do you want to play something else?"

"You'd better go and find them," he said.

"What about you?"

"I've got an ice cream."

"Don't you wish you could play?"

Melted ice cream dripped down his hand and ran between his fingers. He stopped smiling, "Go on," he said with a mild irritation in his voice, "stop fussing, go and find them."

"Four grey walls and four grey towers,
Overlook a space of flowers,
And the silent isle imbowers,
The Lady of Shalott."

I wandered through the keep, looking up chimneys, swinging round doorways, leaping into chambers.

"But who hath seen her wave her hand?
Or at the casement seen her stand?
Or is she known in all the land,
The Lady of Shalott?"

They were nowhere to be found.

One chamber was different from the rest; one end of the room was raised like a step and the stone floor was covered in red tiles. Somehow it felt different, quieter than the rest of the castle. A sign in the middle of the room read 'CHAPEL' and I stretched out my arms swearing my allegiance to God and the King. I drew nearer to where the altar must once have been and sensed a presence in the room.

Perhaps I was going to have a vision like Saint Bernadette. I closed my eyes for a moment and knelt on the cold stones.

"Please," I whispered, "make Peter's legs better."

There was a noise, a shuffling sound; a flapping of angels' wings heralding the appearance of Jesus or one of the saints. I might see a vision who would speak to me kindly,

"You are my chosen one. I will give you miraculous powers."

And I would raise my head until shafts of light streamed from heaven into my hands, my eyes and my heart like the pictures of saints in the library book.

"Lord, I am not worthy," I said and waited for the voice.

"Go where I send you and heal him," and I would stand up and float across the castle, down the steps and lay my hands on Peter's head. He would look up at me, his face radiant and joyful, and leap from the chair and run with us, singing through the castle.

"What's she doing?" the whisper came from an alcove.

I stood up, embarrassed, then got back down on my knees and crawled towards the wall.

Up two little steps into a room marked 'SACRISTY', I saw four feet. Gabriel and Jessica were huddled together behind a pillar.

"Found you!" I said, hoping they hadn't seen me kneeling on the floor.

"It took you ages," Jessica said, "we thought you'd given up."

Gabriel smiled, "Do you two want to hide now?"

"We ought to go and find Peter," I said, "he'll be bored."

We passed down a staircase, Jessica leaning on Gabriel's arm as she pretended to lose her balance on the worn steps.

"That was good fun!"

I nodded, "James would have loved it. It's a shame he couldn't come."

"You can see for miles," Gabriel said, pausing to look out over the river.

I smiled, "We should have brought our bows and arrows. We could shoot for miles from here."

Gabriel closed one eye and rested his forehead against the stone, "It must have been hard to get an accurate shot through such a small opening."

"James could do it," Jessica said, "he won a medal for archery."

"James?" Gabriel laughed.

"Yes."

"Did he tell you that?"

"No," Jessica said, "he never boasts. We just found the medal, didn't we, Georgie?"

I shrugged. I didn't want her to embarrass him.

"Where?" He didn't sound embarrassed. He sounded interested.

"It was in his box of records."

"Is it gold?"

Jessica nodded

"And there's an inscription on it?"

"Yes, something in Latin."

Gabriel walked on, rubbing his fingers along the walls, "I knew he had it," he murmured.

"What do you mean?" Jessica said.

"Nothing," Gabriel's nose twitched as he spoke, "I didn't mean anything."

Jessica reached out her hand and touched Gabriel's arm, "Why don't you like him?" she said but he didn't reply.

Chapter 14

A woman was sitting in the dining room talking to Peter and Gabriel.

"Who is she?" I whispered to Jessica as we spied through a crack in the door.

"Go in and find out."

"You go," I said.

She pushed past me and I followed her into the room where I sat inconspicuously behind the arm of a chair from where I could look closely at the stranger without being seen.

What struck me most was her size: she was *huge,* and the longer I looked at her the bigger she grew. A fluff of white hair lay like a mobcap on top of her head and little curls danced around her cheeks. On one arm lay a baby who had nuzzled into her flesh as though she were made of marshmallow.

"So you see," she told the boys who stared at her eagerly, "anything you can do would be greatly appreciated."

The baby gurgled and made a whimpering noise and at once the woman bounced him around so vigorously on her spongy biceps that I thought he would be sick. He gurgled again and she stood up, still bobbing him up and down on her arm, and she grew so big that I hardly dared come out from behind the chair. And yet, when I looked at her face, I realised she was quite short in stature; her head barely reached the top of the clock on the mantelpiece, but she seemed so big, immense in fact, because her voice was so loud, too loud for her size and she waved her hand as she spoke to take up more room than she needed.

Mum smiled politely and said she was sure that Peter would be glad to help and it was lucky that Gabriel was staying as he also played the guitar and sang.

The stranger paid little attention to Mum; the baby was awake and had absorbed her full concentration.

"Here he is," she said, "here's Matthew! You can see him now!"

Mum nodded and made cooing noises.

"Look," the woman said as though she wanted a round of applause, "he's smiling!"

She held him towards Peter and Gabriel for their admiration, then, catching sight of me behind the arm of the chair she waved him in front of my face, "Come on, I know you want to see him."

I put out a finger and Matthew's little hand curled around it.

"Isn't he lovely?" she beamed. "Do you think he looks like his Grandma?"

He looked like any other baby; a little bald head and tiny ears, bow-legged and kicking in a stripy romper suit.

"No," I said. He looked nothing like the huge woman who held him.

Ignoring my reply, she told Mum, "Everyone says he takes after me, but I can't see it myself. You never can, can you?"

Mum said, "Yes," but shook her head at the same time as though she didn't know what she was supposed to say.

The woman's big hand came down on my head, "I'll bet," she said, "you don't think you look like your sister, but I could spot the resemblance a mile off."

"Ugh," Jessica said, "I don't look like her."

The woman laughed and the baby burped and she threw him over her shoulder patting his back and telling us how clever he was. I wandered into the kitchen and Gabriel followed me, "Who's she?" I said.

"Mrs. Howland. A 'Friend of Brakenfield Hospital'."

"What does she want?"

"Peter wrote to her last week asking if we could busk to raise money for the hospital."

"Busk?" I said. I thought it was something to do with cleaning.

"Singing in the street. We sing and people give us money and they'll use it to buy kidney machines."

Excitement tingled my toes, "Did she say you could?"

"She's checked with the police and they said it's okay as long as we have an adult supervisor."

"Wow! Can I help you?"

All week they talked about Saturday, practising non-stop in Peter's room.

"What can I do?" I asked them over and over.

"They'll find something for you," Mum promised.

Even Jessica caught the excitement. She picked up a tambourine and jingled it in the choruses.

"That sounds good;" Gabriel said, "we could use that!"

"Can I have a go?" I said but I jingled out of time.

Gabriel handed me a triangle, "Try this."

It was no use. No one could hear my ping above the guitars.

"What can I do?" I said to Jessica.

She tried to be kind, "You're not very good at this sort of thing. You're good at other things. Maybe you'd be better in the audience."

I didn't want to be in the audience. I wanted to be a star and when Jessica said that James would be coming to listen, my desperation increased. For the first time since I'd snapped the bow I wished I'd taken more care of my violin.

"What can I do?" I asked Mum as Jessica became increasingly involved in their rehearsals.

"Join in the chorus," Mum said.

"I want to play something. They've all got musical instruments."

"I'll tell you what," she said, "we'll make some maracas."

She rinsed out the Fairy Liquid bottle, dried it with the dishcloth and filled it with rice, "Shake that," she said.

It didn't make too much noise no matter what they said.

"Leave it for the first day," Peter told me, "and maybe you could bring it next time."

Gabriel looked at me with pity in his eyes, "She could play in one or two songs," he said.

Peter relented, "Okay, but wait for us to tell you when."

Jessica prepared a poster:
    HELP US TO RAISE MONEY
    FOR BRAKENFIELD HOSPITAL

I filled in Jessica's letters with red felt tips.

"Don't go over the lines," she said.

"We need a name," Peter frowned, "we have to call ourselves something."

"*Brakenfield Boys*," Gabriel said.

"And girls!" Jessica insisted.

No one liked that idea.

"Folk Groups have names like pubs," Peter said, "*Yard of Ale* or something like that."

"*The Counting House*." I said.

Jessica shook her head, "That's no good for a group."

"I think it's good," I muttered.

Gabriel put his hand on my shoulder, "I think so too."

"You can't be called *The Counting House*," Jessica said, "that's what James is going to call his wine bar."

"It was my idea."

Gabriel's nostrils flickered, "It's brilliant, but let James keep it for his wine bar."

I went upstairs and put one of Auntie Lucy's records onto the turntable to drown the sound of their singing. Verdi's *Anvil Chorus'* rang out loudly and clearly. I closed my eyes and stood on a cloud with a huge metal rod in my hand. I waved it across the sky and played the tune on the stars.

Brakenfield Town Centre was crowded on Saturday morning, bustling with shoppers who packed the pavements and moved like weather people in and out of doorways, carrying plastic bags and armfuls of groceries. The streets seemed wider and more exciting as I climbed over guitar cases, passing papers to Gabriel and Peter while they tuned their instruments and set their lists in order. Dad had nailed the poster to a board that leaned against Peter's guitar case on the pavement.

HELP US TO RAISE MONEY
FOR BRAKENFIELD HOSPITAL
PLEASE GIVE GENEROUSLY!

I hopped around and got in their way, looking up and down the street, waiting for James to appear.

Peter strummed the strings of his guitar, launching the opening song and the shoppers walked more slowly. One or two stopped and smiled and began to listen. Peter's face was glowing with excitement, delighting in the music and applause as a crowd began to gather.

I held the bag where people dropped their money and stood beside the poster hoping everyone knew I'd helped to colour it in.

"We're trying to raise money for the hospital," Peter's voice was confident, "so please drop what you can into Georgie's bag."

I waved my hand and waited for the onslaught. Children came first, pushed forward by parents, dropping their coins one by one into the bag.

Uncle Max came by carrying a shopping bag that clinked as he walked, "Aye, aye," he winked, "what's all this?"

"It's Peter and Gabriel," I said, "and I'm collecting the money."

He stuffed a dirty hand into his pocket and pulled out a coin. He held it up and bit it like a pirate before handing it to me and embarrassingly pretending to dance.

"Still writing poems?" he said.

I nodded and drifted away from the stench of stale whiskey and dirty clothes.

I joined the applause and waited to be called to play my maracas, hoping that James would appear in time to hear me. There was a pause while Peter and Gabriel chatted together and when, at last, the music recommenced, they sang in harmony and something strangely gelled.

'I went to an alehouse
I used to frequent,
And I told the landlady
My money was spent...'

I looked up at Mum who nodded and smiled to Dad, "They're great!"

"I've never seen Peter so happy. I didn't know he had it in him."

"He's a different person up there."

A hand came down on my shoulder and I turned at the sound of a nasal voice in my ear, "Georgie."

"Hello, Alan."

He looked Gabriel up and down and I shook the moneybag in his face.

"Get lost," he said, "I'm not paying to listen to them."

"Why did you come then?"

"For a laugh."

I growled at him but he didn't hear above the music and traffic in the street.

"Hello, Alan," Mum said cheerily, "is James with you?"

He pointed across the street, "He's over there with his friends."

Four boys sat on a bench, laughing and pointing at Peter and Gabriel.

Jessica, shaking her tambourine, hadn't seen them.

"Mum," I said, "can I go and talk to James."

She nodded and took the moneybag from my hand.

I skipped between elbows and shopping bags but James didn't see me approach. A crowd of old people stood talking in front of the bench blocking my route and forcing me round the back.

"What a load of crap!" one of the boys on the bench said and James laughed.

"I can't believe he'd do it! What an idiot!"

They were pointing at Gabriel.

I waited for James to defend him but he carried on laughing.

A song ended and they pretended to cheer, "Hurrah! Hurrah!"

"God!" one of them said, slapping his hand on his forehead, "I don't believe it! People are actually giving them money!"

"They look like they need it," another shouted, "look at him in the chair. What's he got on? His mother's blouse?" he pointed to Peter's check shirt.

"No, it's a table cloth."

"Hey! You in the table cloth, can you dance as well?"

They rolled about laughing, laughing so much there were tears in their eyes. There were tears in my eyes too, but I wasn't laughing.

"James," I whispered, leaning over the bench and tapping his shoulder.

I startled him and when he jumped the others turned round, "Oh no, one of them's come to get us!"

They pretended to duck down and hide their faces. I stared at James who was still smiling but looked decidedly uneasy and wouldn't meet my eyes.

"Do you want to come and talk to Jessica?" I said to him.

He looked at his friends and then up at the sky, "Tell her to come over here," he said.

"She can't. She's playing the tambourine."

"Tambourine!" one laughed, "It's the bloody Salvation Army!"

His hair was dark and curled at the front in a quiff above bright green eyes. Jessica would say he was handsome; he looked like the knight on the cover of my book of *Medieval Castles*, but around his chin and neck were huge pimples, swollen as though their white heads were about to burst.

James stopped smiling and stood up, digging his hands into the pockets of his jeans, "I'll see her later," he said and turned to his friends, "Come on, let's get out of here."

They didn't move.

"Come on!" James said impatiently.

The knight caught his elbow and dragged him back onto the bench, "We're not going yet, the fun's just beginning. Look Weasel's singing."

His lips curled like an upside down smile down and when he laughed I could see all the fillings in his teeth.

A blonde boy, tall and tanned, leaned back on the bench, spreading his long legs before him across the pavement, "I'll bet he can walk. He's just sitting in that wheelchair so the old biddies feel sorry for him and dish out their money."

The knight laughed loudly and lifted his hands to his mouth like a megaphone, "Hey, table cloth, get up and dance!"

I clambered up the back of the bench and with the whole might of my body whacked him across the head with the palm of my hand. He jumped up and stood for a second stunned by my blow.

"He's my brother," I cried, "and he can't walk. Tell him James!"

James looked away as though he hadn't heard so I lashed out again but this time the knight stepped back and I missed, hitting only the air in front of his face.

"Get her off me!" he swished his hand across his face as though I were a fly.

The blonde boy took hold of my wrists and swung me away from the bench, "Go back to your mummy," he said as my feet landed on the floor.

"James," I said, trying not to cry, "are you coming?"

His lips twitched but he still wouldn't look at me, "Go on, Georgie," he said, barely opening his mouth, "go back to the others."

I couldn't stop staring at him. I couldn't believe this was James.

The boy I had hit sat down again, rubbing his head, "Is she the little witch you told us about? The one that fancies you?"

James stood up suddenly, "Come on," he said, "let's go."

He glanced at me for a second. His forehead was furrowed into a frown and he moved his mouth as though he wanted to say something but didn't dare. He wanted to say, 'Sorry,' but he couldn't. I wanted him to say it. I needed him to put his arm around my shoulder and say, 'Sorry,' like he meant it but he turned away and I hated him.

I sat cross-legged between the plant pots on the floor of the shed. In front of me, balanced on a petrol can that Dad used for the motor mower, rested the Sacred Heart whom I had pulled from his hiding place behind the seeds tubs. The crumpled pages of an exercise book wrinkled between my fingers,

"POEMS AND SONGS BY GEORGINA MEADOWS'

*The Hero, The Lionheart...*It wasn't James, not the James on the bench in town. I couldn't tell anyone; Jessica wouldn't believe me, Peter would be hurt and Mum and Dad couldn't understand.

"I love you James,
You join our games,
And your strong arms,
Keep me safe from harm..."

I pulled the night light in its case from a turned up plant pot and was about to light it in front of the image when Gabriel wandered barefoot in the garden. He looked happy, smiling to himself, sucking something yellow and juicy. I uncrossed my legs and kicked the door wider open. He heard the creak and peeped in.

"It was good wasn't it?" he said, wiping his sticky fingers over his shirt.

I nodded and slipped the Sacred Heart back into his hiding place.

"We made twenty-five pounds! We thought we might make ten if we were lucky, but twenty-five!"

I tried to smile but I wanted to cry.

"Do you want some melon?" he crouched down beside me, holding out the huge yellow slice.

We sat on the wooden floor taking it in turns to suck the melon till our faces grew sticky and juice dripped down our chins. It had been in the fridge. So cold! So refreshing! So much better without cutlery or plates; so delicious and watery like a mountain spring.

"I'm sorry you didn't get to play your maracas," he said.

"It's alright."

"Next week we'll play again and we'll make sure you get your chance."

I shrugged.

"*The Counting House* is a brilliant name. If James wasn't going to use it for his wine bar, it would have been great for our group."

"Thanks," I said.

Gabriel punched my arm playfully, "You'll have to think of another name for us," he leaned back and smiled very brightly. "It was brilliant today, I can't remember the last time I enjoyed myself so much. Peter loved it. Did you see his face?"

"You were both really good," I said.

"Do you remember when we went to Bransden Wood and I said that I wished I could fly?"

I nodded.

"That's what it's like when we're singing. When Peter's playing his guitar, watch him. He isn't walking, Georgie, he's flying!"

I forced a smile but the sadness wouldn't go away.

Gabriel was quiet for a few minutes as though waiting for me to speak but I couldn't think of anything to say.

"Georgie," he said at last, "what's the matter?"

I had to tell someone. It was bursting inside me. I dug my hand into my pocket and pulled out the bright shiny medal, "This is yours," I said and handed it to him, "isn't it? You won it, didn't you, not James?"

He ran his fingers over the inscription and smiled to himself, "Yeah. I did. I was really proud that day."

"Why did he take it?"

"Because he was jealous. He's no good at archery. He couldn't even hit the target."

A dark red butterfly flew in through the open door and fluttered around our heads and faces. Gabriel lifted his hand to catch it but it moved too quickly, battering itself on the glass.

"James came to watch you today," I said, "and I went over to him but he wouldn't talk to me. He was with his friends."

Gabriel sighed and laughed at the same time.

"They were laughing at Peter," I said and looked straight at Gabriel wanting to see his reaction.

"Take no notice of them, they laugh at anything," he said carelessly. "They're just a bunch of idiots."

"James isn't," I said, "I've known him all my life. He's not really like that."

Gabriel reached up to the window and wafted the butterfly towards the door. It fluttered against his hand then escaped into the sunlight, hovering over the flowers and skimming the top of the lawn with its delicate wings.

"I'll tell you what he's really like," Gabriel said, "he's a spoilt little kid who thinks because his Dad's rich he can do what he likes."

"No," I saw the Lionheart leaping through the trees, "he isn't. He's not like that at all."

Gabriel threw back his head and looked up at the sky, "He's a bully and a coward and I don't know why you and Jessica bother with him."

I shook my head, refusing to believe it.

Gabriel rocked himself forward and stood up on the step of the shed. He put his hand into the back pocket of his jeans and pulled out a small leather wallet.

"Do you want to see a picture of my Mum and Dad?" he said fidgeting with the press-stud. He slipped a black and white photograph out of the transparent cover and held it up to my eyes. The faces were disfigured by blue biro; spectacles and moustaches disguising the features and huge black spots like pimples over their faces.

"Every single picture I have of them looks like this," he stared at it then shoved it back into the wallet. "Guess who did it?"

I shook my head.

"Only three months after they'd died, he went into our dormitory one lunch time and ruined every photo in my album."

"It wasn't James," I said. "It couldn't have been. James's Mum died. He knows what it's like."

"I saw him," Gabriel's voice was almost fierce and it frightened me, "I saw him standing there sniggering behind the door, laughing because I cried."

He sat down again on the shed floor, digging his nails into the discarded melon skin, "Do you know why he did it?"

I didn't speak.

"Because I came first in class and he came last. He can't stand it. He can't bear it when anyone's better than him at anything."

I didn't know what to say. I looked at my exercise book and tried to shake the thoughts from my head; thoughts of the Lionheart, the King, the hero, laughing and passing my poems around the lawn.

"It's an awful thing to do," I said feebly, "but I'm sure he didn't mean it."

"You can't do something like that by accident."

"I'll bet he's sorry and if we ask him about it, he'll say sorry."

Gabriel's face had softened when he turned to look at me, "I'm sorry, Georgie. I know he's your friend and you really like him."

I shook my head but didn't say a word.

"I know," he hesitated, "I know you think he's wonderful and he can't do any wrong but if you could see what he's really like you'd know he's not worth the bother."

I stared across the garden and tried to understand. The devil comes in many disguises. Through the window I could see Mum busying herself around the kitchen. Peter wheeled his chair to the sink and diluted a glass of orange.

"Here," Gabriel said holding out the medal, "do you want this?"

I looked at it. It was tempting, "No," I said, "you have to do something brave to win a medal."

He turned it round in his fingers and his lip curled slightly, "Give it back to James," he said, "I don't want it now."

"I hate him," I said. "He was laughing at Peter."

The records were stacked in the box where Jessica had left them. She was singing in the bathroom. The water splashed into the basin; she was going to be some time.

I took a blue biro from my box on the desk and held it like a knife in my fist. I picked them out at random, the first that came to hand, and dug the biro deep into the vinyl. The nib buzzed and scraped and bounced on the surface and I pressed it even deeper until half the records were lined with deep crevices.

The water glugged down the plug hole and I stuffed the records back in the box, deliberately ripping some of the sleeves.

"What are you doing?" Jessica said.

"Just looking at this medal."

She took it from my hand and slipped it into the box, "It doesn't belong to you. Leave it where you found it."

I found Auntie Lucy's *Anvil Chorus* and put it onto the turntable.

Jessica frowned at me, "Now what are you doing? It's bed time."

"I want to listen to this." I said, and turning to the window with my eyes closed, I stood on a cloud and smashed all the stars.

Chapter 15

"Bless me, Father, for I have sinned. It's two months since my last confession and these are my sins..."

The outline of Father Paxton's head moved towards the grille.

"Can you speak up a bit?" he said.

I stood on the kneeler and moved my mouth closer to his ear, "Bless me Father, for I have sinned..."

I wished I hadn't decided to come that Thursday evening. It was Dad's idea but he didn't force me to go. It was only because Peter and Gabriel were busy practising and I couldn't think of anything better to do.

"I have been cheeky to my parents. I have told lies."

It was better to start with the mundane sins that I always confessed but couldn't recall committing.

Jessica was sitting on the end of the bench outside the box. More than I feared the wrath of God, more than I feared hell fire or thunderbolts from heaven, I feared Jessica hearing what I was about to confess.

"And I spoiled something," I said, disguising my voice so he wouldn't guess it was me, "something that belongs to someone else."

"I see," he said with his head so close to the grille that little bits of his hair poked through the metal.

"I scratched someone's records."

"Was it an accident?"

"No. I did it on purpose."

"Why was that?"

I didn't want all these questions. I wanted to confess my sins and have my soul washed clean and the whole thing be forgotten.

"He laughed at my brother."

"So you wanted to get your own back?"

"Yes."

He moved away from the grille, "Do you think Jesus would have done that if he'd been in your place?"

"They didn't have records when Jesus was alive."

He sniffed or laughed - I wasn't sure which. "Do you think Jesus would have tried to get his own back?"

"He'd have sent them to burn in the fire of hell," I said. "People who laugh at other people should go to hell."

"The soldiers laughed at Jesus. They mocked him, they dressed him up as a king, they spat at him and hit him and then they crucified him and do you know what he said about them?"

"He said they'd be thrown into hell with weeping and gnashing of teeth."

Father Paxton's voice was gentle, "He said, *'Father, forgive them, they don't know what they're doing.'* We all make mistakes and do things we shouldn't and if we want God to forgive us, we have to forgive other people. Can you do that?"

I didn't answer. It was easy to forgive other people who hurt you, but to forgive someone who laughed at my brother...

"If we want to be forgiven we have to learn to forgive. Can you do that?" he said again.

I wanted to get out so I said, "Yes."

I'd confessed enough and was feeling more uncomfortable the longer he spoke. Jessica would be wondering what I'd done if I stayed in the box too long.

"So what are you going to do to make up for it?"

That was for him to decide; it was his job to give out the penance. I shuffled about putting one foot on the floor and one on the kneeler, gripping the ledge in front of the grille with the tips of my fingers and swinging to and fro.

"Have you told the person you're sorry?"

"No. He doesn't know I did it."

"Can you replace the records?"

"I haven't any money."

"In that case you should tell him you're sorry and do something kind for him to show him you mean it. Will you do that?"

"Yes."

I looked at the cross hanging above the grille; the nails and the thorns, "*Father forgive them,*" I thought.

"Right," Father Paxton said, "to show God you're really sorry, I'd like you to say three *Hail Marys* for the person whose records you broke and see what kind thing you can do for him. Now make your Act of Contrition."

"Oh my God, because thou art so good..." I mumbled the prayer while Father Paxton whispered my absolution.

Jessica stood up as soon as I opened the door, "You were ages!" she mouthed.

I shrugged and walked to the front of the church where I knelt and said three *Hail Marys* for James.

"What was your penance?" Jessica said when we got in the car.

"Three *Hail Marys*."

"You must have done something very bad. I only got one *Our Father*."

"You probably didn't say all your sins," I said, "you missed some out."

"If you said all yours you'd be there all day."

"Stop bickering," Dad said, "you've just come out of church."

Jessica and I looked out of opposite windows of the car.

We stopped at the traffic lights in front of our old house and I stared down the drive at the roof from which Peter had fallen. The house was dark and quiet. The new people didn't seem to be in. They'd stripped the pebbledash from the walls and replaced the coloured glass in the windows. Everything was different, even the garden wall had been pulled down; the flags on the drive, the fence between us and Hoagey, the trees in the front garden; *everything* had changed.

Something ached inside me; a pain of remembering and wishing it could be the same but knowing it never would be again. The Lionheart had been slain and lay buried in the garden. The lame King of France couldn't ride into battle and the heathens had destroyed the castle. Something had happened. Something had spoiled the whole world, the house, Peter's legs; something unfeeling and cruel stepped in and crushed it without even a thought.

"Where are we going?" I said when Dad missed the turning home.

"To James's. To take his records back."

I gripped the edge of the seat and stared more intently out of the window. Jessica hadn't noticed what I'd done but James would see; he'd see as soon as he pulled them out of the box in their ripped sleeves.

"Shall I stay in the car?" I said when Dad stopped in front of the house.

He turned round, "Don't you want to see James?"

"I'm not bothered."

He got out, unlocked the boot, and handed the box of records to Jessica. She tottered down the drive and Dad followed a few steps behind. They stood for a while at the front door until Mr. Radcliff appeared and they went inside.

I wriggled between the seats to the front and sat behind the steering wheel switching the indicators on and off and trying to reach the pedals. I zoomed round corners, screeched the brakes at hairpin bends, chased by policemen from *"Z' Cars'* with sirens and blue flashing lights.

Jessica and Dad were gone for ages then Jessica appeared at the car window.

"Come on inside," she said, "Mr. Radcliff has poured you some orange juice."

I followed her up the drive and met James in the hallway.

"Georgie," Jessica said seriously and James's eyes were fixed on me like the eyes of an interrogator, "did you touch James's records?"

"What records?"

Jessica tutted impatiently, "The ones James lent me, you know."

"I didn't go near them," my absolution was nullified, my guilt remained. "You said I hadn't got to touch them."

"She didn't do it," James said shaking his head and turning away, "but I know who did." He looked at Jessica, "Come on," he led her into the front room.

I started to follow.

"Your orange juice is in the kitchen," Jessica said, pointing me in the other direction.

From the dining room I could hear Alan's nasal voice asking lots of questions as Mr. Radcliff described his new wine bar to Dad. Dad was grunting, 'Yes' and 'No' but I could tell he was bored. From the lounge came the sound of jumping records:

"Now the car...now the car...now the car..."

Somebody nudged the needle.

"We may nev..we may nev...we may nev..."

The orange juice was too sweet and tasted of tangerines. I blew bubbles in it and looked out of the window to see if Uncle Max was in his garden.

"Georgie," James came in smiling; it wasn't the James I saw on the bench in town. "Do you want to win a medal?"

I shrugged. I couldn't hate him when he stood in front of me like that, *"Father, forgive them."*

"Why did you laugh at Peter?" I said.

He shook his head as he sat down beside me, "I wasn't laughing at Peter. I wouldn't do that; he's my friend. It was the others, but they didn't mean it. It was just a joke. Peter would have thought it was funny."

"Would he?"

"Yeah," he nodded very quickly, "I thought Peter was great. We all did!"

"Honest?"

"'Course we did."

It was my three *Hail Marys* - they'd changed him back into the Lionheart.

He put his hand into his pocket, "How would you like to win this?"

The low evening sun shone on the gold medal and dazzling beams shot into my eyes. He pulled it out of the plastic and held it in front of my face.

"Is it yours?" I said.

"I won it at school."

He smiled at me, his bright flashing smile, but the devil has many disguises.

"You only have to do one simple thing and it's yours."

"What?"

"You know," he said thoughtfully, still dangling the medal in front of my eyes, "you know how good Peter is at singing and playing his guitar?"

"Yes."

"Well, last Saturday when they were singing in town, you must have noticed that every time Gabriel joined in, it really ruined Peter's playing."

I wrinkled my nose. I hadn't noticed at all.

"Peter's good. He's great. He's got loads of talent...but Gabriel just spoils it. You can't hear Peter over Gabriel's guitar, can you?"

I wasn't sure.

"You've seen all my records," he leaned back and nodded at me as though I were a grown up sharing an adult conversation. It made me feel important and proud but I looked at his feet, hidden by white pumps; how can you tell it's the devil?

"I listen to a lot of music. My Dad sometimes hires bands for his wine bars and I always help him choose because he's taught me how to recognise what's good and what's rubbish."

That much was true. Mr. Radcliff discussed everything with James.

"Peter's good; but Gabriel..." he shook his head and twitched a nostril, "well, you know, yourself, Georgie, he's spoiling everything for Peter."

He placed the medal in my hand and I turned it over pretending I'd never seen it before. If he knew I'd found it, he'd know I had been in his records' box.

"You want me to tell him, don't you?" I said. "You want me to tell Gabriel that you think he's no good."

"No," he shook his head quickly, "no, you can't do that. It would...it would upset him, wouldn't it?"

"Yes."

"I've thought of something else. Are they going to play in town again?"

"They're going to play every Saturday all summer."

"Right. All you have to do is get Gabriel's guitar and hide it somewhere. He'll think he's lost it and he won't be able to play."

"I can't. It's too big to hide. There isn't a space under my bed anymore."

He smiled very brightly as though everything was going to plan, "Tomorrow morning I'll come round to your house. All you have to do is find the guitar and put it in your shed and I'll collect it on my way out."

I remembered photographs disfigured by blue biro, "What will you do with it?"

"I'll bring it home and look after it until Sunday, then I'll bring it back to your house and you can put it back where you got it from and he'll never know you touched it."

"You won't break it or draw on it or anything?"

He opened his eyes very widely in amazement, "I wouldn't do anything like that!"

I wasn't sure.

"Have you told Jessica?"

"No," he said, "you know she can't keep a secret, but you can. You're good at it, aren't you? And then," he took the medal from my hand, "you get this! Will you do it?"

"I don't know."

"Come on, Georgie," he said, squeezing my shoulder and shaking me gently, "do it for Peter and for me."

I had to do something kind for James to earn absolution for my sins.

Peter whizzed through the kitchen to meet us, "Guess what! We're going to be in the paper!"

Mum, standing behind him, nodded to affirm his story, "Mrs. Howland's just been on the phone. She's coming round tomorrow for the money and bringing a photographer from the *Brakenfield Review*."

"Wow," I said, "we'll be famous!"

Jessica looked at me, "You won't be. You didn't do anything."

I looked at Mum but she was busy talking to Dad. I looked at Peter and Gabriel but they were talking to each other.

"I collected the money," I said to Jessica.

"Well they might mention that, but you won't be on the photo."

"Peter," I said, "can I be on the photo?"

"It's just the singers, Georgie, but I'm sure you'll get a mention."

"Gabriel," I said, "don't you think I should be on the photo?"

He raised his arms to say it was out of his hands, "It's not up to us. Mrs. Howland said the newspaper men wanted Peter and Jessica and me."

"I don't want to be in a stupid newspaper," I said, "and nobody reads the *Brakenfield Review* anyway."

Jessica spent the rest of the evening deciding what to wear. She spread four different sets of clothes across her bed, "Which do you think?" she said.

I sprawled on my own bed resting on my elbow with my head on my hand, "I don't know."

"Help me decide."

"Couldn't I just be on the end of the picture? I'll wear my dress."

She busied herself more and more with her clothes, "It's not up to us."

"Please," I said, "please let me be on the picture. I'll keep the room tidy, I promise. I'll share my pocket money with you."

"Oh Georgie," she said with pity, "it's not an important thing. It's just people who can sing or play instruments and you can't, but you're good at other things."

"Like what?"

She raised her eye brows and rearranged the clothes on her bed, "Other things."

"What other things?"

"I don't know," she said impatiently, "you must be good at something. Bones and that, you know a lot about bones."

I huffed.

"And praying. You're always praying."

It was a waste of time; no one was going to let me be on the picture. I drifted downstairs and found Peter and Gabriel sitting in the dining room with Mum and Dad. They were all talking about what they'd tell the newspaper man.

"Do you think we should be holding our guitars?" Peter said.

"Yes," Mum nodded eagerly, "you want to look like a proper group."

"Why don't you take the sign that Dad made?" I said, "I could hold it for you."

No one paid any attention and I walked out of the room.

"Georgie," Mum called after me, "it's time you were getting ready for bed."

"Yeah," I said gloomily and saw Peter's bedroom door open and Gabriel's guitar leaning against the wall, "I won't be long."

From the dining room I could hear their voices, no one was near the door. Lifting the guitar carefully to avoid twanging the strings, I carried it through the kitchen and across the garden to the shed where I leaned it on the lawn mower as I reached behind the plant pots for the Sacred Heart. I stood him up on the petrol can and fumbled behind the plant pots for the candle and matches. It was all I was good at; praying and knowing about bones.

"Please God," I said, "let James be kind to Gabriel and please make them change their minds about the photograph."

The back door opened and rubber wheels squeaked over the ramp.

"Georgie!"

I blew out the candle and stuffed the image back in its hiding place.

"Georgie! Come out we want to tell you something."

I turned around quickly, trying to escape before Peter opened the shed but Gabriel had his hand on the latch and he pulled back the door, looking beyond me to his guitar. He looked at it, then at me, then at Peter who had wheeled himself to the doorway.

"What are you doing with that?" Peter said sharply.

"Nothing."

Gabriel reached past me and lifted it over my head, examining it closely to check nothing was broken.

Peter said, "That's awful! Did you take it just because you can't be on the picture?"

"No!"

"You'd better not have broken it."

I shook my head and Gabriel looked at me sadly, "It's okay," he said but he sounded hurt, "it's not damaged."

"We came to tell you can be on the photo, but I don't think we should bother now," Peter said.

They went back to the kitchen.

"Please let me," I said, "I wasn't going to break it."

They didn't turn around.

"Gabriel," I said, "I'm sorry. I was only going to lend it to someone."

He paused at the back door.

"Father Paxton said I had to do something for James and then James told me to get it and..." I shook my head, confused.

"What else did James tell you to do?" Gabriel said.

I sat on the side of Peter's bed twisting my T-shirt between my fists.

"I can't believe it," Peter said, "I can't believe you'd be so stupid as to believe him. You know what he's like! You know how he treats Gabriel. Did you really believe he'd just bring it back without a mark on it?"

"Georgie!" Mum called from the other room, "I told you half an hour ago. It's time you were in bed."

"I had to do it," I said. I was nearly crying. "I scratched all James's records and Father Paxton said I had to do something for him to make up for it."

"For heaven's sake!" Peter said.

Gabriel ran his fingers over the guitar strings, "Never mind, it's not broken or anything and I've got it back."

"No thanks to Georgie."

"I'm sorry," I said again.

Gabriel smiled at me, "It's not your fault, it's him. He just uses people all the time."

Peter shook his head and looked at Gabriel, "Why do you let him do it? Why don't you stand up for yourself? You're stronger than he is."

Gabriel's lips twitched as he looked down at his guitar, "He's not worth the bother."

"If you let him get away with it, he'll go on doing it and when he's bored with doing it to you, he'll do it to someone else."

"It's not just him. It's all his friends, there's a whole crowd of them."

"You've got friends, too," Peter said very firmly, "and you should teach him a lesson."

"How?"

Peter frowned thoughtfully, "I have a plan."

"You won't hurt him, will you?" I said.

"No but I'll need your help."

"Georgie," Mum opened the door, "come on, bed!"

Chapter 16

I knew what I had to do. I had my instructions: top secret and organised to perfection. When James arrived I must tell him the guitar was in the shed and wait for him there until he decided to leave. As soon as he came outside, I had to run out shouting, 'Hiya James!' as a signal to Gabriel who would be hiding ready to pounce. Once James was in the shed, Gabriel would bolt the door from the outside and James would be his prisoner.

"Then what?" I said.

"Then we don't let him out until he admits what he's done and tells Gabriel he's sorry and promises not to do anything like it again."

"I don't believe his promises," Gabriel said doubtfully, "and when we get back to school and he's with his friends, they'll probably be worse than ever."

"That's why I've made these," Peter smiled triumphantly as he held out three sheets of paper, "we'll make him sign them before we let him out."

Three written confessions and promises.

"He can pass them out under the door and I'll hide them in my room. We'll warn him that if he ever bothers you again, we'll send one to his Dad, one to the headmaster of your school and one for spare."

Gabriel read them aloud and laughed, "He'll just deny it or say we forced him to do it."

"That doesn't matter," Peter said, "at least we'll have shown him you can stand up to him. That'll probably be enough to stop him."

"Okay," Gabriel said, "it's worth a try," and he and Peter looked at one another with pride and excitement.

I wasn't sure. I went through the details over and over again. Everything seemed fair but something wasn't right. James was still James whatever he had done. Bully or coward he may be, but his smile was as bright as the sun and I was happy even to touch the leaves his breath brushed as he passed.

"What's the matter?" Peter said.

"I don't know if it's right."

"You're not going to back out now! Just remember what he did to Gabriel's photos."

"We're not going to hurt him," Gabriel promised, "just teach him a lesson."

"I won't back out," I said but there was still my debt to pay; my penance and absolution from Father Paxton.

Jessica had two reasons to be careful to look her best: first James was coming then the newspaper photographer. She stood all morning in front of the mirror moving her hair one way then another, standing sideways and backwards and examining her face very closely.

"If you have to be on the photo," she said, "you'd better tidy yourself up. You're not going to show me up."

I sprawled in my shorts and T-shirt, "The photographer's not coming for ages and anyway, Peter says I can wear what I like."

"Well if you want to look like a boy..." she said with one eye on the window looking out for James, but I saw him first and I flew downstairs to open the door.

"I've done it," I said. "It's in the shed."

His finger flew up to his lips, "Hush! We don't want everyone to know."

Gabriel, who was passing through the hall, winked at me without acknowledging James.

Jessica floated down the stairs like a lady in a grand stately home, "Guess what! We're going to be in the paper, in the *Brakenfield Review*!"

"Great!" James's smile shone like a star in the night and my penance might have been a pleasure had the opportunity to do something kind for him come my way.

He followed Jessica into the front room where I heard her effusing about the newsman and I left them alone to take up my position in the shed. I had not been there long when Gabriel tiptoed over the lawn with his guitar in his hand, "Okay," he whispered, "you know what you're doing?"

I nodded.

"We'll put this at the back to make sure he goes right inside."

He leaned over me and his shirt smelt of washing powder; clean and fresh like newly changed sheets.

"Right," he smiled at me again, "I'll hide round the back. He'll probably be a while yet but we might as well be prepared."

Gabriel disappeared, closing the door behind him. For a few minutes I heard thumping on the wood and the whole shed shook as he slithered between the wall and the fence. Then everything was still and in the silence I was afraid.

James would hate me if he knew what I'd done. He'd never forgive me for scratching his records, but to be a party to *this*...Father Paxton's words ran through my mind, "We have to forgive other people if we want God to forgive us."

Would I go to hell and burn in everlasting fire, weeping and gnashing my teeth?

I lifted out the Sacred Heart and rested him in his usual place on the petrol can then reached for the night light and matches.

"Please don't send me to hell," I said, placing the lighted candle in front of his image, "and I promise I'll never do anything like this again. I'll do something really kind for James and I'll save up my pocket money and buy him some new records."

The mournful eyes of the image in the frame stared back at me.

"Jesus, we're not going to hurt him, but you were angry when you threw all the people out of the Temple. We have to teach him to be kind."

I wanted the image to speak but he gazed at me in silence.

"Sacred Heart of Jesus, I place all my...."

The back door opened and through the slats in the shed I saw James hurrying towards me. It was too soon. I wasn't prepared. There was no time to hide my picture and candles. I leaped up and pushed open the door.

"Hiya James!"

Like Judas in the Garden of Gethsemane, I betrayed my Master with a greeting.

"Where is it?" he whispered urgently.

"In there," I pointed into the shed.

"Get it out and bring it round the front."

He was going to ruin everything but this might be my liberation; it wouldn't be my fault if the whole plan failed, yet somehow the words slipped out of my mouth before I had time to stop them, "I can't; it's stuck behind the lawn mower and it's too heavy for me to move."

I spoke loudly as I heard a scratching sound from the side of the shed and I knew Gabriel was emerging from his hide out.

"For God's sake," James said impatiently, moving me out of his way, "can't you do anything right!"

He had passed me and had one foot in the shed the other on the step as he leaned over the Sacred Heart to reach for the guitar. A leap and a crash and the door closed behind him. Click. The bolt was across.

There was more crashing inside the shed and James calling out, "What the hell..."

But Peter was banging on the kitchen window, "Quick!" he called, "Mrs. Howland's here with the newspaper man."

"They're not supposed to be coming till this afternoon," Gabriel said.

Peter shrugged, "They've come early. Come on; they want to take our photo in front of the house."

"What about James?" I said as the banging and cries from the shed grew louder and more frantic.

Peter glanced at the door, "Leave him there for now. We'll sort him out when they've gone."

Jessica was posing on the front lawn.

"I thought you were bringing your guitar," Mum said to Gabriel.

"Peter's got his," he shrugged, "one will be enough."

Mrs. Howland was very busy organising everybody. She moved people around like ornaments then stepped backwards to view them from a distance.

"Move a little to the left, dear," she told Jessica, "and put your arm around your brother."

The sun shone through the leaves casting shadows on the ground speckling the velvet green grass. The man from the *Brakenfield Review* waited patiently, turning the dials on the camera that he held to his eye.

"Are we ready?" he said but Mrs. Howland wasn't satisfied.

She looked at me and raised an eyebrow, "Are you in the picture, too, dear?"

"Oh, Georgie, look at the state of you," Mum said. "Run upstairs and wash your face. You can't go on the picture like that."

"You'll have to get washed in the kitchen," Jessica said, "because James is in the bathroom."

"No," Peter said, "he isn't. He's gone home. I saw him outside."

"He never said good-bye," Jessica frowned and I grew more uneasy.

"Georgie," Mum shouted, "wash your face or you won't be on the picture."

Afraid that they'd take the photo without me, I ran to the kitchen and turned on the tap, splashing water over my cheeks. Reaching for the towel, I looked out of the window.

Clouds of black smoke billowed through the cracks in the shed door. A crack, like a branch breaking. I stared for one second certain I must be mistaken then a yellow flame shot through the roof. The shed was ablaze!

I screamed at the top of my voice, "Help! Help! The shed's on fire! The shed's on fire!" and ran up and down in the kitchen not knowing where to run.

Someone, I'm not sure who, came into the kitchen, and I flew out through the back door. James was burning in hell!

Thick black smoke rushed into my face, stinging my eyes. I tried to inhale but there was tightness in my chest as the smoke caught my lungs and I panicked, breathlessly gasping and blinded in the heat.

"Georgie, get back!" Dad yelled.

I screamed, "James is locked in the shed! James is locked in the shed!"

The fire was raging and crackling. I heard sounds of shouting but no one was moving. The metal bolt stuck to my fingers but I felt no pain and pushed it with all the weight of my arm.

The door flew open and a ball of flames rolled out in a mountain of yellow and orange; and there in the middle lay James.

I stood with my back to the window listening to the rhythmic squeaking of the nurses' shoes up and down the ward. Days had passed and still James lay there motionless and oblivious of our presence. I sighed deeply, inhaling the pure disinfected air of the hospital, and turned my head to and from the disfigured features of his face.

Drip...drip...drip...I watched the steady flow of fluid from the bag and followed the tubing to his arm. His eyelids were swollen like two huge boils and his cheeks were barely visible beneath the dressings and raw wounds. A dark gunge formed in the corners of his mouth, and his bulbous lips were pursed as though to whistle.

"Don't die...don't die...don't die..." I said in my head.

The doctors had done all they could; it was only a matter of waiting. I remembered the wild heroic deaths of the Lionheart on summer lawns, but the reality lying in the hospital bed held none of the excitement and dignity of our games.

A tube drained his bladder and the smell that came through the curtains when the nurses came 'to change him' destroyed every image of courage and valour. It wasn't like this in films. Heroes weren't fed by tubes through their nostrils, they didn't lie in sheets soiled by their own excrement.

"Suffering," Auntie Philomena used to say, "is the surest way to heaven. We must learn to use all our sufferings, offering them for the salvation of the Holy Souls in purgatory. See how the saints suffered!"

And James was no better than Auntie Philomena now. He had no more dignity, no more control than she had.

I leaned over the bed and looked at his face. "There is beauty in everything," I thought, "if we take the time to look for it," but stare as I might I saw no beauty here.

I turned back to the window and looked across the car park as rain began to fall.

Alan came to stand beside me. His face was pale and his eyes were red, "It's busy isn't it?" He sounded desperate to speak.

"He will be alright, won't he?" I said.

Alan shrugged and lowered his eyes to hide his feelings. He looked at the bandage on my hand, "I suppose you've earned a medal for getting him out."

I looked at him and he almost smiled. It was the first time in my life I'd ever seen him smile. I'd heard his nasal laughter and I'd seen his mocking grin, but this was a real smile, a genuine expression.

"I saw the picture in the paper," he said, "they said you're a hero. They said you saved his life."

I didn't feel like a hero; I didn't even feel proud. There was no point in being a hero if James wasn't there to see it. I felt sick and disgusted. I needed to breathe fresher air and pressed my head on the window. This wasn't how it should be; I saw blue cornflowers, delphiniums and spring mornings in a garden; castles and heroes in bronze armour reflected by the waters of a moat around a shed. My hand hurt. It itched and irritated and I wanted to poke around beneath the bandage and scratch it. An itch! Battle wounds didn't itch; they made you cry out in agony, uttering unforgettable last words. I wasn't a hero. I had no reason to feel proud.

"It's at times like this," Mr. Radcliff told Mum, "that you realise what really matters. I was always so busy, all those afternoons when he asked me to go to the park or play football in the garden and I was never there. Always too busy, always working..."

Mum put her hand on Mr. Radcliff's shoulder and drew him down to a chair, "He'll pull through. You'll see, he'll pull through."

I closed my eyes and heard the crack, the sirens and the shouting; saw the ball of flame; a body in the garden.

Drip, drip, drip; the drops fell slowly, mechanically, rhythmically and the crash came again and again; the crash of a hero falling from his pedestal; the smashing of an icon, now in pieces on the floor.

I opened my eyes and gazed at the living world outside, still hearing myself praying for a miracle, "Hail Mary, full of grace, the Lord is with thee…"

But everything was crystal clear; so simple and straightforward: there were no heroes and no devils, only children, spinning dreams on summer lawns. There were no answers to prayers, just an eternity of hoping against hope and a drip, drip, dripping of words through the silence of the night.

The squeaking shoes moved closer to the bed and the nurse pulled back the curtains.

"I'm sorry," she said, "we only allow two visitors at a time."

"Any news?" Dad said at teatime when he came home from work. Mum shook her head.

I wasn't hungry but picked through my tea, searching for the onions beneath the potatoes and spreading them like slugs round the side of the plate.

"He looks awful," I said, "I wouldn't have recognised him."

Jessica sniffed into her teacup but no one tried to comfort her.

"It's my fault," Peter said. "It was all my idea."

"I locked him in," Gabriel said.

"And I left the candle burning," I thought, but didn't say it.

I wandered outside and poked through the soggy ashes in the garden. A twisted frame caught on the end of the cane and I lifted it high into the air; the image of Satan or the Sacred Heart - whoever it was, whatever curse it held, it was gone now, burned to a cinder with only the wrought gold frame to show it ever existed.

"It's not fair, God!" I stamped around the damp cinders. "It's not fair!"

But somebody had to do something. Somebody had to help. The doctors couldn't do it, they hadn't cured Peter; there was no alternative.

"Mum, can I go to church on my bike?"

"It'll be getting dark soon."

"Please," I said, "I promise I won't be long."

It was raining when I crossed the churchyard and the damp air refreshed my face as I leaned my bike on a headstone and sat down on a grave stone. Beneath the tapping of raindrops on the path and on the tombs, the August evening was still. I stared across the graves to the place where the haunted lodge once stood. Here I was in a Maximum Red Alert Zone, but I wasn't afraid. The devil wasn't here in the graveyard. He was out somewhere in a burning shed, on a roof at the end of a rope.

Drops dripped from the branches and tapped like music on the graves, bouncing and rebounding in front of my eyes. The rain fell in torrents into streams on the pathway, extinguishing the candle I'd carried from church.

"Please make Peter walk again," I thought, "please let him walk!"

I dared not even say the words in church, "Please don't let James die!"

My faith was as dead as the candle. I had had to come outside.

"How can something like that be anyone's fault? It was an accident," Gabriel said in Bransden Woods when I told him of Peter.

But God could have stopped it if he'd wanted to. A stone crucifix stood in the middle of a grassy island before the church door. Rubbing my eyes to wipe away the raindrops, I looked up at the thorns tearing into the flesh of the man whose ribs protruded through his skin. His veins wound their way down his arms like snakes. His eyes were closed and his mouth drooped with sorrow and pain.

" *'Without beauty, without majesty we saw him,*
no looks to attract our eyes;
a thing despised and rejected by men,
a man of sorrows, acquainted with grief.
And yet ours were the sufferings he bore,
ours the sorrows he carried.' "

Again I remembered the words from the Good Friday readings. I thought I had never seen such a sad face and I had never noticed before the words carved on a plaque beneath the wooden beams:

FATHER, FORGIVE THEM THEY KNOW NOT WHAT THEY DO

Faces flashed before my eyes; the mocking laughter of children reading poems on the lawn; the sour features of Auntie Philomena; Gabriel's tears at Christmas in Brigthorpe Hall; and the boys making jokes on a bench in town.

"Father, forgive them," I read the words aloud. In the face of the Messiah I saw too, James's disfigured face and the battered body of Peter lying on the concrete of the drive.

"I'm sorry, I'm sorry, I'm sorry," I said.

Tears burned my eyes as I looked at the bleeding wrists and pierced hands of the Saviour on the cross and in his suffering saw the tears of the child crawling with the woodlice round the shed, kneeling in the garden, lighting candles in the church. I slipped my hand into my pocket and pulled out my rosary beads, "Father, forgive...."

A moth, moving suddenly, fluttered onto my hand then darted about my face. I didn't flinch but watched it, fascinated by the delicate intricacy of its wings. Its eyes glowed in the darkness and I was drawn to the fragile creature fluttering desperately in search of the light.

The tread of footsteps coming nearer distracted me. They stopped and for a few seconds there was silence then the gate creaked open. I didn't move as the moth, seeming to sense my fear, fluttered frantically against my face.

"Georgie, your Mum sent me to find you."

I didn't answer and Gabriel sat down beside me on the grave.

"Mr. Radcliff phoned from the hospital," he said but I didn't want to hear his news.

He could see that I was crying and reached his arm to touch me but I turned away, rubbing my hand across my eyes.

"Go away," I said, "I don't want to know."

"It's getting dark. You can't stay here on your own."

"I'll bet you're really glad," I gasped as the tears began to fall, "you've got your own back now."

"No," he said, "I wouldn't wish this on him. I wouldn't wish this on anyone."

"Not even after what he did to you?"

I wanted to hate him; I had to hate someone; the Archangel Gabriel, the devil in one of his many disguises. But I couldn't hate him just as I could never hate James.

"Why," I said, "*why* does everything have to go wrong?"

"When my Mum and Dad died, Aunt Marie said that suffering can affect people in different ways. It can widen our hearts and fill us with understanding or it can turn us in on ourselves and leave us cold. She quoted a French writer called, Victor Hugo, "*Sadness is a fruit; God doesn't let it grow on a branch too weak to support it.*""

"God?" I said. "Do you think God really loves us, Gabriel?"

He stared at the cross and nodded as though he were listening to my words but hearing another voice inside his head, "There's a kind of beauty in everything," he said, "if we take the time to look for it. That's what Aunt Marie says."

I gathered a handful of soil, "There isn't. There isn't anything beautiful anymore. It's not true."

He turned and looked into my eyes.

"There are miracles, Georgie."

"No there aren't. God never healed Peter and now James..."

"There are different kinds of miracles. Music is a miracle. Love is a miracle."

I leaned back on the grave and looked up at the moon. Its face was lined with craters like scars and gaping wounds. I wondered what caused the giant crevices; bruising from some careless passing meteor or explosions in the galaxies of stars?

"I love James," I said. "No matter what he did to you, no matter what he looks like now, I love him. I'll always love him."

Gabriel didn't move.

"I know you think I'm silly and little but everyone believes that Jessica loves him, well I do too. I love him much more than she does because he's always been kind to her. She doesn't know that he can be cruel and mean, but I do and I love him anyway."

He put his arm around my shoulder and pulled me towards him then lifted his hands to my face as Aunt Marie had done.

"And that's why I believe that God loves us," he said, "no matter what we do, he always loves us."

I cried into his sleeve, "I don't want him to die, Gabriel. Please, don't let him die."

"He's not going to die," he said, "James is going to be alright."

"You don't know that. Nobody does."

"His Dad phoned from the hospital."

"You mean he's better?"

"Well," he smiled and shrugged at the same time, "he's awake."

"And he won't die?"

"No," he whispered, "he won't die."

Chapter 17

Autumn came and Christmas. All winter the world was dark and filled with desolation; dead flowers and broken branches crackling underfoot, grass brittle with frost and trees like skeletons tearing at the white blank sky, desperately searching for the sun. Mum took Jessica and me to visit James every week and he never said a word about the fire. I kept waiting, waiting for him to hate me for tricking him into the shed, but he hardly spoke at all and when he did he wouldn't look at us, as though he was too ashamed of his face to let us see him. '*Without beauty, without majesty we saw him, no looks to attract our eyes.*'

"Will it never heal?" Jessica said.

They shook their heads and she turned her face away.

She wouldn't look at him. She couldn't look at him. She cried at night but less often as the nights went by.

"Jess," I whispered through the darkness, "do you still love James?"

She didn't answer. She pretended to be asleep.

"Jess," I said, "shall we save up and buy a present for James?"

"His Dad takes him everything he wants."

I looked at her face, "Have you gone off him?"

"Silly baby," she said, "of course I haven't, only..." she looked away and fingered her curls, "he shouldn't have done what he did to Gabriel."

She didn't love him anymore.

Winter dragged on and on.

The raw wounds on James's face were fading slowly or familiarity made them seem less severe, but they would never disappear and he wasn't handsome now. Jessica came less often to the hospital. She had homework. She had exams in school. She had music practice, netball matches...she had anything to keep her away.

Mum and I still sat there every week beside his bed. His first few steps were painful. He was dizzy and sick and it took time to find his balance, but the doctors were pleased with his progress and eventually sent him home.

Then suddenly it happened. The world was real again; alive and colourful and where once darkness filled the parks and gardens, vast masses of blues and greens emerged; colours and shades too numerous to count. Frozen puddles burst back to life, strangers, walking their dogs, took off their coats and put on T-shirts; everything made new.

People began to smile as though the weather took them by surprise.

"Morning!" they called, "Lovely day!" like it was the first spring ever.

One afternoon as I sat in the Radcliffs' kitchen sipping a sweet still orange juice that tasted of tangerines, James came through the door and sat down at the other side of the table.

"Georgie," he said, "my Dad wants to ask you a favour."

"Your Dad?"

"He's been trying to think of a name for his new wine bar and I told him your suggestion, *The Counting House*. Would you mind if he uses it?"

Would I mind? They were James's words!

"We thought...well, I thought, that when we're older, when we grow up and leave school, maybe Gabriel and Peter would like to sing there."

"Gabriel?" I said and I wanted to say, "Weasel-face?" but it would be too cruel when James sat there in front of me all scarred and ugly.

"If he wants to," he said. "And you can come too and read your poems. We can all work there, like we used to say we would."

I nodded a lot. I didn't speak. I remembered the warm goose with a gungy eye in Bransden Wood Farm. I moved my hand onto the table and touched the end of James's fingers.

"Can my Dad use the name?" he said again and his voice was more gentle than I'd ever heard and I knew that what Aunt Marie had told me was true, "There is beauty in everything if we take the time to look for it."

"Will we really do it?" I said, "Because when Peter plays his guitar, he doesn't need to walk, he's flying!"

James nodded, "One day we will."

"Even Gabriel?"

"Yeah, of course, there'll be Gabriel."

"Can I tell Jessica?" I said, jumping up from the chair and hurrying to the door.

"Before you go, there's something else," he dug his hand into his pocket, "I wanted to give you this."

He pulled out Gabriel's archery medal and held it in front of my eyes.

"Gabriel doesn't want it back so I told him to give it to you but he said you wouldn't have it until you'd earned it."

I put out my hand and he placed it on my palm where it shone in the light of the afternoon sun.

"You saved my life, Georgie, surely that earns a medal."

My Hero, *my* Lionheart - I saved his life!

It was evening, the first day of the week. The moon, like a giant toffee, dripped across the sky where stars shimmered and twinkled, winking at me. I stood on a stool at the bedroom window and pinned the medal to my jumper. Auntie Lucy's *Favourite Opera* record crackled on the turntable. I threw open the window and played Verdi's *Anvil Chorus* on the stars; each star had a different chime and the moon made a loud clash like cymbals. I played gently and they jingled like bells and tinkled like a wind chime in the breeze.

I stretched my arms into the night sky and, standing on tiptoes, reached for a jagged edged star to carve a name across the moon:

THE COUNTING HOUSE

286

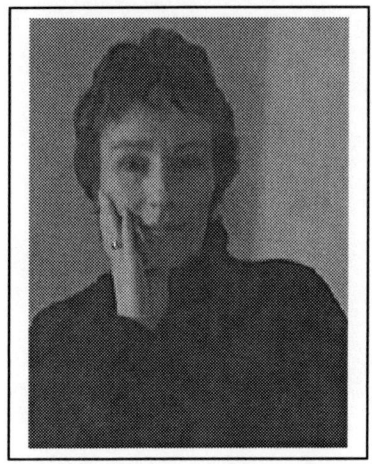 **Christina Croft** studied Divinity and English in Liverpool and has taught English, R.E. and history to children of all ages. After working as a private tutor in France, she qualified as a nurse and worked in a variety of medical settings, in hospitals and the community. .

Co-writer of two musicals, she has previously published poetry, song lyrics and a biography of Grand Duchess Elizabeth of Russia. At present she is working on further novels and a study of the relationship between the granddaughters of Queen Victoria.

Printed in the United Kingdom
by Lightning Source UK Ltd.
120650UK00001BB/21